CINCO PESO

THE JACK LANDERS WESTERN MYSTERY
BOOK SIX

G. WAYNE TILMAN

WOLFPACK
PUBLISHING
— EST 2013 —

Cinco Peso
Paperback Edition
Copyright © 2022 G. Wayne Tilman

Wolfpack Publishing
5130 S. Fort Apache Rd. 215-380
Las Vegas, NV 89148

wolfpackpublishing.com

Paperback ISBN 978-1-63977-961-1
eBook ISBN 978-1-63977-960-4

Appreciation to Denise Kearns
for her contributions as Beta reader.

CINCO PESO

CHAPTER ONE

THE SHOOTING WAS OVER and the acrid smell of one rifle shot had cleared in the south Oklahoma breeze. An ambulance had arrived to check on legendary Texas Ranger Zack Bodeway, stunned from his truck's airbag. They completed the rather unnecessary paperwork on the shooting victim. The cause of death was obvious, but a medical examiner had to certify it.

After chasing multiple murderer Bertie Ingles across the Red River into Oklahoma, the ranger had pitted Bertie's stolen truck. The truck had come to rest in a field. The ranger hit the truck again and toppled it over, his seatbelt unhooked to make a quick approach to the murderer.

His airbags deployed and hit him square in the face at four thousand feet per second. As he sat stunned, Bertie had staggered out, a Glock pistol in each hand. The pistols had belonged to two Texas deputies he had just shot. Those two deputies were a large part of why Bertie's capture had become very personal to both the ranger and the young Oklahoma sheriff's investigator close behind him.

Warrior County investigator Sergeant Rich Ammon watched the scene unfold in slow motion. The name for the phenomenon is tachypsychia. However, he did not act in slow motion. He bailed out of his police truck ready to do business. Rich shot Bertie from what was later measured to be one hundred twenty-three yards. In the forehead. The former Army ranger knew instantly it was a kill shot. It was not Rich's first distance kill by a long margin. Afghanistan flashed as he felt the recoil of the .30-30 against his right shoulder.

While the EMT's and another responding Texas Ranger huddled around Bodeway, the local sheriff, an Oklahoma Highway Patrol lieutenant and an OHP sergeant questioned Rich Ammon and several troopers who had been witnesses. Sufficient senior officers were present to convene an on-site shooting board.

By midday, Sergeant Rich Ammon had passed his second shooting board this week. He, later Bodeway, and the several troopers who were witnesses all told the same story. Bertie Ingles was approaching the stunned ranger from twenty feet, two guns raised. He showed every intent of killing the ranger. There was no other option to save the ranger but deadly force.

Once the board was completed and their finding made, the members all commented on the sergeant's accuracy. A head shot from one hundred twenty-three yards with an open-sighted Winchester lever action deer rifle introduced in 1894. Under stress. They just shook their heads wondering if they could have done the same. Nobody admitted it, but each knew he could not have made the shot.

The ranger, as macho a male as ever born, had

grasped his friend's hand then held him in a long embrace. The others watched approvingly, some nodding their heads. It was a moment only warriors would understand. Men who compartmentalize their emotions, but silently share it with other warriors.

Tough but kind men, all regretted a human life had to be taken. All knew Bertie Ingles had killed a judge and his wife and shot two Texas deputies, killing one and wounding the other. He had murdered the judge's son-in-law in Oklahoma. Rich had come down to charge him with the crime and was returning when Bodeway called him about the shooting and escape during Bertie Ingle's prisoner transfer. Bertie had been looking at life or a lethal injection after years of court cases and appeals.

He had forced justice to visit him in a millisecond from the muzzle of a rifle and destined a young lawman to more dark dreams for the rest of his life.

As Rich's mentor, eighty-four year old retired Texas Ranger Bud Carey, later told him, "Boy, the dreams happen once you hang a badge on your shirt. You can't get rid of them. So, you gotta tell yourself 'he forced it. It was his choice. I was in the right and he was in the wrong.' Then, son, you have to believe what you are telling yourself. 'Cause it's God's own truth."

BY TWO O'CLOCK in the afternoon, Rich had his special order dark green Ford Responder sheriff's pickup moving northbound on Interstate 44. Ranger Bodeway was fully recovered. The push bar on his ranger truck took the hit against the stolen vehicle without showing a scratch and he was headed back to the ranch which had been in his family since the first Ranger Bodeway had homesteaded it in the cap 'n ball revolver days.

Rich had called his boss, Chief Deputy Rose Custalow. Once the nature of his call was established, she had Sheriff Jack Landers join her on the call.

"The questions about the shoot are over and the shooting board is agreeing on their decision. The sheriff and OHP lieutenant are smiling and giving me a thumbs up right now."

"Rich, how is Zack doing?"

"Zack is okay, Jack. He's walking around and says his nose has stopped bleeding and his neck is a little stiff. He promised the EMT's he would get it checked out."

"How about you, Rich?" Rose asked.

"I feel like I am back in Afghanistan. What I did was righteous though. The man was a multiple murderer walking towards our friend with two pistols ready to kill him. Zack was still stunned and in no condition to fire first. Mine was a lucky shot."

"Where did you hit him, Rich?" Jack asked.

"Uh, it was between the eyes, maybe a half inch closer to the left eye socket than the right."

"How far?"

"One of the troopers used his wheel they use for car crash measurements. One hundred twenty-three yards."

"Lever action or your AR duty rifle?" Rose asked.

"The Winchester 94."

There was silence while the two senior members of the Warrior County Sheriff's Office looked at each other. Rose mouthed "Wow" soundlessly.

"Are you headed back now?" Jack asked.

"Yessir, Boss. About two hours unless I stop for a hamburger. I have not eaten except for a drive-through breakfast real early."

"Unless you want to talk with us about it, you can head back to your place. We can talk this afternoon if you need it or in the morning if you could use some quiet time."

"I think I will go for the latter and see y'all in the morning."

"Be safe. See you then."

After he hung up, Jack Landers called the county sheriff who had led the shooting board and got an all-clear for a righteous use of deadly force. Then, he called the ranger. Zack Bodeway was probably his best friend.

"I hear you had a busy day and got quite a smack in the face," he said without needing to identify himself.

"Yep. Like a mule, but with more surface area. I had no idea how hard an airbag hits you. The more important thing is your boy Rich is one helluva shot. I had a murderer coming at me and I was not even able to focus, much less shoot. I owe my life to Rich," Zack said.

"Welcome to the club. I do, too. I inherited him from the previous sheriff. I knew from the first he was a good lawman. I had no idea until recently he had been a ranger sniper in combat. I guess that chicken came home to roost today."

"Thank God it did, Jack. This takes care of four murders. I don't know if Rich had a chance to tell you, but his target was Bertie Ingles. Bertie, as you know, killed the judge and his wife as well as Bill Strauss in your county. He also killed a deputy here in Texas and wounded another badly when he escaped custody. He was a bad one, Jack. Real bad. The world is a better, safer place without him."

"So you have three Texas murders, one malfeasance with the state employee who fed information illegally to Ingles, and one wounding solved. I have one Oklahoma murder resolved today and another somewhat related one solved by Rich earlier in the week."

They continued to chat.

Rich called Isabella Munro. She was the daughter of the judge and his wife who were murdered by Ingles and the sister-in-law of Bill Strauss, also murdered by Ingles. A former Tulsa police officer, tomorrow was to be her first day as a Wichita Falls, Texas sheriff's investigator.

"Hi, it's me," he said when she answered.

"Do you know what happened down here? Nobody's talking but I know Ingles escaped. He killed a deputy and wounded another. All I am hearing is a Texas officer chased him across into Oklahoma and there was a shootout. I heard Ingles died."

"All true, Isabella. How is the deputy who is in the hospital?" Rich asked.

"Out of surgery. The sheriff is there now and word is the deputy, who I don't know except by name, is going to recover. The other poor guy died on the scene. Bastard! I hope the rumor of Ingles being dead it true!"

"It's true. I was there. Let's get Myra on the line with us and I will make the official victim notification to y'all, okay?" Myra had not only lost her parents to Ingles, but also her husband, Bill Straus.

"Myra? It's Rich. Isabella is also on the line. I wanted to speak with y'all at the same time about something which happened today. I guess it's a closure notification for both of you."

"Hi, Rich and Bella. What happened?"

"Murderer Bertie Ingles escaped custody today and killed a deputy in Wichita Falls and seriously wounded another. He stole two handguns and a county truck and escaped into Oklahoma, where he subsequently was killed."

"I should have guessed you were there, Rich. How about the ranger. Was Zack there, too?" Isabella asked.

"He and I chased Ingles into Oklahoma. Zack did a beautifully executed PIT maneuver and ran Ingles off the road into a field. He could see Ingles with a gun in the stolen truck and hit him again, rolling the stolen truck. I was just catching up. The second blow activated his airbags and stunned Zack. Ingles crawled out with both deputy's pistols and came at Zack. He died before he got to the ranger."

"Who killed him?"

"Me."

"Want to talk about it?"

"No. Not right now. Maybe later. A shooting team declared it was a good shoot."

"Are you okay?" Myra asked, still stunned at the news.

"I'm going home tonight and so is Zack. Two of your deputies are not. So, I feel for their families and for the one who was wounded.

"Rich, thank you. Myra and I did not expect closure on our parents and her husband so quickly. I know it's been a really violent week for you. I am here for you, day or night. Just call or come down, alright?" Isabella said.

"I will. It won't take me long to decompress. Not my first rodeo, Isabella. Bye ladies."

It appeared closure had occurred all around. It would take longer for one deputy's family in Texas though.

He went home to his apartment and took a shower. Then, bed. His mind raced for an hour, then he slept on and off until his normal five o'clock in the morning. He got up, exercised on his Peloton, showered again and dressed for work.

White shirt and Resistol cowboy hat, creased jeans

and boots and a brown holster and belt. His badge was on his belt in front of his gun. Today, he skipped the tactical Kevlar vest outside and wore a thinner one under his shirt.

At five forty-five, he pulled into the café down the block from the sheriff's office. The sheriff's and the chief deputy's vehicles were already in front.

Coffee called to him. Food. Not so much yet. Maybe later.

Sheriff Jack Landers motioned him to a corner table. He also motioned the server to bring a coffee pot and cup over.

"You okay, Rich?" Rose asked.

"I'm fine, Rose, thanks. I just needed a good night's sleep," he said.

"Did you get it?" Jack asked.

"Not particularly. Yesterday was a long stressful day. I keep this crap up and I'll have white hair by thirty-two."

"Beats no hair, I guess."

"Not really, Jack. Bald is the new sexy," Rose threw in. Both grinned at her. They knew to never try to guess what she would say next because it was generally a surprise.

Rich took a sip of coffee.

"Need a breakfast menu? I suspect you know it by heart," the pretty server asked.

"Just some whole wheat toast, please," Rich responded.

"How about a quick summary?" Jack asked.

Rich gave it to them. He played down his role. Jack had already gotten the full story from Bodeway and shared it with Rose before Rich arrived.

"You might get another Officer of the Year for your actions yesterday," Rose said.

"No, please. Awards for saving people like last time are fine. I don't want any recognition for killing someone, regardless of the circumstances." She nodded affirmatively, as did the sheriff.

"So, our case load just lightened with our two murders and Zack's several solved," Jack said.

"I'm sure something new will pop up," Rose said. "It always does."

"The most pressing thing for the three of us is to hire two new deputies. I have slots for another deputy and another sergeant. I would make the latter a patrol sergeant and free you up for investigations only, but I am not sure we have enough to keep you busy all the time yet, Rich."

"I don't think we do either," Rose added. "Let's hire two deputies and hold the sergeant title of whoever is the strongest over the next year or so," she added. Both men agreed.

"How about Polly Antrim? What's her status getting her degree?" Rose asked.

"Polly…" Jack paused. The young woman was one he had saved from a kidnapper and who, with Tac, had killed the ex-con who had shot Jack at his wedding. She had been madly in love with him since he rescued her. Her last words to him before the wedding had been she was coming back to marry him, his then-fiancé notwithstanding. She was twenty. Fifteen years younger than Jack and ten years younger than Rich.

"She has been doubling up on her classes. She's really smart and driven. She can graduate with a Criminal Justice degree in three more semesters, she tells me in her too-frequent communications." Both the chief deputy and the sergeant knew about her crush on Jack.

"She says she can join now if we sponsor her for the

academy and finish online. She can go back to Texas for the graduation."

"You better grab her before someone else does!" Rose said mischievously.

"Yeah, grab her hard!" Rich added.

"I don't need enemies with friends like you two," the sheriff said.

"Hell, Jack. You are so lucky to have the two of us. We are good cops, good shots and damned good looking!" Rose said.

"Yep. You two are all of that and more."

"What more?" Rich asked.

"I was thinking Rose left out 'wise asses,' but was not going to volunteer it until you pressed me.

"If it was not for the romantic thing, Polly would be a great deputy. She is dead set on wearing a badge. I don't think it's a frivolous fantasy either," he said.

"I don't either, Jack. I interviewed her after you were shot at the wedding and offered her and Zack both some counseling. She answered me the same way your great uncle would have," Rose said.

"I talked with her, too, Jack and got the same feeling. I would endorse her wholeheartedly," Rich said.

"Well, let's let her graduate on a normal schedule and see if her ardor has cooled by then. I have enough on my plate with an upcoming election to avoid unnecessary problems," Jack said pensively, "I don't want Rich's next murder case to be where my wife shot my deputy."

"A scenario sure to spawn another movie made about you, Jack, but one neither of us would want," Rose said.

"Helluva gunfight scene though. I'd put my money on Lily and take odds."

"Can we change the subject?" the sheriff asked. From his tone it was obviously an order couched as a question.

"Do we have anyone in mind for either deputy slot?" Rich asked.

"There's a patrolman with Oklahoma City PD who took me aside last time I delivered a prisoner there," Rose said. "He said he was tired of urban patrol. He's a country boy and wants to come back. He grew up here."

"What's he like?"

"He's real good looking. Did I mention he's my second cousin?" Rose asked.

"No, I don't believe you did. Age?"

"Twenty-eight. Degree in Criminal Justice. I checked him out with some of the folks at OCPD. Everybody seems to think he's pretty good. I played the relative angle. Nobody knew my real motive. Six years on the beat and vying for a sergeant shot. My sources say he will likely get it."

"Go ahead and arrange three interviews with him. I will be last." Jack said.

"Any more, Rose?" Rich asked.

"I have several employment query letters and emails. Why don't I send them to the two of you and let me know if anyone should have an interview set up?" she said.

Both men agreed.

With help from the county commissioner who works most closely with the sheriff's office, Jack began the fundraising and marketing planning for his upcoming election. He had been appointed sheriff after the previous sheriff was killed in a stupid move during a robbery in a crowded branch bank.

While not a political person in the past, the sheriff's winning looks and personality and ability to speak clearly and with credibility on a moment's notice promised he would be a tough competitor.

Nobody from his own office ran against him. A retired trooper from another county campaigned, but ineffectively and had little local knowledge or appeal.

Jack's main campaign event was attended by several hundred voters and media from outside Warrior County.

One of the three Warrior County commissioners introduced Rose Custalow.

Rose, who hated public speaking, welcomed Rich as the master of ceremonies. She then moved to the crowd around Jack behind the microphone and Rich Ammon.

Rich eloquently recounted Jack's history as a Coast Guard coxswain fighting drug smugglers in the Florida Keys, an OSBI agent who solved every case assigned him, a new sheriff who met the serial bank robber who killed Jack's predecessor in a Dodge City-style walk-down. He spoke about Jack rescuing teenaged Polly Antrim from an Armageddon-believing prepper and single handedly decimated a gang of escaped convicts.

Ranger Zack Bodeway, and Jack's legendary uncle eighty-four year old retired ranger Bud Carey stood with Jack, behind Rich as he spoke. With them were Jack's striking wife, Rich's friend, Texas Investigator Isabella Munro, and Polly Antrim.

Rich had included film clips of the feature film made of Jack's tracking of one of the few female serial killers in US history. Rich also included clips from Jack's press conferences at a tornado scene, getting off the helicopter carrying Polly Antrim in his arms, and his interview after taking on the gang of escaped federal convicts. These played on a large rear screen as Rich spoke.

"I have spoken enough about my boss, my friend, the nationally respected Sheriff of Warrior County. It's time for you to hear from the man himself. Ladies and gentlemen, welcome the current and next Sheriff of Warrior County, Jack Landers!"

There was heavy applause and the news video cameras scanned and recorded.

"Thanks, Rich. You all probably already know Rich was Oklahoma Police Officer of the Year last year. He also saved my life several weeks ago in a very tense situation. Please join me in thanking Rich Ammon."

Another round of applause erupted and Rich walked back to the front and the beautiful blonde investigator took his hand and walked out with him possessively. He flashed his superhero cowboy grin, doffed his white hat, and they stepped back behind Jack.

"You heard my wonderful Chief Deputy, Rose Custalow, before Rich. You just saw Rich's friend Wichita County, Texas investigator Isabella Munro. Say hi to my beautiful wife, Dr. Lily Landers, my great uncle retired Texas Ranger Bud Carey and my close friend current Texas Ranger Lieutenant Zack Bodeway. Also greet the kidnap victim, Polly Antrim. My parents could not be here tonight, but these folks on stage with me, along with the whole staff of the Warrior County Sheriff's Office, are my extended family. Each one of them has dedicated his or her life to making the world a better, safer place.

Being your sheriff is the greatest honor I have ever had. I ask you to please vote for me and give me the chance to continue spending every single day with the express purpose of making Warrior County a safe place for you to live, work, raise your families, and worship. Nothing really matters more than those things, does it? Thank you very much."

Over the next month, Jack reprised the campaign rally without Bodeway, Polly, and the county commissioner. The plan had been for Rose and Rich to alternate staying at the office as the senior sheriff's official, but the initial reception Rich received, along with Rose's discomfort at public speaking, made her volunteer to remain behind each time.

On election day, Jack won by a landslide and his senior staff returned to their duties with a renewed vigor.

AFTER THE ELECTION, things calmed down. The months leading up to the election had two murders within several days, so the break in felonies was welcome.

Rose Custalow brought in several candidates, including her cousin who was hired. As an Oklahoma certified police officer, he was able to start once his two week resignation period ended.

Jack brought him in as a deputy with the promise, all things being equal, of promoting him to sergeant within six months.

He, and another new deputy who had been a patrolman with the Norman Police Department, were assigned to Rich as their field training officer or FTO. They rode with him for a week and he assigned them to ride separately with deputies from each patrol district.

They were exposed to traffic accidents, bar brawls, domestic disturbances and traffic stops in their first week away from Rich. In the second week, they rode with him again and discussed each call for service, how they reacted and how they thought they might have performed better.

Rich received a call from the gunsmith in Texas who

was rebuilding his newly acquired old .45 automatic. He took a Friday off and drove down in his personal car.

It had been a long time since he took the Saleen Mustang on a road trip. Both his four hundred horse-power Police Responder pickup truck and the Mustang were powerful, with great handling and fast acceleration. He felt he was blessed, being a car buff.

He called Isabella several days before.

"Hi, it's me," he greeted her.

"Hi, 'me.' How are you?" she said.

"I'm okay. How's the job going? Catch any good cases?"

"Nope. Just a bunch of child abuse cases. They make me so mad, I want to have the perpetrators resist arrest so I can put them on the ground. Painfully," she said.

"I know. I feel the same way. But judges punish, we just investigate and arrest. A hundred and fifty years ago, our predecessors might have done more. We cannot."

"I know. It just gets to me. I wish I had a crime against adults or property."

"I'm sure you will soon enough. On another subject, I am heading to Wichita Falls and over to where my gunsmith is a few miles away on Friday. Plans for dinner?" he asked.

"Not currently. Depends on what the phone or radio says. Let's plan on it and play it by ear. Either way, stay at my place. Soon to be our place. Myra is selling her family home and investing the proceeds. Since our parent's home is large, we are going to share it."

"Hmm. Could make overnighters awkward," Rich said.

"Not really. We'll take bedrooms on each end of the hall. You remember the house. It's mega large."

"Whatever you say."

"You sound like a placating husband."

"My mistake. I'd never intentionally want to sound like a placating anything. Especially a husband."

"My turn to say 'hmm.' What time will I see you?"

"Anytime you want after about two. I am going to arrive at Smith's at one and he wants me to shoot the .45. He says he can tune it up after watching me shoot. You know, change the sights if necessary. Heavier or lighter springs. Buff a little off the grips if he thinks I am unconsciously holding it a bit to one side."

"Can't do those things with my issue Glock. Change the springs, but it would be against regulations."

"The majority of police agencies in the world carry stock Glocks. I love the dependability but I tend to shoot them low. I don't care for the grip angle."

"Well, Sergeant Ammon. It sounds like we should have a shoot off one day. One with a bit of money riding on it."

"Deal!"

"It wouldn't make your testosterone level drop if I outshot you?" she asked.

"Not in the least Investigator Munro. It would just make me more comfortable with you on my arm."

"How about prone?"

"Shooting prone?" he asked.

"Not necessarily. You work it out and I'll test you on the answer around six on Friday."

"See you then."

She hung up. Rich asked himself aloud, "What am I going to do about Isabella?" Then he realized he asked himself the same question virtually every time he spoke with her and never seemed to come up with an answer. It perplexed him a great deal.

ON FRIDAY, Rich fired up the Saleen for the first time in a while. He headed east, then south on I-44 towards Wichita Falls, Texas.

Just before the bridge over the Red River, he looked to his left. The tire furrows were still in the grass, though not very clear. Bodeway had pushed the stolen county truck off the road here.

Just beyond was the small rise where he had hit the truck broadside and rolled it over, initiating his own airbags.

Between the two vehicles was the spot. The place Rich had shot Bertie Ingles between the eyes from over a hundred yards.

Rich shook his head to make the memory disappear. The kills in Afghanistan and other places in the rangers had not affected him. Probably. Maybe. The ones at home had and he needed to deal with it. His own way. No shrinks.

He crossed into Texas and drove east from the city, then south again. He arrived at the gunsmith's on time.

The gun was perfect. It looked like what it was. A Colt 1911 older than him. Older than his father. The bluing was pretty much gone. The sights were new. The tip of the barrel and the part showing through the ejection port were shiny and new. The mag in the butt was new. The shiny blue of the sights and barrel were the giveaways. The real giveaway would be the way the action felt when he racked it. When he fired it.

Smith watched his customer appreciate what would be his last custom .45. He was in his eighties. A contemporary of Bud Carey. A shooting mentor for Zack Bodeway.

"You ought to walk around back and try her out," he told the young deputy.

Rich nodded and went to the Mustang and got out a box of target hardball and a box of Gold Dot hollow points.

He loaded a magazine with each and rang the swinging steel as fast as anyone Smith had ever heard. This one was going to be hell on wheels with his masterpiece.

"Guess I don't have to fine tune anything," Smith said rhetorically.

"No, I don't think so. I think she's perfect as is."

Rich got an El Paso holster out of the Mustang and replaced the Sig on his belt with the Colt. He put double mags in the mag holster.

Smith had cleaning gear on the table and Rich quickly field stripped and cleaned the Colt. He reassembled it while talking to the gunsmith and looking him in the eye. Not at the gun he was putting back together. He loaded fresh Gold Dot ammo into the gun and two extra mags. He replaced the gun and magazines on his belt and thanked and paid the gunsmith the remaining balance.

"It's absolutely perfect. I cannot imagine any pistol being smoother than this one. Thank you so much!"

The old man nodded and proffered his hand. Another generation of lawman would go forth with a Smith masterpiece .45.

"Wear it in safety and good health young man. It will never fail you if you do your part."

Rich got back into the Saleen Mustang and called Isabella on the way back to Wichita Falls.

"Want me to come to your office? Or to the house? I am about ten minutes out from downtown now."

"I am stuck here for a little while, so come to the

office. Park in the police lot. Your truck certainly looks like a police vehicle to all of us," she said.

"I will, but I'm in my personal vehicle. I have a wind-shield placard I can use though."

He pulled into the police lot at the county sheriff's office later. He set a 4" x 9" laminated sign in the wind-shield. It said "Sheriff Official Business."

Rich walked to the reception and identified himself. The deputy was waiting for him and directed him back to the investigative bull pen and Isabella's cubicle.

"Pretty luxurious, huh?" she asked.

"Yep. Just like mine."

"Have a seat. Or, get a cup of coffee behind you. There's a Keurig and a selection of flavors."

"You want one?" he asked. She shook her head.

He made a cup of Columbian and returned to his chair.

"Happy with your new old gun?" she asked.

"Sure am. You will like it, too."

"Same man who worked over Bodeway's and Uncle Bud's?"

"The same. He says this is his last. But, I bet he'd make one for you."

"Well, there is a precedent for a 1911 here where I work. Someone at a very senior position…"

"Where do you want to eat tonight?"

"I am so tired I could do with take-out and an early night."

"We can get take-out. How about the rough looking barbecue we met at once before?"

"Perfect. I have to finish some paperwork. If you want to get some food and take it back, Myra is already home. Of course. She doesn't work. She's a thirty-eight year old retiree."

"What would she like?"

"She and I are easy. Whatever you want, multiply it by three. I'll let her know you will be there in a half hour or so."

"Isabella?"

"Yes, Rich."

"How safe will I be with her?"

"You are armed and trained. I suspect she could not molest you unless you let her. And, I doubt you would. Because I am armed and trained, too."

"Right. See you whenever." He slurped down his coffee and left the building.

He bought a pound of pulled pork barbecue, a pint of Cole slaw, and a pint of baked beans. He added cornbread and a half pie to the order, paid and left.

Myra, who looked more like Isabella's twin sister than one who was eight years older, met him at the door with her normal big hug. He avoided the kiss on the lips without offending. He quickly kissed her beside the mouth like he accidentally missed. She was an active participant in the lifestyle. Something formerly referred to as being a swinger.

"That smells delicious!" she said as she took the bags of food from him.

"It should. I slaved over the smoker and stove all day. Crime in Warrior County went over the top without me on patrol," he told her with a serious look. She caught him off guard with a direct lip kiss this time.

"Damn! My timing is off," he thought. "Am I going to have to add 'what am I going to do about Myra Strauss after every meeting like I do her sister?"

"You go get comfortable and I'll set the table with this and reheat anything needing it."

"Thanks, I will. I am so glad the Boss won and the

politicking is over! I gave more and longer speeches than he did," he said.

"You will be sheriff before you know it and will have to be giving your own speeches in four years. I know these things. I have second sight, you know," Myra said.

"No, I didn't know. How long have you been clairvoyant?" he asked.

"All of my life. Luckily for her, Bella did not get it. Our mother was born in Italy. But, she was really a Romany."

"A Gypsie? Your mother?"

"Yes! I had an eerie feeling foretelling our parents death and my Bill's. I knew both would be violent even."

"Pretty spooky, Myra. Did you tell Isabella?"

"No. She's the uptight one. About my sexual proclivities, my second sight. A lot of things. I'm the fun one, she's the straight up and down cop!

"If you had met me first and not while investigating my husband's murder, you'd have never taken a second look at her!"

"Indeed," he said knowing word meanings like beauty can be in the mind of the beholder. Or, listener.

"How about a glass of wine?" she asked.

"Maybe a half glass. I may get a call in the middle of the night and have to run back to Oklahoma at a zillion miles an hour," he admitted seriously.

"A zillion miles an hour. Pretty darn fast. What's it like?" she teased.

"It makes your eyelids flutter and your cheeks flap."

She walked over to him and jutted a hip out, slapping herself hard on the left butt cheek.

"Not these babies! Peloton keeps them nice and firm."

He had already used 'indeed,' and was at a temporary loss for a response, so he went with an appreciative

'Umm.' It seemed to satisfy Myra and she walked back to the kitchen table like a Vegas showgirl, one foot in front of the other, sans the five foot feathers on her head.

They heard the door and Isabella called before coming deeper into the house. *What prompted the warning?* Rich wondered. These two scared him, but not in an unpleasant sort of way.

"We're in here," Myra called out. Isabella walked in and unclipped her holster and badge from her belt. She put her running shoe on the chair and pulled up her left pant leg and released the Velcro holding her ankle holster. Rich recognized her late father's Colt Cobra snub nose .38 in it.

Yep. Don't tick this one off, he thought.

"Dinner smells great! Like the barbecue at Jack's ranch."

"It does, baby sister! All we need is an outdoor shower and a small herd of buffalo," Myra retorted.

"You could probably get by with the shower, given the large fenced yard" Rich said, "but, I doubt the herd of buffalo would fly in this neighborhood."

The Western dinner was as good as everyone expected. They chatted and retired to the library which served as their den.

Within an hour, Isabella was curled up asleep on one of the leather sofas. Myra bid Rich good night and retired.

She returned with a throw and covered her sister, now deeply asleep and padded off.

Rich was a bit unsure whether to find a bedroom, which was not a problem in this large house, or to leave and go to a hotel. He decided to save the money and walked upstairs carrying his boots.

He knew which bedroom was Isabella's from his one

past stay. He heard a shower running from through the door of another. Using his keen detective skills, or so he told himself, he deducted it was Myra's room. He opened the door of one. It was obviously the master. Their late parent's room. He quietly closed it and found another room and chose it.

Rich put the .45 and his tactical flashlight on the bedside table and his clothes and Kevlar vest on a chair and climbed into bed. He wondered it Isabella would seek him out in this dark room.

He was almost asleep when he saw a splinter of light widen in his door. He saw a tall blonde, the light shining through a sheer nightie, enter and approach the bed.

Rich decided to pretend to sleep for a second. The woman approached him. He smelled shampoo and soap. She smelled really good. She was also most certainly Myra.

She leaned over and kissed him on the cheek, turned and went out, closing the door behind her.

Close call!

Damn, she smelled good, he thought as he tried to fall asleep. It was a long time coming. Isabella apparently slept on the sofa.

Rich woke up Saturday morning at his usual five AM. He dressed without showering. He would clean up at home.

He hoped the alarm was not set, since he did not know the code. It was not on, so he quietly slipped out the door and hoped the raucous exhaust of his muscle car would not awaken the sisters.

The visit had been nothing more than a pleasant dinner together. It was okay. It was far from what he expected. It was also probably a blessing in disguise.

Particularly since the sister had not acted on her strong libido and crawled in beside him.

The morning was cool and his jacket covered the gunbelt and badge. He was just a cowboy in a white hat as far as the world knew.

Rich found an open restaurant on the edge of town and pulled into the lot.

Seated, he immediately ordered coffee and looked at the menu.

Myra might be an acceptable eight years older than he. The cute waitress flirting with the young cowboy however, was an unacceptable eighteen or so.

He ordered a Western omelet with hash browns and biscuits. He was on the Interstate heading to Warrior County thirty minutes later.

CHAPTER TWO

OVER HIS COUNTY LINE, but with no police radio, he saw one of his deputies in his Charger running Code-3. Weekend or not, the sergeant knew he should backup his deputy. He pulled in behind the Charger and accelerated to within a hundred yards and maintained the distance.

He saw Bob look in the rear view mirror and wave, recognizing Rich's car. His POV, or personally owned vehicle, was known and admired by the members of the sheriff's office.

They were going to add two more deputies in addition to the two new ones. But for now the rural county had little backup outside the nearest OHP trooper, so Bob was glad to have Rich behind him.

Bob was pushing hard for a two-lane county road. Rich looked down for a second and saw 105 on the Mustang's speedometer. He turned on his full headlights and emergency flashers as he followed at the hundred yard distance. Rich wished he had a blue dash or sun visor LED for the car.

Bob doused the siren, indicating to Rich they were

near the call for service location. He saw the Charger's brake lights and applied his own brakes maintaining a safe distance.

They pulled into the yard of a mobile home. It was fully involved in flames. Both bailed and Bob got a fire extinguisher from his trunk.

"Fire truck is on the way!" Bob yelled as he approached the house. The front door was locked. Rich kicked it. It buckled some on the first kick and flew open on the second. Both entered, Bob spraying a path, sweeping the spray ahead of them.

There was an older man slumped in a chair. The fire seemed to be at the stove, which had a coffee pot on it. Bob tried to extinguish it to no avail as Rich picked up the man and carried him towards the door.

"Come on, Bob! The fire is getting ahead of us! No need to die in here. We have the likely victim. Just look in the bedroom and make sure he doesn't have a wife or pet."

Bob kicked the bedroom and bathroom doors open. They were the only other ones in the trailer.

"Nobody here, Rich!"

"Good! Now let's get the hell outta here!"

Both made it outside, Rich carrying the man. Unfortunately, he was not a skinny octogenarian, but one who had not passed up desert in a long time.

Rich staggered with him to behind the Mustang and set him on the ground. He had a pulse but it was extremely weak. He looked a bit blue under the soot on his face, so Rich commenced CPR.

They could hear the fire truck in the distance, its tinny siren and occasional air horn sounding.

The salaried deputy chief and one salaried firefighter arrived. Volunteers would be on the way. The latter handed Rich an oxygen apparatus. The deputy chief had already run the hose to the trailer and looked back.

As Rich and Bob gave the man oxygen, the firefighter turned the truck's pump on full and joined the deputy chief holding the hose and laying a heavy stream of water from the pumper truck on the roof of the trailer.

The trailer was fully involved with fire and they turned the stream on surrounding land to prevent the fire from spreading. The trailer was too far gone to continue wetting down.

The rescue squad arrived and took over the resuscitation efforts. They maintained the faint pulse but nothing more and transported the man to the hospital. Despite the fast response and on-scene efforts, he died at the hospital. The smoke inhalation before the two deputies arrived had been too much. While the firefighters were still watering the surrounding area, Bob got a radio call saying to secure the area for one of the deputy state fire marshals since a death had occurred. He and Rich ran yellow tape around the trailer once there were no flames anywhere. They did not secure until almost noon.

Jack came by and surveyed the scene.

"You two did as much as was humanly possible," he said. "Head home and drop your uniforms off at the cleaners later. Be sure to expense it to the office."

Both smelled like they had spent the night in a smoke house and Bob took his advice.

The four first responders left knowing they had done their jobs but felt hollow. They simply had not been there fast enough to save a life.

Rich found a voicemail from Isabella questioning why he had left without a word. He called her and got her voicemail.

"Hi. You and Myra both went to sleep. I slept a bit and decided to not awaken you. I've been at a fire scene where another deputy and I tried unsuccessfully to resuscitate the elderly victim. Not a good night or day so far, generally speaking. Catch you later." He left off the "or not," he was thinking as he spoke the final words of his message.

The phone rang as he was out of the shower and shaving. It was the sheriff.

"Rich, head back over to the burnt trailer and meet the fire investigator. He has declared it a homicide based on accelerants at the location where the fire started. Also, the hospital said there were suspicious wounds in the back of the victim's head. Sounds like he sustained a heavy blow there causing blunt force trauma."

"There was no, blood on his head, Jack. I would have gotten it on me from carrying him," Rich said.

"I'm only sharing what I know. Head over and open a homicide investigation. The fire inspector already asked for criminalists from the OSBI to respond. I have the weekend dispatcher working on next of kin. You and I just need to be careful when we get the information and make the requisite notifications. We may be notifying our principal suspect."

"I'll text or bring the information to you at the scene," Jack said and hung up.

A third homicide in our big rural county in a matter of month. This could almost be construed to be a crime wave, Rich thought as he strapped on and grabbed his hat.

When Rich arrived at the scene of the morning fire, the fire investigator was still there. He was in his truck writing a report on his laptop.

"Hi, I'm Rich Ammon, investigator for Warrior County."

"Hey, Brad Crenshaw. I'm a state fire marshal agent."

"Nice to meet you, Brad. Can you give me a quick summary of your findings?"

"The first thing ties in, but it's not one of my findings. The doctor who tried to resuscitate him after you did found he had been hit in the head. The skin was not broken, but at the very least he was knocked unconscious. I understand you did not notice any blood when you carried him out?"

"Correct."

"I found traces of accelerant near where the fire started. Which was the stove. It was made to look like a senior citizen forgot and left the stove on when he made coffee. Not the case. The stove was on. It was a gas stove with a flame. A bottle with gasoline was placed on it and when it heated enough to break, the gasoline hit the fire and 'poof!' Off it went. I believe the murderer moved the body to the side chair by dragging him unconscious over there."

"I see the criminalists are inside. Any chance of them finding prints after the place was pretty well scorched?" Rich asked.

"It would be a long shot. A real long one. The aluminum shed out back had the door ajar. I looked in there without touching anything. There was a lawn mower, but no gas can. I have to assume whoever did this did not come prepared and took the gas can from the shed and used the gas as an accelerant. They must have taken it with them. It does not appear to be around here."

"Brad, did you instruct the criminalists to look for prints on or around the shed?"

"No, I was waiting for you to handle the shed part while I was thinking about writing my report. Thank heavens I don't have to write homicide reports very often."

"Okay. I'll tell them then ride up and down the road for a while and see if I can find an empty gas can which was maybe thrown out of a vehicle."

"Good idea. Here's my card in case I'm gone. Give me one of yours so I can send you the report, okay?"

They exchanged, Rich spoke with the criminalists about the shed and started driving. He met Jack in his first half mile and they stopped.

"I'm running down the road to look for a discarded gas can, hopefully with prints on it. I'm going to follow this to the next intersection," Rich told him.

"How 'bout I do the same the other way?" Jack asked. Rich nodded and they both drove off, much slower than they usually transited rural roads.

About the time Rich reached the intersection and was ready to turn around, Jack called him on the truck radio.

"Warrior-1 to Investigator-1?"

"Investigator-1. Go."

"I have a discarded old gas can somebody threw twenty feet into the brush about a mile from the fire scene. I have not taken the cap off to protect prints, but if the small amount of gas in it is still fresh, it may be the one."

"Roger that. I'm done this way. I'll meet you back at the scene. Investigator-1 out."

They met at the scene and Jack had already bagged the gas can for the criminalists.

"Okay, Rich. We have a start. With some luck we'll get prints and maybe have a suspect."

"With luck! I am going to have Tac do some research on the property. Once he gets a description for the tax collector, I am going to go over there and research a couple things. Does the land itself have much value? How much? Has anybody else inquired about it? Are there oil or gas rights? What do they add to the value?

"Then, I will start on the victimology. Who was this guy? What do his neighbors say? Who is his doctor? Does he have a will filed in the county? Who is the beneficiary?

"But first, I am going to reprise our gas can efforts and look for a murder weapon. I wish I had the ME's opinion on what it was. A tire iron? Hammer? A club? But since I don't have the info at hand, I am going to give it a best efforts search."

"Good plan. If I think of anything else later, I will call you," Jack said. Before leaving, he walked over and paid his respects to the fire inspector, a man he had never met.

Rich drove to the western intersection, slowly scanning the right side of the road. When the road was built, trees were cleared about fifty feet on either side. Rich figured an escaping murderer who had thrown the gas can out going in that direction would not stop and he or she had thrown it through a car or truck window. Which is why Jack had found it relatively close to the road. The murderer might have been able to throw a club or hammer or other blunt object a bit farther, so he pulled the truck off onto the red clay mud and grass, engaged four wheel high and slowly drove twenty feet off the road, then paralleled it. He drove to the approximate location where the gas can was found and focused. He would have thought the person would have gotten rid of the murder weapon first, but it did not appear so. He searched for several miles with no success.

Rich stopped off road and called Tac on the radio.

"Investigator-1 to Radio."

"Go ahead Rich."

"Anything from the property tax folks about the identity of his ID's?"

"Roger. I have a name and the property number. Are you heading back to the office?"

"Roger. Hold the information. I'll be back there in ten minutes."

Now his truck looked like an Oklahoma ranch truck. Covered with red clay mud.

He parked at the office and went in.

"What do you have, Tac?" he asked. Tac spun the black wheelchair around and grinned his million dollar grin.

There were civilians in the office, so he shared his legal pad notes with Rich.

"Thanks, buddy. Great job," he said as he perused the page quickly. It had all he needed to know to get started.

He went to his cubicle and sat down after getting a mug of coffee. Law enforcement and the military ran on coffee in his experience. Actually, so did his college, rushing through a Criminal Justice degree in three years.

Tac had done the research and accompanying notes on his computer, so Rich punched two holes along the top edge and got out a hard cardboard case file. Since they reused the case folders, he put a peel-off label on it and "Cliff Bronson, Age 71, Homicide trailer fire" and the date.

Rich put the printout of Bronson's driver's license and a number of photos he took of the scene in a sleeve he inserted.

"I'll be at the courthouse," he said as he walked out the front door.

The first trip was to the Property Appraiser's Office. He learned Bronson's property was a quarter section of one hundred sixty acres. The updated appraisal was awaiting results of some natural gas exploration by a company active in the county. His next step was to go to their offices which were down the street.

He apprised them what had happened and asked about the status of the explorations. In return, they wanted to know who the beneficiaries were. Bronson had signed a contract to allow exploration for gas fracking, or the use of high pressure hydraulics to reach gas so it could be piped up. Fracking rules had tightened with an increase in earthquakes in the state which may have been related. The engineer Rich spoke with said the quarter section could possibly yield over a million dollars to the owner if all went as expected.

He and the manager showed Rich a plat with the fracking plan for Bronson's property and gave him a copy.

The company wanted to know if the sergeant knew who would ultimately own the land. They told him they had already paid Bronson thousands of dollars for the right to explore and sink some holes on his land. They had already drafted an agreement but had not presented it to Bronson for his signature yet.

Rich told them he did not know, but the identity of heirs was his greatest quest at this time. He offered them a deal.

"If I find out who the beneficiary is, or are if there are more than one, I will let you know. If someone presents themselves to you first, you let me know. Okay?

"In a majority of the times a murder occurs, the closest of kin either did it or knows important facts about it. At least one of the these is present in most murders: motive, opportunity, or means. I always thought motive was the most significant of the three. Several million dollars of gas money is a really significant motive, gentlemen. If the heir or heirs present themselves here, let me know right away. I don't know who killed Cliff Bronson. All of us here know who stood the most to gain—the most motivation—from his death. It is imperative I talk with them right away!"

He went to the County Clerk's office to see if a will or trust had been filed there in Bronson's name. None had been filed with the court, though not filing did not automatically render a will null and void.

His next stop was each of the two bank branches in town. He knew both local managers.

Bronson, he found, had not banked at the first.

He hit pay dirt at the second. Bronson had a checking and savings accounts there as well as a safe deposit box.

"I'm sorry, Rich. I cannot give you any more information than I already have without a warrant or a subpoena if it came to court," the manager, Gwen O'Keefe said.

"Gwen, this is a murder case. Doesn't the fact your customer is dead alter your duty to hold his information?"

"Nope."

"May as well put together a summary and get ready to drill a safe deposit box. I will be back."

He walked out and went straight to the Clerk's office.

"Do you have a magistrate or judge in? I need a warrant in a murder trial," he said.

The clerk made a few calls and directed Rich to the chambers of the senior judge resident in the county.

He explained his case and the judge agreed, signing him search warrants for the bank.

The bank had already closed by the time he walked back, warrants in hand.

There were several lawyers in town, but only one

advertised as specializing in wills and trust. It was none other than Jack's neighbor's partner, Cindy Bouvier.

"Hi, is Cindy in?" he asked her receptionist or paralegal. He doubted she had both at this juncture in her local practice.

"Who's calling, officer? I will check to see if she can see you." He identified himself and she called.

Cindy, a beautiful blonde in her thirties, immediately walked out and embraced him.

"Liza, did you formally meet Rich Ammon? You need to know him. He'll be sheriff one day. He's currently the most eligible bachelor in Warrior County. If I didn't have Julie, I'd be chasing after him myself."

Her admission seemed sincere and surprised both of the listeners. Since he did not know what to say, Rich flashed both his very best superhero grin to date.

"See what I mean?" she said to Liza and took Rich by the arm and led him into her office.

"How's the gorgeous Isabella?" she asked.

"Okay, I guess. We are at a relationship standpoint right now. She is starting a new job and I am trying to figure whether I want to get stuck between her and her oversexed sister."

"The sister is not chopped liver. I noted it right away at Jack's barbecue. Is she after you?"

"I think so. May we shift to business for a moment? I have a bit of a murder case."

"Hell! You just solved two in the county."

"Number three looked like it was going to be simple bad wiring. Now it is surely a homicide."

"Do tell!" she said.

"I understand Cliff Bronson is one of your clients."

"Yes. I read he died in a fire at his single wide. He is

my shortest tenure client. I only met him two weeks ago."

"I sure hope it was for you to write a will or trust," Rich said. "He was murdered then the single wide set afire. I need to know the beneficiaries. One of them could be my murderer."

"When I found out about the fracking deal, I insisted he do a revocable trust and a pour-over will. I have both final copies right here as yet unfiled."

"I will need copies. Do they have the beneficiaries" names and addresses?"

She pulled through several legal folders on her desk and found the one with Bronson on the tab.

Opening it, she said "Yes! Mr. Bronson's next of kin is a niece who gets ninety percent of his estate and a third cousin who gets ten percent. The niece lives in Oklahoma City. The third cousin lives in West Virginia."

"Cindy have you reached out to them or vice versa?"

"No, I just figured it out."

"Let us do it as law enforcement first. It's not only a notification of death, but of opening a homicide case," Rich said.

"I am primarily a trust and real estate attorney, though I used to do divorces. Which is how I met Julie. I was her divorce attorney. So, I am not up on this criminal stuff. What's the chance of one of them being the murderer?" Cindy asked.

"When you consider the gas fracking contract on his property could be worth millions, both have sufficient motives to kill Bronson. The cousin would also have to kill the niece to get a worthwhile piece of it. Whether they did is the question. I hate to give you and the gas exploration company the wrong idea. Both may be as pure as spring rain. Or, not. I need to find out which very quickly.

"Is your intent to call them both in for a reading of the will?" Rich asked.

"With only two people, it's not totally necessary. But I can if it would help."

"It might. How about if I tell them in the notification process about a will being in existence and you being the attorney who will be contacting them?"

"Good idea. Will you be present at the will reading, I hope?" she asked.

"It might be prudent."

"If not, I have a Walther PPK in my desk drawer and an Oklahoma concealed license for it."

"Also prudent. I have shot enough people recently."

"Indeed. But they all needed to be shot."

"True."

"Let me know after you talk with them."

"I surely will. Thanks, Cindy. Oh—may I have a copy of the will to put in my case file? I promise I won't spill the beans to either beneficiary."

"Hmm. Not usual, but I don't see what it would hurt, being a murder case and all." She made him a copy for his growing file. He noted she included contact information for both.

"What's next for you?" she asked.

"I have to serve a search warrant on the bank tomorrow to get Bronson's financial information and to drill his safe deposit box."

"If I bring the key to the box, may I be present as the decedent's attorney?"

"The key would save the estate several hundred dollars and me a lot of time waiting for a locksmith, so sure."

"Which bank and when?" she asked.

He told her the branch and the time.

"Thanks for everything, Cindy. I'll see you at nine tomorrow."

He doffed his white hat at the person he determined to be a paralegal on the way out and got an interesting smile. One he may have to investigate further.

———

AT SIX CENTRAL TIME, he called Shawna Bronson, the niece.

"Ms. Bronson? This is Sergeant Rich Ammon with the Warrior County, Oklahoma Sheriff's Office."

"Warrior County? Where my uncle lives?" she asked.

"Yes. It is your uncle I am calling about. I am afraid I have bad news."

"Did something happen to Uncle Cliff?"

"Yes, Ma'am. There was a fire in his single wide. He was taken out alive and given CPR on site and on the way to the hospital. I am sorry to tell you, he passed away at the hospital. This occurred yesterday. It took us a while to find out his identity and his next of kin."

"Omigod! Did he suffer?"

"No. I am afraid he had received a heavy blow to the back of his head and was unconscious when the fire was set. It was a homicide, Ms. Bronson."

"Somebody killed Uncle Cliff? He never hurt a soul in his life. He was an introvert, didn't go out, go to church. Anything. Who would do such a thing?" she asked incredulously.

"I don't know. But I am going to find out.

"There is a will. His attorney will be contacting you. Do you have something to write with and on?"

She did and he gave her Cindy's name and number so she could recognize it when it came up in the caller ID.

"When you get over here—or I can come there—I have some basic questions for you. Things like the last time you saw your uncle. His state of mind, et. Cetera."

"Sure. Is his attorney in McKenzie where he lives? I guess lived?"

"Yes, she is. Do you know an Eddie Buchanan? He is a cousin of your uncle's and the only other next of kin I can find."

"He's the only other one, I am afraid."

"Afraid?" Rich asked.

"He's from the trash side of the family, Sergeant. Drugs, alcohol, in and out of jail for a variety of offenses."

"I see. Any prison time?"

"You mean over a year? Yeah. A couple of times."

"What type offenses?"

"Trying to con people. Some drug dealing. And one attempted murder."

"Pretty serious stuff. All in West Virginia?"

"I think so."

"If there's a will reading, he will be invited since he is one of the two next of kin's. How do you feel about him being there?" Rich asked, learning a bit about the person he was getting ready to call."

"He scares me. The way he looks at me. He undresses me with his eyes. He's a damn creep! Will you be there?"

"I can be," he said not offering he already planned to be.

"I hope so. I will ask the lawyer to invite you."

"I will see you then, I am sorry for your loss."

His next call would be interesting, he thought. Assuming he even reached Buchanan.

He dialed and a man answered. It did not stretch his deductive abilities to figure out immediately he was drunk.

"Hey, is Eddie there?" Rich asked.

"Naw, who's this?"

"This is Rich. I need to talk to Eddie real bad. When will he get back?"

"I dunno. He's in Oklahoma or somewhere."

"Yeah? I'm in Oklahoma. He didn't let me know he was coming."

"Why you need Eddie?"

"I got bad news, man!"

"What is it? I'll tell him if he calls me. He might, you know."

"His cousin Cliff died in a trailer fire. Yesterday. It was awful."

"Damn. Well, I'll tell him if he calls." There was a click on the line and the drunk was gone.

So. The ex-con cousin of the victim was here in Oklahoma. Very interesting. He just rocketed up the short list of suspects. To the very top.

Rich would update the sheriff and chief deputy tomorrow after the visit to the bank and he could report on the balances, possible indebtedness and the contents of the safe deposit box.

Sometimes, murder investigations were boring as hell, he thought.

He dressed down and got on the Peloton and got in a heavy workout.

His phone rang at eleven. It had to be Isabella or the office. He really did not want to talk with either. If the latter, he'd have to rush off somewhere.

It was not. It was Shawna Bronson.

"Sergeant, it's Shawna Bronson. I'm sorry for calling you so late, but my scuzzy relative called me.

You'll never guess where he is!"

"Oh, Oklahoma maybe?" he said.

"Yes! He's at an Indian casino hotel somewhere. He called me on a funny area code. It may be a cheap cell phone from Walmart or somewhere. Said a friend of his just talked to a guy he didn't recognize and told him Uncle Cliff had died in a trailer fire."

"So! My message got through the guy's drunken haze," Rich said.

"It was you? The guy did not identify himself as a policeman. Eddie's friend thought it was somebody Eddie knew.

"Good. Sometimes one can learn more when he pretends to be someone like the person on the other end of the line."

"I told Eddie the lawyer was going to call me and I'd call him with the time and location on the number he used from the casino. He said fine, he'd keep it on and with him."

"Shawna, handle it just like you told him. But, please give me his new cellular number."

She did and he wrote it in the file. The first thing in the morning, he would have Tac run a full police report on Eddie Buchanan.

He hit the sack again, and to his relief, nobody called him during the night.

———

HE WENT in early and by eight-thirty had a full federal run on Cliff Buchanan. The guy was a low end lifer. He never seemed to do anything well, even crime. He always got caught early on. Rich read a meanness into what he saw. Buchanan could be dangerous if backed into a corner. He had tried to kill someone once before, but had not done a very good job at it. He also resisted arrest with violence on the West Virginia troopers who came to arrest him. He did not resist very effectively and arrived at jail with a broken nose and dislocated shoulder he deserved.

He walked over to the bank at eight-forty-five and saw Cindy arrive. It was Cindy's first time in this bank as she dealt with the other one in town. They went in together and he introduced her to the manager and presented the search warrant for the safe deposit box. The three went into the vault and opened the box with Cindy's key and the override bank key.

The box had a couple of insurance policies made out to Shawna, his trust and will, and a few gold Kruger-rands. There were also a couple old photos of himself and a brother, who was probably Shawna's father.

Cindy and Rich both photographed the contents with their smart phones and returned the locked box until Shawna and Eddie's arrival.

"I missed breakfast. I'll buy if you will go," he said to Cindy who agreed.

They sat and got Rich's automatic coffee as Cindy read the menu. Rich could have recited it to her but spared her.

"So. What's your story Rich? I know you dated Lily's nurse Eleanor. She departed. Now you date one or both of the gorgeous Texas sisters. I don't know anything more about you beyond your growing reputation as a top cop."

"Ha. I can fill in the rest in a couple of sentences. I've been an Army Ranger all over the place, got out and let the government pay for a Criminal Justice degree and became a deputy sheriff right here in good old Warrior County. End of story."

"I rather think it's the beginning of the story," Cindy said.

"Myra Strauss thinks I have a rapid and ascending career here. Says she has second sight. I don't put much credence on spooky powers, Cindy. Other than the horrible desk job of chief deputy, where can I go? Jack is only five years older than me. He loves his ranch. His wife has a great, and I am sure very profitable, medical practice."

"Do you know about his legacy to return to the Cinco Peso Ranch in Texas and run it one day? It's been in his family for five or so generations. He is the sole heir."

"I heard a bit about it. He's pretty close-mouthed. I suspect it's worth a lot," Rich said.

"It is really large. It was a land grant his three or four times great grandfather bought from the original Spaniard for an unknown number of buckets of gold cinco peso coins. They fought Indians, Yankees, outlaws and speculators to keep it intact. Jack would never walk away from it. Shortly after Jack's mom married his dad and Uncle Bud had time to develop a trust for his dad, Bud gave it to her. Clear deed."

"Interesting. How'd you learn all of this?"

"Jack is private. Julie and I are kind of like his aunts. Julie met him the day he moved into Doolin's Cave Ranch. He had a crush on her. Then, he saw me and his ardor cooled and he adopted us and was our protector, too."

"What did Julie think of the amorous part?" Rich asked with hesitation.

"She loved it. What woman wouldn't? She's only

seven years older than him. I am the same age as Jack. We initially moved in as roomies. Both of us still like men just fine."

"We knocked out Jack's and my stories. What's yours?" Rich asked.

"I grew up in south central Texas on a small ranch. After high school I went to the University of Texas and on to their law school. I met a fellow student and we fell in love. We married after we graduated and became members of the bar. His practice became his life.

I wanted his world to revolve around me, but saw it never would. So, I divorced him and became a divorce lawyer. I met a woman who had the same problem with her rich physician husband. I got her a dream settlement. We became friends and moved in for a bunch of reasons more housekeeping than romantic. Her husband's brother had perpetually stalked her and she wanted to be out of his reach.

He was batshit crazy and became a rustler. He stole some of Julie's Morgan horses and killed a young rancher while stealing his remuda. After the brother kidnapped a couple women, Jack solved the case. The man ran for Texas. A stupid thing for a horse thief to do!"

"And Zack Bodeway killed him at a roadblock," Rich finished.

"I see you know the case."

"Somewhat. I was a patrol deputy with his own district to worry about, but one of the horse thefts was in my district. This is the first I knew he was related in any way to Julie other than stealing her Morgans. Jack held it close to the vest apparently. The current chief deputy might have known. She organized the horse trailers to transport the horses back to Julie."

"Julie is still very guilt ridden about someone related to her past causing so much pain to innocent people. She still is not comfortable talking about it."

"I can understand it. Jack was looking out for her when he kept a lid on it. I'd like to think I would have done the same thing."

"I'm sure you would have Rich. Julie and I had quite an enjoyable talk about you. You and your two knockout dates at the barbecue. We figured out the sisters."

"You have done far better than I. I have not been able to figure them out together or separately."

"Want some help?" she asked.

"Lord, yes!"

"Let me start with what we concluded about the wild aspect. Isabella can be wild if she lets herself. Myra can be less wild if she lets herself."

"Pretty thought provoking wording. I cannot argue with it. What else do you have?"

"They are seriously competitive when it comes to you. I could see them fist fighting over you."

"Isabella would win. She's trained in taking people down."

"I disagree. So does Julie. We believe Myra would win."

"Why?"

"She's an alpha predator. Isabella is more normal. Myra does not live by rules."

"Interesting. Rules lose fights alright. Which is why in special ops we were trained in Krav Maga and bar or street fighting. No rules. The organized martial arts have rules. Rules get you killed instead of the other guy."

"You see, Rich, you are an alpha predator, too. I had no idea you were a ranger. Were you ever a sniper? An exfiltration expert? A LRRP?"

"I was all of those. Cindy, where on earth did you learn those terms. Not practicing trust or real estate law. Not even carnivore divorce law," he said.

"I dated a SEAL before moving in with Julie."

"What team?"

"Three, I believe."

"He would have been the same tier operator I was. Tier 2. The old SEAL team six, has another name now. They, another Army organization and, of all things, an Air Force group are the only US Tier 1 operators."

"Air Force? Really?" she asked with some surprise.

"Yep. And they are some pretty tough motor scooters."

"Motor scooters?"

"It's a polite substitution for a term which is not polite."

"Oh. See? We have both learned some things today," she said.

"On a more business subject, any idea of when you might have the will reading?" Rich asked.

"If the Buchanan person is in-state now and the niece just lives within an hour, we might want to try for Wednesday. That gives us a few days. Maybe at ten in the morning?" she asked.

"I'll make note of it. If I get enough on Eddie Buchanan to arrest him, I will let you know as soon as possible."

"Thanks for breakfast. The next one's on me."

"You have a deal," Rich said as he put a seven dollar tip on the table and took the bill to the register to pay.

CHAPTER THREE

THEY WALKED OUT, shook and went a block in opposite directions. Rich thought it was a shame Cindy was not on the dating market. She was smart, funny and very pretty. So was her older partner. Cindy had given him some helpful female insights into Isabella and Myra.

He was getting increasingly concerned about furthering the relationship with the former. She was part of a package. A package which was full of problems. He decided to ease away. Maybe date Isabella every now and then.

In the meantime, he had no local options to explore, so he would focus on the job.

Rich caught both Jack and Rose. Each had a few spare minutes to spare, so he brought them up to date on the case.

"And, it looked like it was going to be a straightforward, easy one," Jack lamented after Rich finished.

"What I thought, too, Boss. Looks like I was wrong."

"Do you have a next step planned?" Rose asked.

"Several, Rose. I need to go through the financial

documents I picked up at the bank on the warrant this morning and see if the victim was paying anyone. Particularly either beneficiary. Shawna did not ask anything about whether I knew if there was any money in the estate either time I spoke with her over the phone. Either she figured he was an old guy living in a run-down single wide who didn't have a pot to pee in, or she knew about the value."

"Or, didn't care?" Rose asked.

"No, I don't buy anybody not caring about money," Rich replied. "I want to enlarge the picture I took of the safe deposit box contents and read them closely.

"Oh! Did either of you hear from the criminalists? Did they get any prints off the gas can or the shed?" Rich asked.

Both said they had not heard yet.

"I'll follow up with them and see if I can get a copy of the autopsy. I thought he was a lot older when I brought him out. My initial impression of his age is irrelevant I guess. I am going back to the scene and begin to interview neighbors. There are a few trailers and shacks tucked up in the woods off his main drag."

"Where are you going to interview the beneficiaries?" Jack asked.

"Here if at all possible. I am trying to keep all my conclusions flexible until I have more, but the motives seem to lie with the beneficiaries."

"Okay. You have a full plate. Need any help from Rose or me?" Jack said.

"Not at this moment. I will let you know," Rich said as he rose and headed back to his cubicle to study the financial records and make larger copies of the safe deposit box contents.

He learned nothing from either, so he logged out verbally with Tac on the way out the door.

Still in his detective garb, which meant he left the equipment and Kevlar vest on the seat and wore his sidearm on a holster on his pants belt behind his badge, he spoke with every neighbor he could on the road where Buchanan lived.

Some of these single wide modular home and cabin dwellers had a wealth of land behind their modest homes. He came away from the series of interviews thinking they just wanted to be away from people. Which was something he thought had merit.

Most knew Cliff Buchanan. All liked him. One mentioned he, too, had signed an exploratory gas drilling contract. Rich learned that, while there was a modest bar in the area, Cliff did not go to it. He kept to himself, was friendly to folks and minded his own business.

"Did you ever see anyone around his place? He has a niece and a cousin," Rich asked prompting every neighbor. Nobody reported ever seeing any visitors.

Cliff Buchanan was universally reported to be a pleasant but solitary man. One who smiled and nodded when he saw a neighbor but who did not stay to chat convivially.

Today's efforts with studying the financials and interviewing neighbors had only given him insight to the victim. It had not brought him any closer to solving the homicide. Nor had it reinforced his feeling Eddie Buchanan was the prime suspect. He hoped Cindy would be able to gather both relatives for the will reading the day after tomorrow and he would learn more from interviewing them in person and watching their body language. He would also look for verbal cues.

Until then, he would go out to the eastern edge of the county where Jack, Rose, and two deputies were running two radar operations on the Labor Day holiday.

Rich relieved Rose as one of the two chase cars. One deputy would take speed readings, while the other two, now including Rich, would be a half mile down the county road to stop speeders picked up on radar.

He got his summons book out of his briefcase kept in the front floorboard and made ready. He backed in a grassy area hidden by some trees and waited.

Bob, the deputy who was at the Buchanan fire with him was the first chase car. He heard the radar operator call on a tactical channel.

"Bob, you got a maroon Ram pickup coming to you. Got him at seventy-eight in a fifty-five zone. Take him!"

The truck passed Rich at a normal highway speed, having seen the radar too late. At this point, he thought he was in the clear. Rich saw Bob accelerate past at speed and hit his lights and siren. He pulled the Ram over several hundred yards west of Rich.

"Sarge, I have a blue Camaro with loud exhausts. It's gonna blow past you at any time. Write him for ninety miles per hour!"

Rich watched knowing this would not be a warning but a summons.

The metallic blue pony car blasted by, having slowed down after running the radar, then sped back up. Rich pulled out and accelerated the twin turbo four hundred twenty five horsepower truck. He hit sixty in about five seconds and kept climbing. Rich caught the Camaro at once and hit his lights and siren at about eighty five. He saw the white male look in the mirror.

"Don't do it, man! Don't be stupid!" he said aloud. The Camaro would have a considerably higher top speed, but it would be foolhardy on this two-lane road and he would not pursue at speed. He already had the license plate number.

The driver did the smart thing and turned on his right turn signal and began to slow down. Without screeching brakes, the two vehicles slowed to thirty in about a half mile and the driver pulled onto the red clay shoulder.

Rich called in the plates and stepped out of his vehicle. He knew domestic calls and traffic stops were about the two most dangerous things in law enforcement.

He walked up to the Camaro.

"Good afternoon, sir. Your license and registration please."

"What if I refuse?"

"Then I will have to take you to the sheriff's office in custody and we will find out all about you from your fingerprints."

"I am a lawyer, you hillbilly asshole," the man said haughtily.

"Congratulations. License and registration please."

"You drag me out of this car and I will sue you."

"You have every right to take whatever legal action you wish. This conversation is being videoed and audio recorded, so I suspect the suit won't go well for you."

"Do I finish up your ticket quota for today?"

Rich stepped behind the door of the car so it wouldn't hit him when he demanded the next thing.

"Step out of the car slowly. Do it right now."

"Make me."

"Units at the radar locations, Investigator-1 has a problematic suspect. Be advised this is getting ready to become fight," Rich said quietly with no anger nor nervousness in his voice. His unworried tone should have been a clue to the driver, but it was not.

Rich could hear an engine accelerating in the distance. Bob. He knew the sheriff and Bob would both be responding and probably Rose.

Not ready to wait for reinforcements, the driver yelled "Damn you!" and threw the car door open, getting out quickly, manifesting extreme anger.

As he exited the car, bent to clear the roof, Rich grabbed his collar in his left hand and the back middle of his belt in his right. He jerked the man forward over his extended cowboy boot and flat on his face in the red clay. Rich went down on the man's shoulder with a knee, pinning him as he cuffed his hands behind his back. Bob pulled up and radioed to the rest the driver was restrained.

Jack came in hot. Rich was already lifting the subject up and putting him over the hood of his Camaro to be searched. In addition to his wallet and a money clip with several hundred dollars cash, he had a baggie with what appeared to be well over the "intent to distribute" guideline of two grams of cocaine.

Bob got out his field test kit and it tested positive.

Rich and Jack spoke for a minute and Rich returned to the man, already pontificating.

He already knew the man's name and his car was not stolen. He knew the man had numerous traffic offenses, but no criminal ones. Until today.

"Mr. Carmine, you are under arrest for suspicion of cocaine possession, driving ninety miles per hour in a fifty-five zone, and resisting arrest with violence."

"I want to see your supervisor!"

Jack walked up and stared at the man.

"Who the hell are you, deputy, looking at me like that?" Carmine demanded.

"You wanted to see the sergeant's supervisor. I am his supervisor. County Sheriff Jack Landers. Rest assured we will examine the tapes of your performance this afternoon with the Assistant District Attorney and see if there are any other charges to be levied on you. I am thinking assaulting a police officer for one. Bob, please read Mr. Carmine his Miranda rights. All of us will witness it in case he chooses not to sign the rights statement before we lock him up."

Jack added "let's call the radar quits for the day and return to the office. Rich, help put Attorney Carmine into the back of Bob's car for transportation to jail."

Jack called the ADA on the way back to the office and told him about the incident and who he was bringing in. The ADA said he would like to review the tapes of the incident and throw the book at Carmine. He knew him and said he was known as an ambulance chaser in the Oklahoma City area and was not held in very high esteem by most of his peers. The cocaine arrest would come to the attention of his bar association and likely prompt a disciplinary action and possibly disbarment.

Later in the office, Jack sat down with Rich and Bob and the Assistant District Attorney to review the tapes.

"These show he was unrealistically belligerent, gave you reason to think he was assaulting you, and showed you removing a large quantity of white powder in real time. You tested it on film and it tested as cocaine.

You guys were professional today and your professionalism was recorded for posterity and the court."

The ADA added assault on a police officer to the list of charges. He said the video and audio "will back up your actions, so don't lose any sleep, Rich."

"I hadn't planned on it. Thanks for getting there so fast, Bob and Jack. Things could have gotten worse. However, generally on a guy like Carmine, the action seldom lives up to the mouth," Rich said.

"In view of the assault on an officer charge, I would like you guys to re-read him his rights. I will be present and ready to testify my presence if he refuses to sign. My guess is he will try to defend himself. His ego would not consider anyone else is as smart as he is," the ADA said and the group went to the holding cells to re-Mirandize Carmine. As surmised, he refused to sign the rights agreement and to say anything else until he decided upon an attorney.

Cindy came by the office later in the afternoon and confirmed the Wednesday, ten AM meeting to read the will. They decided Rose would be present in civilian clothes, waiting as a client just after the two beneficiaries arrived for the will reading. She would provide security for the somewhat worried Cindy.

Rich would wait in his truck outside Cindy's office to make his initial in-person contact with the two after the reading. Rose would back him up from the doorway in case Eddie Buchanan ran upon seeing the sergeant.

Carmine bonded out and a trial date was set. As suspected, he decided to serve as his own attorney.

The rest of the day was uneventful. The three senior members of the Sheriff's Office all went home around six.

Jack met Lily for dinner and Rose went home to her usually absent husband, back from his latest job on a Louisiana offshore oil rig.

Rich worked out for an hour on his Peloton and made a roast beef sandwich for dinner and watched a French detective show on his cable Acorn channel. He turned in early. *Five AM will come only too soon*, he thought.

The three met at the diner at six. It was not official, but ended up being a usual occurrence. Rose seemed like she had something on her mind, but did not address it. The two males left breakfast with concerned looks which neither voiced, but both noticed on the other one's face.

To be ready for the visit at the lawyer's office, Rose wore plain clothes today. Luckily the cool weather allowed a covering jacket to camouflage her off-duty hideaway gun and badge.

Rich decided to drive back to the scene of Carmine's arrest and take a few still photographs to accompany the dash camera photos for the trial in two weeks.

At nine o'clock, Rose walked into Jack's office.

"Rose, you seem preoccupied. What's up, my friend?" he asked.

"Jack, it's the toughest talk I have ever had to have with you."

"Sounds ominous, Rose. Spit it out."

"Howard just got back from a Louisiana rough-necking job. While there, he got the offer of a lifetime. It's for two years with the probability of an extension. Maybe more. An Irish platform in the North Sea. They will pay him the equivalent of three times what he makes stateside, fly us both over and provide housing and a vehicle. We can't turn it down, Jack.

"So, I guess I am resigning. I have prepared a formal letter," she said as she handed an envelope to him.

"Rose, you have been fantastic. There is no way I would do anything but wish you and Howard the best. It's a great offer and you almost have to take it. What an adventure for both of you! You will be sorely missed."

"Thanks, Jack. I will miss you guys and the job. I gave the requisite two weeks, but he has to leave in one."

"You leave whenever you need to. It's only a couple days into the month, so you will get the full month's pay. Modify your letter and resubmit it for October 1st," he said.

"Thank you, Jack. I will. I know I am catching you cold on this. But, it seems to me Rich is the only real option for Chief Deputy."

"I agree, Rose. He will like the extra money and prestige, but I fear he will hate the job as much as I would. He's an action guy and loves the new investigative role."

"My nephew, Hank, is already aboard and being oriented. What if you made him the office deputy? It would give you an experienced law enforcement officer from another jurisdiction to cover the office like I did. Rich can investigate as chief and do his admin duties, too," she suggested.

"Without any thought on my part yet, it seems to work. I will speak with both later this afternoon. Let's get this will reading and interview of both Buchanan beneficiaries done first," Jack said.

"I agree. I have to walk over in about thirty minutes myself," she said.

Rich returned to town fifteen minutes before the scheduled time for the reading. He parked the Responder on the street. The café was directly across from Cindy's office. It afforded a good view and a third cup of coffee. Maybe a donut, too. His early morning workout certainly earned him a donut or two.

He watched as attractive young woman walked up to the office and hesitated. She looked around, probably for her disliked cousin, and went in. Just before the time for the reading, a scroungy looking guy in worn jeans and a hoodie walked up, looked at a piece of paper in his hand to verify the address, and walked in.

Rich saw Rose walk up, turn to the café and smile. No need for operational security. The two suspects were already inside. Rose saw Rich raise his cup and smile. She grinned and walked in.

Rose walked up to the paralegal who also served as receptionist in the one attorney office.

"I am Mrs. Custalow. I am real early, but I had to drive from the other end of the county," Rose said.

"That's fine, Mrs. Custalow. Let me get you a cup of coffee. There are some magazines on the table. There is a will reading before you, but they usually are fairly brief. Make yourself comfortable.

"Ms. Bronson and Mr. Buchanan? There is coffee in the conference room. Let me show you in there. Mr. Buchanan's attorney will be in shortly."

The paralegal, Liza Mackey, led them in and returned with a cup of coffee for Rose. She had taken the call earlier with the new plan where Rose would be inside and Rich would contact the beneficiaries as they left.

"Good morning! I am Cindy Bouvier, Mr. Buchanan's attorncy," Cindy said as she entered the conference room and held out her hand for both other occupants. Cindy intentionally left the door ajar. Liza and Rose could hear what was said in the conference room.

She noticed Eddie Buchanan did not have the courtesy to stand when he shook with her.

Shawna Bronson was medium height and had light brown hair, pretty and had a very good figure. Cindy observed Shawna's cousin was leering at Shawna, now Cindy. *What a creep*, Cindy thought.

"Is everyone comfortable? Sufficient coffee? Okay, then. Let's get started.

"Mr. Cliff Buchanan came to me some months ago for testamentary advice. I recommended he do a pour-over will and a revocable living trust. We reviewed the fact such an arrangement would prevent his nearest of kin—Ms. Bronson here—from having to go into probate court, pay probate expenses, and so forth. It was important to craft the document carefully since there was the probability of significant value in the gas rights. Mr. Buchanan had already signed an agreement with a gas exploration company and the income picture was very optimistic.

"With the arrangement he selected, the will would dump all of his assets into the trust upon his death. He appointed me the trustee of the trust in lieu of a trust company since there is none in the county. It is a fairly normal situation.

"I contacted the gas company when Mr. Buchanan died and told them, as trustee, to go ahead and commence withdrawing the gas from the property. The rights are owned by the trust and the proceeds will be automatically deposited into it with no action needed by you or by me as trustee.

"The trust provides Ms. Bronson, as the nearest living relative, to be the beneficiary of ninety percent of the trust's income. Mr. Buchanan, as next living relative, receives ten percent of the income. There are provisions in the trust for each of you to request additional payments. Should the gas dry up and the land and dwelling be sold, you will receive the full value at the rate of 90/10.

"Separate from the trust, Ms. Bronson, you are the beneficiary of seventy-seven thousand, two hundred fifty dollars in life insurance benefits."

She saw the cousin grimace at being left out.

"Do you both understand Mr. Buchanan's provisions?" she asked.

"How much do you make on all of this?" Eddie Buchanan asked.

"Good question! I received a standard trust package fee of twelve hundred dollars when I prepared the documents. As trustee, I will receive one and one half percent of the assets managed annually until dissolution of the assets. A bank trust department in Oklahoma City will be the residual trustee should something happen to me."

"How much money are we talking about?" Shawna asked.

"I have not had the value of the house and land valued yet because it is dependent on the gas found. The gas company said they anticipate paying the trust around a million dollars a year, more or less. Nothing is definite until gas is withdrawn and payments start."

"When will the money start?" Eddie asked.

"It will start once the gas is coming out of the ground and the trust starts getting payments. The company estimates several months before the first payment. I will need depository account information from each of you to direct deposit your income," Cindy said.

Shawna tore a deposit slip out of the checkbook she withdrew from her purse. Cindy looked at Eddie.

"I ain't got no account," he said defensively.

"You will need to open one and send me a deposit slip."

"Is this taxable?" Shawna asked.

"The trust is taxed. Your inheritance is probably not. You should check with a CPA on it, however. The good thing about the trust is it's protected from creditors and is *per stirpes* which means 'blood beneficiaries only'. If one of you was to marry, for example, and get divorced, the spouse could not claim anything from the trust," Cindy said.

"Say it's a million a year. How much would I get each month?" Eddie asked.

"You'd get one hundred thousand a year, which works out to $8333.33 per month deposited in your account."

"And, she'd get nine times it or nine hundred thousand a year. Which is seventy-five thousand a month."

Somebody breathed "holy shit!" but Cindy was looking at the calculator on her iPhone and could not tell which.

"If one of us died, the other would get the whole thing, right?" Shawna asked, as Rose took notes from the adjacent waiting room.

"Right. And become the primary suspect if the death was suspicious of course. I might remind you your relative's death is a homicide and is still under investigation by the sheriff's department."

"Yeah, but they are yokels," Eddie observed.

"We had two murders in Warrior this year. The sheriff's office solved both within a week and a half. One man is awaiting trial and likely to get life. The other, unfortunately was trying to kill a Texas Ranger and died."

"Them rangers are nobody to mess with!" Eddie said.

"True, but the suspect was killed by a Warrior County Sheriff's investigator. From a long ways off. I understand the shot was amazing," Cindy said. Rose nodded unseen to herself in the next room.

"Here are copies of the will, an advance directive which ended up not to be necessary, and the full trust for both of you," Cindy said handing folders and a large envelope to use to each beneficiary.

"Don't forget, Mr. Buchanan, I will need account information like a deposit ticket to begin paying you when the natural gas is flowing." He nodded.

Both got up and left without a word. *Odd people*, the lawyer thought.

Rose ducked out the rear door and walked briskly to the office with notes she thought Rich could use in the interviews.

The two came out of the front door of the office.

"We ought to get married," Eddie said.

"Not in a million years. Besides, even if you were human, why would I want to share my ninety percent with you, jerk?" Shawna retorted.

"Bitch!" he said.

"If you two are finished, I need to speak with both of you," a stern voice said.

Eddie jumped and Shawna flashed a smile at the handsome lawman in the white shirt and pressed Wranglers.

"I am Sergeant Rich Ammon with the Sheriff's Office. I am lead investigator on Mr. Buchanan's murder. Let's hop in my vehicle and ride down the street."

"Isn't the sheriff's office a couple of blocks? We could walk," Shawna suggested.

"We could, but I need to keep my vehicle close by for emergency calls, so we need to take it down there with us."

"We could meet you there, Sergeant," she said sweetly.

"I promise, I am a good driver. You needn't worry. Please get in." Both realized the softly spoken words were an order not a request.

Maybe this guy is the one who killed the last suspect, Eddie thought.

Two minutes later, they were at the office. Rose sent Rich a text to meet her before starting the interviews.

"Both of you take a seat here in the lobby. If you need a restroom, ask our office manager, Mrs. Adams, and she'll direct you," Rich said as he walked back towards the chief deputy's office. On the way, Tac spun around, his back to the people in the lobby, and mouthed "suspects?"

"Yep. All due care please," Rich said under his breath and the chief dispatcher, armed and deputized, nodded assent.

Rich walked into Rose's office and closed the door. She filled him in on the conversation in the lawyer's conference room, making particular note of the question about if one died, would the other get the whole thing. Rich thanked her and went back to the lobby.

"Mr. Buchanan, I think I will speak with you first. You live in West Virginia and may need to get on the road home. Ms. Bronson, do you mind? If you want coffee or water, Mrs. Adams will bring it out to you upon request."

Rich motioned for Eddie to head down the hall. Rich followed rather than turning his back on the man. He would have recognized Buchanan as a career criminal even without the having seen his Record of Apprehensions and Prosecutions or RAP sheet.

"Today is Wednesday, September 8th. This is Sergeant Richard Ammon interviewing Edward Buchanan at eleven AM. Mr. Buchanan has not been Mirandized as he has not been charged with any crime. This is an audio and video recording. Nobody else is in the room. I am starting the recording at eleven oh one."

"Am I a suspect because I have a record?" Eddie asked as soon as he sat down.

"No. The close kin are almost always suspects. If you have nothing to hide, our talk should eliminate you from the list," Rich said.

"Do you have a suspect list?"

"I do," Rich said without amplifying his response.

"Miss Bouvier said the sheriff's investigator shot and killed the last murder suspect. Was it you who done it?" Eddie asked.

"He was more than the suspect. He was the actual murderer. And, yes."

"How far?"

"Let's talk about you instead," Rich said. Something told Rich to be careful so he changed his mind and read Eddie his Miranda rights. Eddie signed the Miranda statement on video. He asked Eddie to identify himself by full name and birth date. Then, he gave Eddie the date and time of his cousin's death.

"When did you get to Oklahoma and how?" Rich asked.

"I drove over from West Virginia and got here on Sunday."

"A long drive from West Virginia. Why did you drive so far?"

"To do some gambling and see my cousin Cliff," Eddie said.

"Where were you?"

"I was at the Indian casino over to Ada."

"Did you have a room there?"

"No, I slept in the truck."

"Did you use a credit card to buy meals or gas or anything?" Rich asked.

"Nope. Ain't got no credit cards," Eddie said in an irritating whine.

"Is there anyone who can verify you were there on the day Cliff was murdered?"

"People seen me."

"What people?"

"You know, the casino employees, the folks at McDonalds where I ate."

"So you think people who don't know you would remember you were there on a specific day a week ago?" Rich pressed him.

"Maybe."

"Did you drive over to visit your cousin Cliff during this trip to Oklahoma?" Rich asked.

"I was gonna," Eddie said.

"But you didn't, right?"

"Right."

"Did you call him?"

"Yeah, I called him the day he died apparently."

"I'd like to see your phone, please."

"Don't you need a warrant?" Eddie asked, getting more nervous.

"To look at it right now, yes. I can get a warrant here in an hour while you wait in a cell. Or maybe charge you with the murder of your cousin. You have no alibi and a million dollars' worth of motive."

"I didn't know about the gas deal, much less how about the million dollars!"

"The phone?" Rich repeated.

Eddie handed him the phone and turned it on. No password was needed on this burner phone from Walmart, obviously purchased with cash.

Rich went to recent calls. There were not many. One was to Cliff. Rich recognized the man's phone number. The call had no duration. It was about the time of the fire. Rich would have Tac try to track down the cell provider to see if they could determine from where the call was made. If it was made in Ada, a good two hours away, it put Eddie in the clear. If it was made in Warrior County, it put Eddie in handcuffs.

Rich decided to ask the best kind of interview question. One where he knew the answer before asking.

"What did you and Cliff talk about on this call?"

"Nuthin'. He didn't answer."

"Okay, Eddie. What did you do then?" Rich asked.

"I drove the truck over to McDonalds and got a hamburger, fries and a Coke."

"What time?"

"It was about eleven or so. Before the big lunch rush."

Knowing he did not, Rich asked, "Did you continue to try to reach your cousin you drove over to visit?"

"No. I got caught up in the gambling."

"So, you drove over a thousand miles to see him, called him on the morning after you arrived and not since?"

"Somebody called me in West Virginia and said he was dead, so why call?"

"Some time had passed before your friend got the message," Rich said.

"How do you know?"

"Because it was I who called your friend," Rich said.

Eddie sank lower in his chair.

"You sit here and don't go anywhere. The interview is temporarily suspended at eleven fifteen in the morning," Rich said.

Once the recording was off and Rich was up by the door, he added "Don't try to run. You do and you will go down hard. Real hard. Understand?" Eddie nodded. Rich was pretty sure he was a consummate liar.

Rich went out to Tac's work station and gave him the

phone. He quietly outlined the parameters needed to prove where Eddie was during the time Cliff was murdered. Rich was quiet because Shawna did not need to know what he was up to. It might be better for her to be a little bit apprehensive during her own interview.

Just as he turned from Tac, Eddie barreled towards the front door. Rich was between him and the door and Eddie lowered his head and charged like a bull.

Rich stepped aside and brought a knife edge hand down hard against the back of Eddie's neck. The fleeing suspect hit the floor at Tac's feet.

Rich squatted and placed a knee between Eddie's shoulder blades, pulled his arms behind him and cuffed him. As he came to, Rich assisted him up.

Shawna looked up, an undecipherable look on her face.

"Be with you in a minute," Rich told her and shot her a superhero grin. He tuned, winked at Tac and walked Eddie back to a cell.

Jack walked out of his office to see what the ruckus was, saw Rich moving a half conscious prisoner to a cell and grinned.

"Tried to get away?" he asked.

"Yep, silly boy. Trying to run from the Warrior County Sheriff's Office. How dumb is he? He just put himself on the top of the suspect list for the homicide of his cousin, Cliff Buchanan," Rich said.

"Charged him yet?"

"No, I want to talk with the ADA before we charge him. I have a recorded interview which was just an interview. No Miranda was necessary, but I read him his rights anyway," Rich said.

Jack nodded and said, "once you get him in his cell

come to see me about a development. I need your buy-in quickly."

"I'll be there in two minutes," Rich said as he had Eddie empty his pockets into a plastic bin and get frisked.

He ran out and asked Shawna to be patient.

Two minutes later he walked into the sheriff's office. Rose was there.

"What's up, Bosses?"

"Rose's husband, Howard, has gotten an offer of the lifetime for them to move to Ireland all expenses paid and him to make a lot of money on a North Sea platform.

"Accordingly, she has resigned. She needs to be out of here in a week and I have agreed to her early departure. She gave us and will be paid for the expected notice period.

"Which leads me to the question of the day: will you accept the title of Chief Deputy. It will be effective immediately. I will re-swear you for the new position. The county executives agree with me you are the one for the job.

"Rose has come up with an idea to let you spend more time on the road. You have been overseeing the orientation of her nephew, as well as one other new deputy. Hank already has several years law enforcement experience. We will put him here in the office for now. It will give us an experienced sworn person to run things during your absence investigating, training or whatever.

"What do you think, Rich?"

"Hmmm…of course I will take it. I ride for the brand, Jack. I have a person of interest patiently waiting to be interviewed, though I suspect she has some serious trepidations after seeing what happened to her cousin after his interview."

"Rose, do you have a second Chief Deputy badge to keep as a souvenir of your service? You do? Great! Rich, stand up and raise your right hand."

Rich was sworn in on the spot and Rose pinned her badge on the belt badge holder he handed her. Unorthodox, but efficient. He hugged her and shook with Jack and returned to the lobby.

He retrieved Shawna and led her to the interview room.

"Sorry you had to wait. Your cousin got stupid over me seeing his phone record and decided to split," Rich said.

"Does running make him the suspect?"

"A suspect. It certainly sped him up the list! I have to record our interview. We even do it with witnesses now.

"This is Chief Deputy Richard Ammon and it is Wednesday, September 8th. I am interviewing Ms. Shawna Bronson regarding the homicide of her uncle, Cliff Buchanan. The time is twelve thirty-five PM." With the recorder on, he advised her of her Miranda rights and she signed the statement.

"Ms. Bronson, please state your full name and date of birth for the recorded record," Rich said.

She did. Rich thought "Shawna" and "Mabel" did not go together very well, but held the thought. Instead, he gave her the date of her uncle's homicide and a two-hour window.

"Ms. Bronson, where were you on the date and within the hours I just related to you?"

"I was at work in Oklahoma City."

"Where do you work?" he asked.

"I work in the city HR department."

"So, I can contact them and someone in authority can verify your presence at the time I just mentioned.?"

"No! Wait. I took a sick day. I am so sorry. I got my days crossed. I was thinking the next day. I was at home ill with a twenty-four hour virus."

"Do you live with anyone who can validate your presence?"

"No, Sergeant. Nobody can."

"Did you make any calls to anyone?"

"No."

"How about any neighbors who can attest to your presence during the time frame we discussed?"

"Let me think...maybe. Nope! She was not there. I guess you just have to take my word on it."

"Did you happen to come over and visit your uncle during the time we are discussing. You were off from work, after all," Rich asked.

"Not that I can think of."

"So you didn't visit your uncle on the day of his death?"

"No! I told you I was home sick."

"Did you speak with anyone on the phone?" Rich asked.

"No, I don't believe so."

"Ms. Bronson, please describe your automobile for the record," Rich asked.

"It is a new model Toyota Rav4. It's the new gray enamel. Not the old metallic gray. The new kind of muddy one." She retrieved her registration and gave him the license tag number.

He copied the VIN on his notes. He would run her and the car through NCIC and print the records for his file.

"Does your car have the navigation package?" he asked.

"Yes. It does." He made note to check to see if he could verify where the car was during the time in which Buchanan was murdered.

"When was the last time you saw Cliff Buchanan?" he asked.

"Oh. I guess about last January. I called him on his birthday. The twentieth. About nine months ago."

"I'd like to review your cell phone, please."

She handed it to him. The "Recent Calls" were all erased.

He made note of the erasure for Tac.

They spoke for another half hour and he released her to go home, saying he may think of more questions later and give her a call. She smiled sweetly and left.

A criminalist from the OSBI called Rich. They had gotten a good print off the gas can used to burn Cliff Buchanan's trailer. There were no hits on the print when they ran it through NCIC.

Unless he had an accomplice, the print virtually eliminated Eddie as the murderer. As a frequent arrestee and a resident of a prison in his home state of West Virginia, his prints were easily available to compare.

This single latent print was of a person who had never been fingerprinted in the United States. It moved the interest back over to Shawna Bronson. Rich's background checks on her showed no arrests, weapons licenses, military service, or other things which would have caused her to be fingerprinted.

During the interview, Jack and Rose had called her nephew in from the road by cell phone.

"Hey, Hank. Jack and I need to talk with you about a

change in duty. Come on in early. I think you will like this a lot."

"Okay, Chief Aunt! See you in fifteen," Warrior-9 said.

"He lives near me and has a wife and two toddlers. He should love the regular daytime hours," Rose said to Jack. Rich walked in and said, "We will be losing a good man off the road. I have spent a lot of time with Hank. He has good cop instincts."

"And, he's a helluva good tracker. I taught him when he was about seven," Rose said.

"Since he is a former Oklahoma City PD officer and is familiar with the area, I may get him to snoop around for me on this Buchanan murder. The cousin is so perfect for the perpetrator, but I just found out from OSBI the print on the gas can is an unknown person. The cousin has multiple arrests and a prison record. His print would have popped up like a covey of quail on a fall morning.

"There's something about the niece worrying me. She was too disinterested in the amount, which could exceed a million dollars a year. And, she has no alibi for the day Cliff Buchanan was killed. She was off work for a sick day but has no witnesses. I am thinking of sending Hank to her neighborhood to do a door-to-door. She'd recognize me in a heartbeat if a neighbor talked," Rich said.

"Makes sense to me, Rich. Rose?" Jack asked.

"I think so, too."

"After you broach the office deputy deal with him, I will keep him for a few more minutes and ask him to do the snooping in OKC," Rich said.

Hank arrived shortly and the three met with him. Rose had already told him she was resigning to go to Ireland with her husband.

He was pleased with the change in career and quickly accepted it without needing to think about it or confer with his wife. He knew she would be thrilled.

Jack and Rose left him with Rich to discuss the side investigative assignment.

Rich looked at the deputy and frankly appraised him. Hank was approximately Rich's age, medium height, and had a stocky, muscular build. Rich suspected he would win most physical confrontations quickly as long as his close combat skills matched his apparent strength.

Rich went through the murder board with him and made him copies of Shawna Bronson's photograph, residential and job information, and her alibi—or lack of one—for the day of the homicide. Included in the folder Rich had prepared was a description and copy of the registration of her car, dark gray Toyota RAV4 she had told him about.

"She lives near the city building where she works. If I were you, I'd cruise by in the unmarked Chevy I am going to give you for now. Make sure her car is there. Since she might come home a few blocks for lunch, do your door-to-door either before or after the general lunch hour. I gathered from her conversation with me she lives among retirees at her apartment complex. So, they are likely to be there when you are.

"As I said earlier, we have a good latent which does not come back to anyone present on the NCIC. Which pretty much gives the primary suspect, Eddie Buchanan, his walking papers. You and I are going to release him when we wrap up here. He has not been charged with anything yet, so it will be clean."

"I will wear a sports coat and slacks and my off-duty gun. I think I will leave here about seven in the morning, get to OKC around nine and check on Shawna's car at the city lot. It may be hit and miss, but it's worth trying. Then, I will start working the neighborhood. I patrolled her area about two years ago, so it's familiar territory," Deputy Hank Custalow said.

The two released Eddie, but told him to stay in touch. After being caught and subdued so quickly, he was meeker than before and left quietly.

Rich got the keys for the unmarked Impala he had driven as an investigator until getting his unmarked Responder pickup and passed them to Hank.

Hank drove the Impala home and Rich left on time. The next couple days would be learning what a chief deputy does. There were a lot of administrative duties a chief performed just as there were a plethora of signatures and decisions the sheriff made of which deputies were unaware. Something told him he better learn both. And, then there was Myra's prediction of him becoming sheriff sooner than later.

HANK ARRIVED at the parking lot for where Shawna worked well after normal work hours commenced. In ten minutes, he located her car by description and verified the plates.

Now it was time to do his detective work. He drove to her neighborhood and parked. As he remembered, it was largely retired folks.

He knocked on doors, smiled an affable smile and showed his badge and credentials.

"We are doing a confidential job background check on your neighbor, Shawna Bronson. I'd like to ask a few questions. It won't take long," he promised.

"Will Shawna be moving away? She's the only looker

around here," one retiree said, dropping his voice as his wife walked up behind him.

"I don't know. I was just given her name and asked to check her out for a security clearance. I was also told to tell people to not tell her about the visit. Apparently she is a finalist and the hiring authority does not want to give her false hopes yet."

His explanation worked so well, he used it several times in his visits over the next hour.

Luckily, the murder date was only a week ago, so some people had memory of seeing her on the specific day. He finally hit pay dirt when he was walking back to his car and saw her next door neighbors drive in from shopping.

Hank went through the routine. He asked about the date, saying she had missed an important interview then to make his story somewhat believable.

"Oh! I saw her in a different car then!" the lady said.

"You are right, she left in her car, came back in a little red car. Then, and she went in the front door like she left something, came out and sped off. She turned up later in the afternoon with her own car."

"Interesting. Maybe she left something for her interview," Hank prompted.

"Well, I'd think it would be like a folder or papers. But she came out empty handed and took off," the retired gentleman said.

Hank had learned early in his police career, retirees often make great sources. They were often at home and watched their neighborhoods for anything suspicious.

"Do you think it might have been a loaner car from a dealer's service shop?"

"I guess it could have been. It was a little Mitsubishi. I doubt a Toyota dealer would give her a competing car.

The dealer here sure does not sell Mitsubishi's. Probably was a rental car. There are a couple of rental agencies about a mile over," he said.

"I suspect you are right. Well, thanks for the help. I have some good referrals and need to go back and write up my report. Remember, mum's the word about our little chat, okay?"

"You got it agent! I was in the navy. I understand these things."

Hank nodded and smiled and walked back towards his car.

His next stop was at the rental car offices nearby.

It did not take him very long to learn Shawna Bronson had rented a small red Mitsubishi Mirage. He verified the out and return times and the mileage. The mileage equaled what he estimated the roundtrip from the dealer to her uncle's and back to the dealer to be. Had she not wanted to use her own vehicle for fear someone might recognize it? Or maybe it had a navigation system which could be checked?

Hank was a thoughtful and careful man who did not jump to conclusions. He drove directly from the dealer to the murder scene and doubled his mileage. It was within two miles of what Shawna had put on the Mirage. He was pretty sure she had driven to the trailer, killed her uncle, and tried to hide the evidence with a gas fire.

He went straight back to the office from the fire scene and reported to a very impressed chief deputy and sheriff.

The decision was made to get a murder warrant for Shawna Bronson. Part of the booking procedure would be to fingerprint her. They would have a fingerprint expert from the OSBI stand by with the latent taken from the gas can to compare with her prints. If it matched, they would have their murderer. If not, she would still have to explain the rental car and her rental car mileage recorded being almost the exact mileage from the rental agency office to the murder scene and back. There was the matter of lying about being sick. They felt they had enough probable cause or PC to convince the judge for a warrant.

The warrant was issued. Murder in the First Degree. Rich picked it up from the judge's office.

As Rose was rapidly transitioning out, he asked her to accompany him to Oklahoma City to pick up Shawna Bronson. Rose would perform the pat down for weapons or contraband.

In order to catch her before she got wind of a detective asking around about her, they left immediately and planned to serve the warrant as she returned home from work. Rich called a contact at the Oklahoma City Police Department and advised they would be serving a warrant in their jurisdiction as a courtesy.

CHAPTER FOUR

ROSE HAD a new Ford SUV which Rich planned to assign to her nephew in his new job. He elected to keep his unmarked pickup since he would retain investigative duties as long as possible.

The two talked about staffing on the way over to OKC.

"Rich, I think we need to have at least one female deputy. Like today, it's nice to have a female for searching other females. It's just the right thing to do, too," Rose noted.

"I agree. Is Polly Antrim, the young lady Jack saved from the prepper who kidnapped her still hounding us?"

"I wouldn't call it hounding. She's in a position in her criminal justice degree where she can go to the nearest state academy for certification and finish her degree in less than a year at night or online. I have liked her from the get go. I don't know if you met her during the kidnapping, but even as a teenager, she was mature.

"It may be a fight with Jack, though, Rich. She has major hots for him and doesn't care who knows. He's afraid his wife will shoot her or something," Rose said seriously.

"Do we have any other female deputy applicants?" Rich asked.

"Nary a one. They seem to be more interested in the areas where they can have a social life with the job."

"Do you think Polly is mature and tough enough to patrol alone?"

"Without prior experience, it's always a chance, Rich. I would hire her if Jack didn't put up a fight. I like her and think you would, too."

"Let's both talk with him after we get back and process and interview Shawna Bronson" Rich said.

They backed into a parking space where they would be able to see her arrive at home. Once they saw her RAV4, Rich pulled in behind her and blocked her in her parking space. Both got out and Rich approached her driver side door.

"Good afternoon, Shawna. Deputy Custalow and I need to speak with you inside."

"Can't we do it here?" she asked.

"It would be more comfortable for you if it was less public," Rose said.

They could see her facial expressions go through several changes as she considered options. Rich hoped none of them was stupid. Like resisting or running. She would loose and everybody would be unnecessarily hyped up.

She nodded them towards the door and they followed her in closely.

"So. What's this mystery all about she asked," trying to appear calm, but not pulling it off.

Rich stood facing her, Rose beside her.

"Shawna Mabel Bronson, you are under arrest for the

murder of your uncle, Cliff Buchanan in the first degree. We have to go through certain standard procedures to keep you and us safe.

"Deputy Custalow will handcuff you from behind then conduct a full-body pat down. This is something done with every felony suspect. You can do whatever necessary to prepare your apartment for an absence. Do you have any pets? A cat? I suspect if you had a pup, we'd know it by now," Rich said.

"Nope. Just me. Lonely little old me." Rose cuffed her and gave her a more than cursory pat-down.

"We want you to know your rights. So, I am going to read them to you now. Listen carefully.

"You have the right to remain silent. Anything you say can and will be used against you in a court of law. You have the right to have an attorney and he may be with you when you are questioned. Should you wish one and not be able to afford one, the court will assign one at no cost to you. You can decide at any time to exercise these rights and not answer any questions or make any statements. Do you understand each of these rights I have explained to you?" She nodded affirmatively.

"Shawna, we will record formal questioning and your answers by video and audio recording. Please keep your rights in mind with anything you say on the way back to the Sheriff's Office," Rich ended.

"Maybe we'll just chat about the weather and so forth in the car, okay?" she asked.

"Sounds fine to me," Rose said. Rich nodded and smiled at her. Both peace officers had dealt with a lot of arrestees in aggregate. Shawna was different. She seemed nice. She was really as scary as hell, both thought silently. She had killed her own uncle in cold blood. She manifested not guilt whatsoever. They thought she must be a psychotic and knew to deal with her with kid gloves.

The ride back was scarily pleasant. Rich drove. Rose and Shawna sat in the backseat, Shawna buckled in securely with her hands handcuffed behind her back. She volunteered a couple of comments about the traffic and being thirsty.

They stopped at a truck stop and bought her a bottle of water. Rose switched her handcuffs to the front. She sat behind Rich. Shawna was across the wide rear truck seat, belted in behind the passenger seat. Rose thought the risk minimal.

Back at the office, Rose and Tac booked Shawna and took her prints and photo. The OSBI tech immediately took the prints to the conference room to compare with the one latent on the gas can. She stuck her head out the door almost immediately and motioned Rich in. She showed him the exact match of her right middle finger pad with the latent. They had their murderer.

Shawna Bronson would receive a more detailed and invasive search and provision of jail uniforms and slippers when booked into the regional jail. While at the sheriff's office lockup cell, her phone and purse and contents were placed in an envelope with contents written with her name and the date on the outside. They provided some disposable slippers to replace the three and a half inch stiletto heels she wore today.

"I would like an attorney. I will choose one of the famous ones from Oklahoma City if you will provide my phone for research or a computer or something," she said to Rich. "I can certainly afford one."

"Shawna, I recommend you speak with Cindy Bouvier as trustee of your late uncle's trust before you commit to spending more than you can currently afford out of your checking and savings.

"Oklahoma has a 'slayer statute' which prohibits someone from profiting from their crime. I suspect you need a lawyer to discuss the statute with you before you count on accessing the money in the trust," he said engendering a look of horror on her face.

"You mean I may not have the millions awaiting me when I return?" she asked.

"I am not qualified to answer your question. I suspect speaking with an attorney is a wise thing at this juncture in your life."

"Will you arrange it for me, Rich?" she asked and he agreed to speak with Cindy. In the meantime, Shawna said she would be happy to wait and not speak about the matter regarding her uncle until the attorney was settled.

Rich called Cindy and told her he needed to speak with her briefly. She told him to walk over right away.

"Hi. We have a suspect charged with your client's murder, Cindy," Rich began,

"Oh, thank heavens, Rich. I knew the cousin was a career criminal even before you told me."

"I released him and arrested Shawna Bronson on murder one today."

"What! She's a sweet young thing. She could not murder anyone!" Cindy exclaimed with agitation.

"We had a latent print on the gas can used to torch the trailer—and, Cliff if we had not pulled him out first. It did not come back to anyone when we ran it through the system. It was someone who had never been finger-printed. We developed some collateral evidence pointing towards Shawna. The ADA said it was enough to go to the judge for a warrant. We did and got it.

"She is calm and not contrite at all. I suspect she is a mental case. Sociopathic. Maybe paranoid schizophrenic. Psychotic. These things are way above my training, Cindy. But, if you look at what she pretty definitely did and how she is dealing with it, she is one scary young lady."

"Boy! I didn't see it coming. I feel like I was just hit by an unseen tractor trailer," she said.

"Me, too. The real reason I am here has to do with the trust. She was under the impression as a new millionaire, she should get a high powered and priced lawyer from OKC.

"I mentioned some concerns about the slayer statute and for her to speak with an attorney to see whether she will get any of Cliff's future money. She wants to talk with you as the attorney for the trust about it."

"Rich, let me think about it. I have to remain a prudent fiduciary. My client is the trust, not the beneficiary. Me talking to her about it may be a conflict of interest.

"Who's available as a public defender?" she asked.

"I checked before walking over. It's Ralph Compton."

"He's not a bad choice for her. He is doing it as part of his bar public service, not as a full-time PD. His practice is as a criminal attorney and he has twenty or thirty years of successful experience. Moreover, he seems completely ethical and committed to his clients.

"Get her to accept him and ask him about the slayer statute. I have never had to contend with it in my practice. Quite frankly, I have not used the term "slayer statute" since law school. My leaning is it does come into play here and I would not consider her a beneficiary to be paid under the trust without a lot of research and overwhelming indications it would be okay.

"Please don't share the trust's position with her. I would share it, with some research, with Ralph and let him tell her."

"I would not mention it. It's not in my area of concern anyway, Cindy. I am having a difficult enough time trying to be fair, but not over condescending because she's so damn nice. It appears she is a cold-blooded killer of the sort which does not come along often in a lawman's career."

"This just prepares you for the next step!"

"Folks keep talking about me moving up. There must be something to it. Jack made me Chief Deputy."

"Where is Rose going?" Cindy asked.

"I'm not sure it has been formally announced, but she is moving to Ireland with her husband who is an oil platform supervisor. It sounds like a killer deal for two years, with the option to renew."

"I didn't even know she was married, Rich," Cindy said.

"He is usually on a platform off Louisiana. She keeps personal stuff close to the vest."

"I guess. Well, more power to her for a mid-life adventure!" she said.

"Thanks for the information on Ralph. I will go and talk to Shawna about choosing him. See ya later!" Rich said as he stood for the door. Cindy gave him a lingering hug. Not the first one. He wondered for a moment as he left her with a superhero grin, but decided he may as well stop trying to figure out women because, as he thought to himself, *I really suck at it.*

He spoke with Shawna, telling her the short version. She should choose the PD. He is an experienced criminal trial attorney. He said she should ask him about the slayer statute as he would be her actual attorney so there was no reason to get Cindy Bouvier involved.

She bought it and he contacted the ADA to get attorney Compton assigned and over to the office to meet with his client. Rich knew he would have his client clam up and make the case tougher. An admission was what he wanted in view of other evidence being circumstantial. Her fingerprint on the gas can was good, but the attorney would probably propose it did not prove she used it to douse the trailer. He could say she happened to throw it away on Cliff's road, but it was her gas can and she never went to the house. The same for the exact distance from the rental car place to the murder scene. He would say if one put the point of a compass on the rental site and revolved it in a circle whose radius was equal to half the distance on her rental car, she could have driven to a virtually infinite number of places and back. Not just to the murder scene. Would a judge and jury buy his questions? Rich hoped so. But he did not have a confession nor a true smoking gun.

He determined his only effort before the interview began would be to search, with help, along the road for the murder weapon used to kill Cliff Buchanan. He and Jack had driven in opposite directions and turned up the gas can. A club or pipe could be thrown farther.

He scheduled the interview for late tomorrow afternoon and began to recruit searchers. The Warrior Sheriff's Office was not of sufficient size to support a police explorer program, but he reached out to the local Boy Scout troop and the Civil Air Patrol.

THE NEXT MORNING, he, Rose, and Hank had a total of forty searchers ranging in age from twelve to eighty.

"Folks, first off, I really appreciate all of you turning out with limited notice to help us search. Mr. Cliff Buchanan was killed at this burned out trailer last week. He died from a blow to the head by a hard round object of several inches in diameter. It could have been a pipe or round wooden club. It may have been a small baseball bat. It could have been a foot to three feet long.

"We don't know which way the killer left—to the right or left. But he or she would have thrown it out of the driver's window across the opposing lane going this way," he pointed "or out the passenger window going this way. It may be a tough toss from the driver's seat out the window. It is possible the driver exited to throw the murder weapon, but I doubt it. It would take time for a scared person who wants to get away.

"If you see a possible stick or pipe or bat, yell out. Don't touch it! The fingerprints on it are crucial and have to be specially handled to protect them. Okay?"

Everybody seemed to understand. The scout master would ride herd on the younger ones to keep them from picking anything suspicious up. Rose maintained a radio watch from the crime scene. Hank went with the CAP and Rich went with the scouts. Both had handheld radios.

Twenty minutes into the search, Hank called Rich on the handheld to come and look at a piece of wood. Rich jogged over to the site, where Rose still was and took his Responder truck the half mile up the road to where he saw Hank.

The piece of wood was stout and about three feet long. It was a piece of 2"x2" lumber. It was worth bagging, though it did not have the round surface the medical examiner said characterized the injury to Buchanan's skull.

Rich put it in the truck and returned to his group, parking the truck well into the shoulder.

They were searching the same section of road where Jack had located the gas can, but were well past where he found it.

Rich heard a young Boy Scout squeal up at the front of the group. At first he feared the boy had stepped on something and hurt himself. But, he responded and found the boy pointing at a brightly colored bat hidden from the road in a shallow trench. Rich guessed the trench was scooped out with a shoe. Some branches lay on top of the two-foot long aluminum T-ball kid's bat. He could see some dark brown stains on the ball end. Blood! He had the scout leader and his young searchers guard it while he sprinted back to his truck and brought it to where the bat had been hidden. Any footprints in the soft earth were trampled by the searchers.

Rich took several pictures of the bat and how it was sequestered out of sight of the road.

He put it in a paper bag, handling it with nitrile gloves.

Rich thanked the boy and wrote his name down. He thanked the leader and rest of the scouts before getting in the truck. He called Rose and Hank on the radio and said to secure the scene and thank everyone. The probable murder weapon had been found by a twelve-year old detective.

He did not have a lot of time to get the bat verified. He would go to the area around Shawna's neighborhood and visit sports stores with a picture of the bat and of the suspect.

He gave the scouts a bit of a show when he powered

the over four hundred horsepower truck off, lights and siren on.

He knew he would have loved it at twelve. Or, thirty...

He had Tac call the OSBI and tell them he was coming in hot to their lab and to tell Rose to call the attorney and put off the interview with Shawna until ten in the morning. He got there in record time to have them study the bat for fingerprints and type the probable blood on it. He gave them his cell phone number and asked he be called as soon as they had anything.

The next stop was the area near where Shawna worked and lived. He did a computer search on "sports stores near me." There were no specific ones in the neighborhood, but both a Walmart and a Target. He went to both.

It would be a long shot. He had no idea what time Shawna may have bought the bat—if in fact she did. So, getting the right clerk who would have waited on her was improbable.

Target did not carry the particular brand. He went to Walmart next. They did and took him to a display of T-ball bats. An identical one was in the display.

The sporting goods manager was able to look up the skew on the bat and find out one had been sold the night before the murder. He identified the clerk who was due to come on in several hours.

Knowing it may take several hours for OSBI to do a comprehensive analysis of the found bat, he decided to wait instead of attempting to make contact with the employee at home.

He spent part of the wait time filling Jack and the ADA in on his progress. A lot hinged on the outcome of the bat as evidence and being able to tie it to Shawna Bronson.

Rich found a decent looking coffee shop and had a cup of French roast and a cream cheese bagel for an early dinner. Neither his sometime girlfriend, Investigator Isabella Munro nor her flirtatious sister would approve of his diet selection.

It actually irritated him he would even think of what they might feel. He smacked his six-pack stomach and ordered a donut and another coffee to go.

He backed the unmarked Ford pickup into a corner of the lot at Walmart to wait for the clerk who sold the T-ball bat to come in.

As a naturally curious person and a cop, he watched people come and go as night encroached and the parking lot lights came on.

He noted a young mother with a stroller and arms full of bags making her way slowly towards a small SUV. A seedy looking male about twenty-five approached her.

The hairs on the back of Rich's head went up and he reached for the start button on the truck and began to move it towards the unfolding scene. The man grabbed the woman's arm and she pulled away. He reached again and tore her purse off her shoulder. At this point, Rich aimed the spot on him and hit the red and blues and siren. The latter was more for calling Walmart security than traffic control.

The man sprinted. Rich jumped out.

"You okay, Ma'am?" he asked the woman, who nodded. "Stay right here. Call 911 and get some OKC officers here," he said as he got back in the truck and drove towards the running man.

The man, not in the best of shape, was breathing hard

after clearing a large parking lot. Rich dismounted and locked the doors, lights still on.

It took him less than a minute to catch up with the man and punch him in the shoulder when he refused to stop. The blow sent him sprawling hard onto the pavement. Knee across his back, Rich pulled both of his hands behind him and cuffed him. He gave him a quick rear frisk and rolled him over to do the front. He took a large folding knife out of the man's pocket.

He heard sirens. It was not surprising especially if the victim said a deputy was in foot pursuit.

Two marked units rolled up as a couple of Walmart security guys arrived. Rich had his vest on, badge and .45 prominent on his hip. There was no question he was a law enforcement officer.

"Joe, what did you do this time to get this big deputy to tackle you?"

"He accosted the woman who called 911 and stole her purse. I saw the whole thing."

One of the three officers, the one speaking, squinted his eyes.

"Damn Joe! This guy is from Warrior County. They shoot people there!" he said.

"Only when they need it," Rich added.

"Oh, this fine citizen needed it a long time ago. I'm Frank Mifflin, I'm sergeant for this district."

Rich stuck out his hand.

"I'm Rich Ammon. I'm Chief Deputy over at Warrior County. I am here to interview a clerk who may have sold a T-ball bat to a woman who killed her uncle with it."

"Chief, if you will give us a quick report to go with the one from the lady, I will do my best to see this idiot goes to jail without you having to testify in court about tonight."

"It's Rich, Frank. I'd be happy to. Then, maybe these gentlemen would like to introduce me to Ms. Smith in Sporting Goods."

One of the Walmart security men, a muscular man about the suspect's age, agreed to wait until the report was done. He needed some of the names for his own report anyway.

They reassembled back where the crime occurred and the sergeant interviewed the victim.

She was a nurse at the regional hospital on the edge of Oklahoma City. It was on the Warrior County side and the one they used for everything except trauma center medevacs. The eighteen month old in the stroller was her niece. She was most appreciative of Rich's fast action and saving her and her purse with much of her life in it. The name on the card she gave Rich was Jenny O'Neill. He saw the handwritten phone number on the back of the card.

Rich knew he would call the number within a week to check on her. Maybe over dinner. He did not see either an engagement ring or wedding band on her hand.

It took a while for two reports and then Rich's hand-cuffs were returned and Joe got new OKCPD ones to wear to jail.

Rich, his back turned to the other officers, mouthed "I'll call you!" to Jenny and was rewarded by the kind of smile guys dreamed about.

He gave the Walmart guys a ride back to the store in his truck and was taken to Sporting Goods and intro-duced to Ms. Smith.

"Yeah. I remember the woman who bought this bat in

the picture last week. It was early in my shift. I was trying to make conversation and asked her how old her boy was who played T-ball. My boy plays. She hesitated and gave me an age five years too old. I knew she was lying, but figured she had her reasons."

"Was this the woman?" Rich asked showing her Shawna's mug shot.

"Sure is! Nice lady. Pretty. But, lying sure as the devil!"

"Your instincts were sound. I cannot go into an open case, but your information really helps us," he said.

Rich took contact information and her full statement and walked out with the muscular young black man who was the chief security officer for the store.

"What's it like being a deputy in rural Warrior County?" he asked.

"It's great. You get to do a bit of everything. Not the gang and drug problems like in a big city. Robberies, traffic, domestics, murders. I picked it over a big city force when I got out of the Army and got my Criminal Justice degree."

"What did you do in the army, Chief?" he asked.

"75th Ranger Regiment. A bunch of deployments."

"I was a 31B," the man offered.

"Military police? I am surprised you didn't go LE when you mustered out."

"I will in the next month or so. I am wrapping up my Criminal Justice degree and working here at night."

"Here's my contact information. Give me a call if you decide to go the rural deputy route instead of a city beat," Rich said.

"I will. You can bet on it." Rich wrote down his information on the notes with Ms. Smith.

Halfway back to Warrior County, his cell phone rang.

He glanced at the face, thinking it would probably be Isabella. It was the criminalist at OSBI.

"Bingo! We have one of her prints on the bat and her uncle's blood type. I will know if it is specifically his first thing in the morning," she said.

"It would really help if it was before ten. I have to interview the suspect with her lawyer sitting there. I'd love to have a smoking gun, or smoking bat maybe, to wave under their noses."

"You got it cowboy!" she said and hung up. Rich grinned. She could be his mother age-wise, but was one interesting proposition. He knew her from a recent murder investigation. Then, this ER registered nurse might be, too.

True to her word, the criminalist called Rich at eight-thirty in the morning and confirmed it was Cliff Buchanan's blood on the T-ball bat.

Rich asked Rose to join her for the interview and had Hank observe and take notes of his impressions from behind the one-way window.

Rich welcomed everyone cordially. He might switch to bad cop later on, depending on need. Rose knew she could assume the role of bad cop at any time, too.

"We are recording this interview both visually and audibly," Rich said after he turned the system on. He introduced each person in the room.

"Let the record show Ms. Shawna Bronson was given her Miranda rights when she was arrested and indicated she wished to withhold any statements until in the presence of her counsel. No questions were asked about the case.

"Now, Ms. Bronson, you stated you had not seen your uncle, Mr. Cliff Buchanan for almost nine months. Do you wish to change your statement?" Rich asked.

She looked at Attorney Compton, he almost imperceptively shook his head.

"No comment."

"Mr. Bronson, you also stated on the day of your uncle's murder, you had called in sick and were not visiting him.

"Let the record show Ms. Bronson did not respond to the question."

"On the day of Cliff Buchanan's death, you rented a red Mitsubishi. The rental agent identified you and we have a copy of the rental agreement. The mileage you put on the Mitsubishi was the exact mileage of a round trip from the dealer to your uncle's residence and back again. Your neighbors have stated they saw you leave, return in the red car and go into your apartment for some reason, return and get something. You left and returned in your own current model gray Toyota RAV 4 several hours later. Did you go to your uncle's?"

"No comment."

"Mr. Buchanan was struck in the head by a cylindrical object and was unconscious when you torched his trailer, igniting it with gasoline which was both on a hot burner on the stove and poured profusely throughout the trailer. Do you acknowledge hitting him, putting a container of gasoline on the hot burner, and spreading the gasoline?"

"No comment."

"The gasoline can was from his shed. After use, it was not returned. Sheriff Landers and I searched the road which runs past your late uncle's residence. The Sheriff located a red two gallon gas can. It was thrown on the side of the road."

"Did you discard the can on the side of the road?" Rich asked.

"No comment."

"In view of you claiming to not have visited your uncle on the day of his death, the use of a rental car for the trip when you own a perfectly good late model car, and you claiming to not have discarded the gas can, will you explain how it got one of your fingerprints on it?"

Rich and Rose watched Shawna's face become very pale. She swallowed and looked as if she was going to say something.

"My client will not respond to the question," Compton said for her.

"Moving on then," Rich said. "On the night before your uncle's murder, you went to the Walmart nearest you and purchased a children's aluminum T-ball bat from a clerk named Ms. Smith. She identified you and showed me a bat in inventory. It was just like the one you bought, she said.

"Do you acknowledge buying the bat?"

"No comment," Shawna said with a bit more composure.

"The bat you bought was located by sheriff's searchers on the road further up from where the gas can had been tossed out. Please review a photograph of the bat buried in a shallow hole and partially covered by twigs."

Shawna and Compton both looked at the photograph and said nothing.

"Ms. Bronson, will you explain to me how both your uncle's blood and your fingerprints got on this bat?"

She got a wild look in her eyes and began to jerk in a seizure-like manner. She drooled a small bit of foam from the side of her mouth.

"Let the record show this interview is concluded at

ten-oh-seven due to the suspect having medical distress," Rich said.

He turned to Rose, but she had already risen and was heading for the door. "Got it!" she said.

The people in the interview room could hear her say to Tac, "Paramedics to the interview room STAT! The suspect is having a seizure of some sort!"

By the time she got back, Rich and the attorney were on either side of Shawna and holding her arms as she flailed about to keep her from falling from the chair.

"We need to lift her off the chair and place her on the floor on her side," Rich said.

"Rose, would you clear a space of all objects and maybe find something we can put under her head?" he said.

The placed her on the floor and Rich rolled her over on her side. She continued to foam and jerk.

"Don't hold her down. We just want to prevent her from injuring herself on something," Rich said.

"Thank God you seem to know what to do! How?"

"Combat first aid in Afghanistan," Rich said, watching for the professionals and wishing they would speed it up.

Paramedics arrived in minutes. Shawna's movements had abated. They checked vital signs and told Rich she needed to be transported to the regional medical center without hesitation as her heart was failing. They put her on a gurney, fastened Velcro straps and rolled her out to the ambulance after putting an electronic defibrillator on the gurney with her.

"Do you want to go? I am," Rich said to the attorney.

"Yes, of course."

"You can ride with me if you want. I will bring you back here when you are ready." Compton nodded, genuinely concerned his young client could die at any time.

The ambulance was pulling off with lights and siren.

Rich and Compton got in the Responder and buckled in.

The chief deputy energized the LED red and blues and the Wail siren. He caught the ambulance quickly and passed it before the first intersection.

He stopped in the intersection to block traffic as the ambulance roared through. Rich accelerated hard, caught the ambulance and passed it again. They did this motorcade dance several times until hitting the Interstate.

Not having direct radio contact with the Fire Rescue ambulance, Rich radioed Tac.

"Tac! Warrior-2!"

"Warrior-2, go."

"Call the ambulance and determine the maximum safe speed he wants to maintain on the Interstate. I'll make sure it happens for him by clearing traffic."

A few seconds later, Tac said "Roughly eighty."

"Roger, Thanks. Let him know we'll run interference to enable it."

As they entered the on-ramp, Rich took the middle between the lanes and merged the same way, hitting the air horn. He moved to the left lane and the ambulance followed him.

Rich eased up to eighty and maintained it until he saw traffic grouped in all lanes a half mile ahead. He sped up and approached the traffic. A couple of slow moving tractor trailers seemed to be the problem. He pulled onto the rough shoulder, ambulance following.

Rich alternated his air horn and the klaxon and moved traffic as far right as he could.

They took the hospital exit and he blocked the first intersection deactivating his siren as they pulled into the lot. He pulled over and let the ambulance lead around the building to the ER entrance.

Several nurses and orderlies ran out, followed closely by a young physician.

Rich and Compton left the F-150 Responder lit up and ran to the ambulance as the gurney was removed. The EMT with Shawna had apparently used the defibrillator during the run and was preparing to use it again. He stepped aside and let the doctor do it as they rolled Shawna into intensive care. The lead nurse gave Rich a quick smile as she tended to the patient while running the gurney in. It was Jenny O'Neill.

THE LAWMAN and the lawyer went to the intensive care waiting room. They made a point of not speaking about the case, only talking about their genuine concern for Shawna.

Rich knew the recording of the interview would bear out the quiet, non-emotional questioning. Either she was spurred by holding back guilt, by being caught with a smoking gun in the form of the murder weapon, or the seizure pushed her into the heart episode and both were unrelated to the case. Rich had had friends die in his arms in combat. He could deal with this cold-blooded person. *She is a total chameleon though*, he thought.

RN Jenny O'Neill came out first.

She smiled at Rich and asked Compton "Are you her next of kin?"

"Better. I am her lawyer. She effectively has no real

97

next of kin. There's a money grabbing ex-con in West Virginia and nobody else," he said.

"I see. Well, Rich. I suspected I would see you soon, but not this soon! Have you saved another damsel in distress like last night?"

"Not quite. This is a situation where, when Ms. Bronson begins to recover, she will need a police guard," he said.

"Like witness protection?" she guessed.

"Like murder suspect," he responded.

"She doesn't look like one."

"Her cousin Mr. Compton here just mentioned did look like a murderer. It just goes to prove one can always be surprised."

"So, she's your prisoner?"

"More like Warrior County's prisoner. But, I am their number two representative, so…"

"I will try to explain this to the doctor. He will be out shortly to speak with you. I suspect he will treat you two like guardians or something."

"A fair assessment, young lady. We kind of are," Attorney Compton said.

Twenty minutes later, the young physician came out. He was young in years, but aged with his five years as a board certified ER physician.

"We have stabilized Ms. Bronson. It appears she has a congenital heart issue. We don't know for sure until we get some more test results back, but she may be epileptic. The heart may have triggered the seizure or it may not have. The heart is the major problem. She will most definitely require a stent, maybe more. I have requested a cardiac surgeon to come by this afternoon and take a look at her and the X-rays we did before as a matter of course.

"I understand from Nurse O'Neill she is a murder suspect and will require a guard? If so, I'd be amazed if she would be mobile enough to need one for a few days."

"Not as something we have reason to be concerned about, but how about self-harm? Do you think she needs to be on a suicide watch? This whole episode took place the instant she realized she had been caught decisively."

"Maybe. I am not sure I'm the one to ask."

"I may ask the court in Warrior to order a psychiatric examination pretty quickly. Would not such an exam give us an idea about suicide?" Compton asked.

"I would think so," the doctor opined. Rich, who probably should not have heard an indication of the defense's strategy, kept his mouth shut. It would take an idiot to not use a mental defense. Ralph Compton must know it and know Rich knows it. Compton's question told Rich the attorney has some integrity and cared more about his client than the case.

"For what it's worth, the Sheriff's Office will pressure the ADA to support this action ASAP, Ralph."

This was the way it was supposed to work, but seldom does, Rich thought. No doubt Compton thought the same thing.

Shawna Bronson's hospitalization insurance with the Oklahoma City covered her emergency heart repair of three stents. Her physician placed her on seizure medication. She was out of the hospital in a week and transferred by the Sheriff's Office to the regional jail to await her psychiatric review by a panel of two psychiatrists and one MD. The court covered the cost of the review.

She was found to not be paranoid schizophrenic or other socially debilitating mental disorder. One of the doctors, the physician, remarked *she was faking mental disorders and was just plain cold and mean.*

The ADA and judge reviewed the finding and set a trial date for murder in the first degree. The trial was two months away and a large bail was set. Shawna had no family, nor collateral upon which to base a bail agreement and settled into the regional jail for the duration.

CHAPTER FIVE

Rose and her husband left for Ireland after a small going away gathering at the office. Hank Custalow moved seamlessly into his new responsibilities. Rich learned the duties of both sheriff and chief deputy. He learned some of the latter in a hectic week from Rose and most from trial and error on the job.

Attorney Carmine's trial was held and he was convicted on all counts. It made regional news and the bar association suspended him pending an investigation which shortly led to the loss of his license to practice. He received some prison time on his four gram distribution quantity of cocaine. He could plan his new career while serving his sentence.

Shawna Bronson's trial was prosecuted with the prosecutor asking Rich questions along the theme Rich had asked Shawna. The circumstantial evidence led up to the gas can with her finger print, the T-ball bat with both her finger print and the murder victim's blood. Ms. Smith was called to testify about selling her the bat. A representative from the car rental agency testified about renting the red Mitsubishi to her.

A jury found her guilty of murder in the first degree. She was sentenced to life without parole for thirty-eight years.

Rich and Jack talked at length about the murderer in the Buchanan case. Rich was blown away a woman could be so pleasant on the outside and mean on the inside. He had experienced deadly women in Afghanistan. Ones with AK-47's and IED vests who were willing to die for Allah. This was his first really cold American woman.

Jack Landers did not share his experience. His first major investigation at the OSBI had been a serial killer who killed only blonde women. A movie and a book, Only the Blondes, had been made about his investigation which led to her capture. His OSBI associates captured her while he was recovering after she shot him. He never blamed her, knowing what she had suffered which triggered her murders.

The movie nor book told the rest of the story. The story of her love-hate relationship with Jack and her prominent father who had deserted her when she needed him the most.

How she had set up her escape from a psychiatric detention facility under contract to the state. How she had used her lawfully earned funds as a successful mutual fund wholesaler to have plastic surgery and had transitioned from attractive businesswoman to looking like a bombshell Hollywood quality starlet. And, how she manipulated the two men, lawman and father. Jack had shot the father in the closest gunfight to a Dodge City draw down in modern history.

How in the end she and the unknowing lawman had fallen in love. She had been murdered by the very female convict who had savaged her as a teen and disrupted her psyche. The lawman had her cremated once he knew the truth and destroyed evidence of who she was. And, never mentioned a word of the rest of the story to a single soul. And, never would. He loved his almost perfect wife, Lily. But, Jack Landers would die one day, still with a hole in his heart about which only he knew.

A TWENTY-FOUR YEAR older version of the lawman also had a hole in his heart, more than figuratively.

John Landers, Senior, Jack's father had been suffering silently from an incurable heart disease for several years. Even his beautiful wife Georgia, the Yellow Rose of Texas as crowned by her famous Uncle Bud Carey, did not have a clue.

Like his son, John was six foot three and had the lean body of what he was. A lifetime cowboy.

He had worked his way up to ranch manager at a spread near the three thousand acre Cinco Peso, owned by Texas Ranger Bud Carey. The ranger's beautiful niece lived on it and ran it as a teen with the help of a full-time manager and Bud part time. The ranch, bought for buckets full of its namesake, gold Mexican Cinco Peso coins in the 1850's, had a lot of Carey blood shed on its dirt and sand.

John and Georgia Carey had fallen in love. Bud did not think anyone was good enough for the niece he had raised from toddler. But, a former cowboy himself, he recognized the best in Landers. His wedding gift to his niece had been the deed to the ranch. As he expected, she hired her new husband as the manager and he did a remarkable job keeping it afloat during hard times and flourishing during good times for almost forty years.

John had a wonderful life. His only failure was the permanent rift between him and his lookalike son, Jack.

In the days when Jack had been a high school rodeo standout, he thought maybe the boy would take over the ranch. The ranch which had been in his mother's family for a hundred and seventy years.

However, his boy followed the uncle he worshiped into law enforcement and was now a nationally famous sheriff in Oklahoma. One who had a movie made about him.

One who moved his beloved great uncle out of a retirement home and to his own ranch in the Sooner State.

Jack had known all his life the Cinco Peso was his legacy. He would have to return to it in Texas and run it one day. His father thought the day was farther off. Now, he knew it would come much sooner.

He had long since replaced himself with a good ranch manager. He was an old friend and respected cowman named Jess Noland. The ranch now only took perhaps thirty hours a week work by the owner. John still put in fifty.

Today, just before lunch he was putting bales of straw into the bed of his F-250. It was cold out but he was sweating lightly from the exertion. He knew Georgia would be there soon with a lunch for them to share out by the barn. They had placed a picnic table there for their ritual lunch years ago.

He heard her Gator four wheeler coming and felt the worst pain imaginable in his chest. It was like a red hot Bowie knife being slowly pushed in up to the hilt. He felt himself falling and somehow heard the Gator stop.

The next thing he knew, his head was cradled in the lap of the blonde angel he loved.

"Stay with me John! Stay with me! I'll call for help."

"No, honey. I'd rather pass right here looking at you than spend twenty years in a wheelchair or worse. Tell Jack it's time for him to begin the life he was born for. Tell him I love him. You don't need to tell him I love you more than anybody or anything. I expect he already knows. I will wait for you on the other side, my Georgia."

He smiled as she reached down to kiss him, hot tears falling on his weathered handsome face. He died with the smile set forever. For her.

GEORGIA SAT THERE for a long time. She fumbled in her jeans pocket and took out her phone. She called her son's cell phone number.

"Hi, Mom. This is a pleasant surprise. How are you?" came the familiar deep voice, so much like the one she had heard for the last time a minute ago. She could not speak.

"Mom, are you there? Is everything all right?"

"Your dad, son," she said with a sob. Jack Landers instinctively knew.

"Is he gone?" She shook her head, then realized she had to answer with words.

"Yes."

"When?"

"A minute ago. Heart."

"Are you sure? Have you checked for a pulse?"

"Yes."

"Have you called the paramedics?" he asked.

105

"No. Just you. His last words were he loved you and it was time for you to come home."

"Hang up. Call 911. When they come, go to the house and wait for me. Make sure Jess, the manager knows. I will bring Uncle Bud and Lily. I will be there in a couple of hours."

"I'll be here son," she said as she hung up.

He knew his wife had taken a day off and was at the ranch with Uncle Bud. He called.

"Honey. It's Dad. He died a couple of minutes ago. Heart probably. Will you and Uncle Bud pack a few things and put Jazz in the carrier? I will be there shortly for us to go to Texas."

"The time has come. We have known it would. You will now run Cinco Peso, right?" she said, her voice breaking.

"I will. With the Red Rose of Texas, the Yellow Rose, a Texas Ranger and the world's most beautiful cat beside me." He heard Jazmine's rolling R "reep" in the phone. She always eavesdropped.

Jack motioned Rich into his office.

"You are now Acting Sheriff. Probably the Sheriff soon enough. My father just died at the ranch. It was probably a heart attack. Lily, Bud and I have to go there.

"You always did a great job of covering my six, even saving it. This may be the last time, Rich. Give 'em hell!"

The big chief deputy walked over to his friend and boss and embraced him unabashedly.

"I'll take you to your ranch. You'll want to drive Lily's German hot rod, I guess."

"No. I am going to ask you to break the rules. Lend me your unmarked truck for the trip. You drive her BMW over for the funeral. I'd really like you there. I don't have any brothers..."

Without a second's thought, Rich handed him the keys to the Responder.

"The tank's full. As you haul ass through Texas, everybody will think you are a ranger."

"Rich, here are the keys to the ranch. We will leave the BMW keys in the kitchen dish cabinet. Will you look after the horses? And, tell Julie and Cindy? And, the team here? Please send Helen and Tac in?"

Rich sent them in and got all of his gear from the unmarked truck. He knew Jack's new marked Responder had much the same police gear. He removed Jack's rifle since the .30-30 had been Uncle Bud's.

He came in as the three finished their goodbyes.

"I put your .30-30 in my truck. Go!"

"Okay, Sheriff!" Jack said as he hugged his friend again. He slipped out the back door. And the legendary sheriff was gone with no more fanfare than the sound of a truck accelerating.

That boy drives like a Texan, Zack Bodeway would say, Rich thought. He picked up the phone in his office and notified the ranger, probably Jack's closest friend.

Zack, Jack, and Rich were all Texans by birth anyway. No wonder they drove and drew fast.

Rich also called the county supervisor closest to the sheriff's office and told him Jack would be away for a few weeks due to his father's death. He advised the sheriff had left him, as his chief deputy, in charge in the meantime. He neglected to mention yet Jack would not be back except to move out of Doolin's Cave Ranch.

In Texas, Ranger Lieutenant Zack Bodeway, the most revered modern day ranger, called the Department of Public Safety, or DPS, to alert troopers his friend as well as retired ranger Bud Carey were transiting to Ranger County on official business in a F-150 Responder. He knew this would significantly reduce the chance of speeding stops.

Rich had promised to let Zack know the time and place for John Lander's funeral. Bodeway would be there for certain.

The distance from Warrior County to the Cinco Peso Ranch was normally over five hours. Bodeway smiled. He was betting on four without sirens or lights.

He called his live-in companion to let her know. She was a senior level Deputy US Marshal and had worked with Jack on a case several years ago. She had also met his wife, Lily, when the two men had met to shoot in a North Texas Single Action Shooting Society match. He was getting close to marrying the forty-year old after a couple of blissful years. Bodeway was considered one of Texas' most eligible bachelors. Virtually nobody outside a small circle of friends even knew about him already having a serious girlfriend. Or, fiancé. Or, partner. Or, whatever.

Rich called a meeting at shift change where the office staff, deputies changing shifts, and available off-duty deputies could all hear the changes.

He broadcast, with Tac's talents, to the deputies still on the road and overall, had an audience of ninety percent of the small sheriff's employees.

"I am going to make this quick. For those of you who have not heard yet, Jack Lander's father died earlier today of an apparent heart attack. Jack, Lily and Uncle Bud Carey are on the way to Ranger, Texas and their Cinco Peso Ranch to arrange for his funeral.

"Nobody is sure what this means yet for the Warrior County Sheriff's Office. As Chief Deputy, Jack appointed me Acting Sheriff. Things will continue to move forward and we will all pull together to keep Warrior safe as we have always done."

"Rich," Bob said, "what about the funeral?"

"I will let everyone know as soon as I know. I would guess it will be in a week or so. With a small department having only sixteen total sworn officers, we will need to hold the number who go to about three or four. I will be as fair about it as I can."

"Hey, Rich. I believe this ranch his father had has been in the family a long time. Do you think Jack will stay there to run it permanently?" a deputy asked.

"Chris, I really don't know. I think his father would want him to move in and take over. But Jack is a lifetime lawman, not a rancher. I suspect he will have to do some real soul-searching over the next few days and weeks."

"Rich, does Rose know yet?" Tac asked.

"No, Tac. She has not sent a permanent address. I will try to send her an email when I get off the phone, but I am not sure what her connectivity is yet. Okay, guys. Some of you are getting ready to head out on patrol, others to hit the sack. Let's cut this one short. I will keep everyone aware of what's happening as soon as I know. Be safe out there!"

He let out a long breath. Longtime manager Helen Adams walked over and put her hand on his shoulder.

"You've got this thing, Rich. And, you are going to run with it. You have the respect and support of everyone on the payroll. Like Jack, you were one of us before being the boss."

He reached up and patted the hand on his shoulder and gave her his best superhero grin. He did not really feel like a superhero right this moment, but he pulled it off just fine.

The phone rang out in the communications area.

"Warrior-6 take the call, Warrior-7 back him up. Report of a rollover traffic accident on County Road 62. Possible injuries. Referred over by OHP. They don't have anybody close. Handle Code-3!" Tac said over the radio.

Units marked underway.

"Tac, did OHP dispatch rescue?"

"Yes, Rich. You want to check it out, too?"

"I do, mark me underway."

He walked into Jack's office and opened the locked cabinet where the ammunition and keys were stored. He found the keys to the sheriff's white, marked Responder and took them off the hook. Rich walked briskly out the door and to the truck. He put his .30-30 in the rack.

Rich pulled out and headed down Main Street. When the powerful truck was in a straight line, he energized the lights. Traffic was light. At the edge of town, he hit some traffic and turned on the siren.

And so it begins, he thought as he accelerated the twin turbo engine and moved towards the accident with great alacrity. There could be bleeding to be stopped, a fire, trapped people, scared children. One never knew. Rich just knew he owed it to the citizens of Warrior County to get there fast and render whatever aid was needed. He and his super truck were up to it.

JACK, Lily, and Uncle Bud were an hour into Texas and had, by Jack's best estimate, two and a half hours to go. Nobody said much. Each was deep in his own thoughts.

His father's unexpected death sped Jack to a decision he had been dreading all of his life. He was a lawman. A damned good one. He knew how to be a rancher. He grew up on Cinco Peso Ranch. He just never had the interest in being one. But, he owed it to his mother and to his legacy. Even Uncle Bud, snoozing in the backseat, had always said, "Boy, one day all of this is going to be yours. It's your birthright. A lot of Carey blood—blood in your veins—was spilled building and defending this land. It has to be protected and passed down to the next generation and the next one afterward. On and on, boy. It's the way things are."

Next to him, Lily sat with her eyes closed. He knew she was awake and thinking. This would be a new life for her. She would have to sell her medical practice and start a new one in Texas. Licenses, an office, an employee or more. Building a patient base from scratch. Stepping into a kingdom which already had a queen. Now, in the role of queen mother. Lily and his mother had bonded instantly. He knew the relationship would flourish. But it would have some bumps in the road.

Uncle Bud would be back to his rightful home. Jack was pleased with bringing him back to his Cinco Blanco for the rest of his days. It was only right. "It's the way things are," his great uncle and best friend on earth had always said.

Bud Carey, before he went to sleep in the back seat with the little black and white cat purring beside him in her carrier, did some thinking himself.

My boy has to be upset by this. He loved his dad though they never really got along. John Landers was a good man. But a man always jealous of how his son favored me. The boy was a natural born lawman. Not a rancher. But he knows his duty and will do it fine. I'm just betting there will still be a badge in his future. People like Jack and me...it's not what we do. It's who we are. He smiled and dozed off dreaming of his early days as a ranger. Of riding a horse after outlaws a truck couldn't follow. Those were the days. The real ranger days.

Jack passed a trooper who nodded at him and smiled. *He either thinks I'm a ranger in this blacked out truck or Zack made a phone call. He knew Rich had already spoken with his friend. Rich had saved the ranger's life a few months ago. It was going to be okay. All of this. It was going to be fine.*

Jasmine, or Jazz, emitted a "reep!"

"Shhh, Jazz. You are going to wake up your buddy sitting beside you. Or the beautiful woman you share a pillow with. Everything's fine. You just have a new adventure facing you."

Jack could hear her circling in her carrier. He knew what she was doing. Spinning around several times to look for danger, then to settle down and sleep, knowing everything is okay in every direction.

Two people and a cat. And, his beloved mother. His family. Like it or not, he was coming home to roost.

Jack drove on. At speed.

CHAPTER SIX

THE ARRIVAL at Cinco Peso was as rough as Jack anticipated. He was grateful for a kind wife and a logical great uncle to help moderate emotions. His parents had shared a long and great love, though only sixty. His mother was at a loss, and for a tough cowgirl, almost non-operational.

Jack and her Uncle Bud finally ascertained her preference for a funeral parlor and the choice of cremation and a simple graveside service at the graveyard on the ranch. Careys and their spouses had been buried there since the original owner, Helmonius "Hell-raising" Carey.

He had defended his ranch from a war party and gotten impatient fighting from inside. In the middle of the fight, he walked out, emptied his single shot rifle and two six shot Colt Dragoons. He used his Bowie knife to finish subduing a literal pile of hostile braves until the rest rode off.

His wife and employees inside watched this fight and saw him curse the remainder of the war party as they departed. He stood cussing with several arrows stuck in his body in places which hurt like hell, but were not fatal.

They were removed and he survived to be ninety-six before his God-given hours ran out.

John Landers would be in fine company. Never friends, but always respectful, Bud Carey would join him there one day and Jack in the distant future.

"Jack, all this dying stuff reminds me of something I want you to know. I'd like a ranger badge cut into my headstone," Uncle Bud said unexpectedly as they left the funeral home.

"Of course. I would have done it even without you suggesting. My only request, Uncle Bud, is you stick around a good while longer. You walked me through being a good lawman like you. I'm gonna really need your help on this ranching."

"You got it, sonny boy. I will correct you on one thing. I was a good lawman. You are a great one, faster, fairer and more famous than I ever was," the old man said to one of the two people he loved more than anyone on the earth.

"If so, it's all due to your influence and a long line of fightin' blood!" The old man smiled at him. The smile said it all. His boy had said the right thing. And, it was all true.

Options from the funeral parlor in hand, the family gathered. They set the date for the Saturday after the upcoming one at two o'clock. Georgia selected a photo and would choose flowers with Lily's help tomorrow. The family had an Episcopal priest and contacted him to conduct the service. Jack paid extra for a headstone company to have his father's completed set and the small urn grave dug in the short time before the funeral.

Bud Carey notified the Texas Ranger Association that

a relative of a ranger had passed, only to find Zack Bodeway had already reached out to them. Both he and his grandnephew knew the famous ranger lieutenant would be in attendance. Other notifications were to the Livestock Association leadership and the heads of other ranch groups.

While Georgia and Lily planned the menu for after the service, Jack and Uncle Bud set up the barbecue.

"Uncle Bud? You still have your ranger holster you wore the 1911 in?"

"I do, but it's back at your ranch. I mean your *other* ranch."

"Is it somewhere Rich could locate it when he goes to pick up Lily's car? He's going to drive it here for the funeral and take his truck back."

"If I wear my old gun, what will you wear? You can't be going to no Texas barbecue unstrapped."

"I'll be fine. It would make me proud seeing you wearing the one I saw you use so fast at the rodeo when I was a teen."

"I will if you have something appropriate."

"Good! You knew the old time sheriff who hired me out of college. You probably told him to. Well, we got close and his wife gave me his old revolver and rig when he died. I have kept it clean, but never wore it. Maybe this is the time to honor a couple of people with it."

"As I remember, it was a Smith & Wesson Triple Screw .44 Special. It was engraved nickel with stag grips," Uncle Bud said.

"Your memory is on target. You described it exactly. He took me out to his ranch to see me shoot the day I started. I did okay. Then he drew and put six rounds on drop down steel plates so fast I couldn't believe it," Jack said.

"I know. You called me and told me about it that night. He was a real old-time gunfighter of the Hickok ilk. You learned a lot from him." Both stared out onto the miles of rolling pasture and sporadic trees of the Cinco Peso. They stood a long time without a word. The old man was bent, but still tall enough to put an arm around "his boy's" shoulder and steady his gun side with a cane as they walked back to the ranch house happy as either could be under the circumstances.

RICH HAD A DECISION TO MAKE. The decision was Polly Antrim. She had fallen in love with Jack as a late teen when he rescued her from a prepper kidnapper. She was now close enough to being finished with her Criminal Justice degree to complete it online while working. About fourteen and a half weeks at the Oklahoma Council on Law Enforcement Education and Training (CLEET) academy and she was ready to be a road deputy. She could actually be a deputy first, but serve only riding along with certified ones. Rose had been convinced she would be a great one. She already showed prowess when she and Tac both shot an assassin at Jack's wedding.

The problem was she still loved Jack and would have provided a lot of discomfort at the Warrior County Sheriff's Office because of it. And, at the Doolin's Cave Ranch.

He knew he needed a couple more deputies. He had already checked out the Walmart security guy who had been an Army MP. He was hired and half through the current CLEET academy class at Ada now.

Polly needed to know about Jack's dad. He needed to

know if she was a viable candidate without Jack present. There was only one way to find out.

He called her on his cell phone. She did not have the number in her Contacts, so might just consider it Spam. If so, he would recall on the office phone. She had spoken to Jack and Rose enough to recognize it.

She answered with a hello, obviously with some hesitation.

"Polly, it's Rich Ammon at the Warrior County Sheriff's Office. How are you?"

"I'm okay, Rich. Is everything okay there?" she asked, still with concern in her voice.

"Everyone is fine. Lots of changes. Listen, I want to apprise you of some news and to pick up where Rose left off with you. Do you have a few minutes?"

"I do. Is Jack okay?" she asked.

"Jack is fine. But, he's part of the news. He, Lily and Uncle Bud had to rush to the ranch in Texas this morning. His father dropped dead, totally unexpectedly. I am sure he and Lily would want you to know."

"I am so sorry. When is the funeral. I will go."

"Probably in a week or so. I would strongly recommend you sit this one out."

"So, sitting the funeral out is why you called me?"

"Nope, good advice to someone I'd like to talk about hiring though," he said.

"I thought you were the head investigator and Rose was the chief deputy who did the hiring with Jack's concurrence."

"Past history, Polly. Rose's husband got a mega job on an oil platform off Ireland and they moved several months ago. I was named Chief Deputy. Now this, and I am Acting Sheriff for now."

"Does this mean he will own the big ranch?" she asked.

"It's too early to know. I do know it is his legacy. It has been in the family since the 1850's and is a three thousand acre working ranch. Certainly too much for his mother to run, even with a ranch manager. I doubt it would ever be sold, in parcel or entirety."

"I see. My guess is you and I both think the same thing. Jack will stay in Texas and give up his badge and you will become sheriff."

"Not definite, but certainly probable."

"I definitely want to speak with you about the deputy job," she said.

"Even," he began, but she interrupted him.

"Yes. Even without Jack. I have seen the handwriting on the wall and now accept it. He is sublimely happy with Lily. I cannot think of a woman alive who could compete with her."

"Me, either, Polly. Look, this is a bit premature. I just wanted to get things going and to let you know about John Landers."

"Thank you for both. You were kind and professional when you took my report after killing the ex-con who shot Jack at his wedding. I liked you then and would like you as a boss. I can finish my degree online in just a couple of months. All I need is a sheriff or chief of police to let the academy know I have a job pending completion. I am fit for the job. I run marathons and shoot regularly. With a .45. If you'd like me to come over and go shooting with you, just let me know."

"Maybe, but I already saw your headshots under pressure. I am pretty well convinced, Polly."

"Should I await your next call? Or, see you at the funeral?"

"Polly, if you see me at the funeral, there won't be a next call. If you are going to work for me, you need to learn to trust my judgement."

"I read you loud and clear. I won't go. But I will wait eagerly for your call."

"And, I will make the call as soon as I possibly can. Talk with you then. Bye." He hung up. He knew she got his message. Whether she would heed it may be quite another thing.

He had spent several years of a young life leading rangers in a more stressful environment than this. The conversation just reminded him of how much easier it was to patrol and investigate than to sit in the chair at the top of the roost.

———

JACK DID what he knew he had to do. He arranged a conference call from the ranch's spacious office to the three county commissioners who had originally appointed him sheriff.

"Good morning gentlemen. Thanks, for agreeing to an impromptu conference call. I know how busy each of you is.

"You all know, from my call to Commissioner Hawken on the way out of town, my father unexpectedly died yesterday at Cinco Peso, the family ranch. It's a big spread, at least by my standards, at over three thousand acres. It has been run by my family since the 1850's. We have a lot of history here.

"I always knew I would have to take it over one day. I thought I had twenty more years before I was forced to. Unfortunately, I did not.

"I am therefore giving you my verbal resignation as

Sheriff of Warrior County effective the end of the month. Two weeks. A formal letter will be in the mail to you each today.

"You showed a lot of faith in me, appointing me after the death of the previous sheriff. I have tried to live up to your expectations and think I generally have. I will admit to you, the passing of my father and the passing of the job I have loved most of all makes for the saddest day of my life."

There was a brief silence, before Robert Hawken spoke. He was the commissioner who unofficially overlooked law enforcement and fire-rescue in the county, while the others oversaw things like roads, tax matters, utilities and other infrastructure.

"Jack, we all knew this day was coming. Like you, we thought we had our famous sheriff for another twenty or twenty five years. We accept your resignation sadly and send our sincere condolences to you and your family. We all met your folks and family at your wedding and think highly of all of them.

"Which brings us to the next part. You have properly appointed young Rich Ammon, the chief deputy as acting sheriff. You called me first and I agreed.

"Rich is young, but has proven himself smart and tough. We learned recently he had led troops in Afghanistan and other places too secret to name.

"Is Rich who you would propose to be your successor? Or, is he too young and we should advertise for an experienced man or woman? I fear we made a horrible mistake when we did it for the sheriff before you. He looked good on paper but was a train wreck in person. The only good thing he did was hire Rich."

"Bob, I recommend you gentlemen swear Rich in immediately as sheriff. There is nobody else I can name who I would rather see in the job. He may be young in years at thirty or thirty-one, but his experience is solid. As you know, both Ranger Lieutenant Zack Bodeway and I owe our lives to Rich's immediate decision making and superb skill."

"Jack, give us a minute to chat. Don't go away. We'll just mute the call for a short time," Hawken said. Jack waited.

"We are back, Jack. Here is our decision. We accept your resignation and will keep you on full salary and benefits like insurance until the end of next month, not this one.

"We will offer the sheriff position to Rich today. If he accepts, we will ask Judge Hartley to swear him in today. Is there a spare gold sheriff's badge anywhere in the office?"

"My top drawer. Thanks, guys. You are making the right decision with Rich. And, I appreciate the salary thing. I am not sure whether the ranch is making money yet or not. And, Lily's pay stopped late today when she stopped seeing patients."

"Well, good luck on the financials. I am sure you will have Cinco Peso rocking and rolling in no time and Lily will create a new, successful practice in Texas. We will arrange to take the judge and visit Rich before the end of the day."

"Thank you, gentlemen. For everything," Jack said and the call terminated. He sat back in his father's office chair. It did not need to be adjusted. The two were identical in weight and height.

Jack let out a long breath as Lily came in carrying little Jasmine and the three began the rest of their lives.

TRUE TO HIS PLAN, Robert Hawken set a meeting with Rich, then arranged for the judge to meet them at the Sheriff's Office in an hour. It was a somewhat worrisome hour for Rich. But if they were going to advertise for his replacement, he knew of one office in Oklahoma and another in Texas looking for chief deputy's.

The four men arrived on time. Rich had warned Helen, Tac, and Hank to expect the three commissioners for a meeting. The judge was a good surprise. It could only mean what they hoped.

After a brief meeting, Rich asked Helen, mother confessor of the office for years, to come in. The judge swore Rich in as Sheriff of Warrior County and Helen was honored to be asked to pin on his new badge. It seemed heavy on his shirt. But he had carried heavier weights in the rangers. He knew he would do just fine.

Robert Hawken said he would draft a press release and let Rich review it before being distributed.

As soon as they left, Rich called Uncle Bud in Texas.

"Uncle Bud. It's Rich. There is nobody I would call about this other than you. The judge just swore me in as sheriff. I had to share it with somebody. I hope you don't mind it's you. I wasn't blessed like Jack with someone who would understand the pride which goes with this."

"Sonny boy. I am honored. You can sure consider me your uncle and call me every damn time you feel like it. You are family, boy. Like Jack's younger brother he never had.

"I will tell him right now. He will love you calling me first. He will understand. It's what he always did, too. Now, you be safe. And, call me frequently to let me know what outlaw you are chasing and I'll give you ranger pointers, okay?"

"Yessir, Uncle Bud! I will. And, thanks."

Rich felt like the gold badge just got a little lighter. Like a tough old guardian angel was helping him hold the weight. He smiled and knew he was going to knock it out of the ballpark.

After speaking with Tac, Rich approved Tac simulcasting a call to the deputy's and related agencies on their simulcast network.

Commissioner Hawken came back for the broadcast and told all this was an immediate need to know broadcast to be followed by an official press release and Jack had resigned to take over his family ranch in Texas and Rich Ammon was the new Sheriff of Warrior County.

Rich did not have any close family. He knew there were five women he better notify before the word got out.

The first was Cindy Bouvier, who would tell her partner, Julie Moran. It was a quick, but happy call.

The second was Jenny O'Neill, who had become very prominent in his life in the past two months. She was excited over the news and asked if she could drive over to McKenzie on Saturday and take him to dinner. She did not have to twist his arm. At all.

The last two comprised two calls. The sisters in Wichita Falls, Texas.

He called his dwindling date, Isabella first. His reticence and her lack of time due to a heavy case load at the Wichita Falls Sheriff's Office had caused whatever ardor they shared to fade.

They had eased into being professional friends, a solution Rich really appreciated. Isabella seemed okay with it also. She was ecstatic with his appointment.

The final call was her sister Myra, who still held amorous feelings for Rich, though they had never even dated.

"Did I say you would be sheriff soon?" she asked rhetorically.

"You did. I will never doubt your second sight again, Myra. In fact, if you have any numbers in mind, please share them. The Powerball is way up in the millions. Way up!"

"Well, cowboy. You will have to earn those kinds of numbers!"

"Guess I'd win the jackpot twice then!" he said, flirting along with her as they always did.

"Yep. And, the money wouldn't be the part you'd think of the fondest!"

"There's no doubt in my mind about it. I called Isabella first, since we actually dated a few months," he said.

"It was the right thing to do, Rich. Always save the best for last. Like desert!"

"Okay, Cherry Pie. I'll talk with you again soon. It's always the high point of my day. But it looks like I have some sheriffing to do. Bye!"

She blew him a kiss and hung up.

Isabella was too intense. Jenny was perfect. But Myra was...well, Myra. There was no one quite like her.

Rich guessed he needed to keep the marked white Responder Jack drove. Like Tac had said when they did the sheriff's office wrap with the lettering and sheriff's star emblems, and exterior lights, "It's kind of a rolling badge of office."

He intentionally did not call Bodeway in Texas. He knew Jack would.

Notifications made, he got back to work, signing papers, reviewing BOLO's and answering phone calls. And, officially being sheriff.

DINNER WAS LATE. The day in Texas had been both strenuous and trying. Jack spent a long time with the ranch manager and his mother going over the books and what was needed for the ranch to move forward successfully.

"The main barn needs some roof repairs. I got a bid for five thousand and am waiting for another. We have to bring in some casual cowboys to round up the cattle on the far north pasture for shots. We are looking at three days. Five riders with their horses and the vaccine and hypodermics will cost around two thousand. We need some salt. Maybe twenty-five blocks of fifty pounds each. I figure about two-fifty for the blocks. We need a blacksmith to come in for some shoeing and trimming. Think five hundred there," ranch manager Jess Noland said in his quiet drawl.

"Okay, Jess. You're talking around eight thousand dollars, rounded up. Those sound like things needed pretty quickly, right?" The older man nodded at Jack.

"Mom, how does eight grand square with the working capital checking account?" Jack asked.

"No problem with eight thousand. Twenty would be an issue, Jack."

"We need to up our profit. Twenty thousand could hit all at once in a three thousand acre spread, couldn't it, Jess?"

"Yep, could come right up on us with no warning."

"What do we need to do to build a war chest with maybe fifty thousand in it?"

"Wal, it would take a time, Jack," Jess said. "We have more horses than we need. I could cull out five nice ones and get five or six thousand.

"Thinking ahead, we have a good crop of winter wheat. We can get around eight dollars a bushel in late June in this part of Texas. We got a hunnert acres planted. Figure eighty bushels an acre."

Jack quickly computed it on his iPhone.

"Looks like around sixty-four thousand gross. I hate to ask, but do we have a combine or is it a co-op situation?" he asked.

"We have one here at the ranch. Figuring Diesel and all, with you and me doing it, you could net about sixty-two three," Jess estimated.

"And, we could harvest around end of June?"

"Yep."

"What major expenses are facing us between now and then? Ones we know about," Jack asked.

"A big one would be supplemental hay. Figure three pounds per hundred pounds of body weight. Say twelve hundred pounds per cow times five hundred. Should be around eighteen thousand pounds of hay. It will cost two hunnert fifty bucks for a ton, so..."Jess was figuring in his head, but the iPhone computer was faster.

"Twenty-two hundred fifty dollars for the hay," Jack said. Jess nodded his assent.

"We can do it," Jack said. "Lily and I have a quarter section ranch in Oklahoma. It's fully paid. I have no idea what we'd get for it. But we both have to go there after the funeral and put it up for sale as well as her medical practice. I will dump whatever we get for the ranch into the Cinco Peso's working capital. Lily will need what she gets to begin to establish a practice here. It's gonna be a busy fall and winter, for sure!" he said.

Later, at dinner, Jack had an informal family meeting.

"I want to say something. I have done some real soul searching and I know each of you has, too. Giving up the badge and coming to run the ranch has been my legacy from the day I came into this earth. It was one, once I became a lawman, I dreaded. Mom, Jess and I had a business meeting today. The immediate costs of running the ranch are pretty small in the whole scheme of things.

"Doolin's Cave Ranch is our old home. With Lily's agreement, we will sell it and deposit the net sales price into the working capital of the Cinco Peso, our permanent home. Lily will have a lot on her shoulders. She has to sell her practice and establish a new one nearby. Incumbent in her decisions is whether she wants to drive twenty miles each way to the city or put the practice in a nearby town the size of McKenzie. It is her decision which way she wants to go.

"I am taking this on as my life's work. I no longer dread this like I did. I was somewhat successful as a lawman. I pledge to the three of you I will be more successful running this ranch as a home for all of us."

"Your father would be so proud, son," Georgia said.

"I'm just sorry he didn't see the day," Jack said as his mother passed a platter of roasted beef and au jus over to him.

The day for John Lander's funeral had come. Bodeway and Deputy US Marshal Ann Ross drove in. Rich brought Helen, Cindy and Julie in Lily's BMW. Tac and his wife drove separately in his handicap-equipped van.

Uncle Bud wore a dark suit and his weather-appropriate Stetson. Rich noted his original .45 in an old El Paso holster when the retired ranger's coat opened. Jack was dressed the same.

Georgia and Lily both wore black dresses. Except for the age and hair color differences, they might have been mistaken for sisters. Lily stayed at her mother-in-law's elbow to provide any help needed.

Members of the area ranching community were there, including the head of the Livestock Association.

After a simple service in the family plot, the group of forty people adjourned to the barbecue. Nary a Texan there was unarmed, though it was not always obvious since the weather kept coats on and often buttoned. So the famous traditional Texas Barbecue Guns were not visible.

The head, Jesse Anderson, and several board members of the livestock association approached Jack and Lily privately. Cy Cozart, a local agent with whom Jack had worked was with them on a horse rustling case in Oklahoma and Texas.

"This might not be the best of timing Jack, but we want to run something by you. We are from around the state and this was the only time in the immediate future we could do this all together."

"Tell me what's on your mind, Jesse," Jack said. He had solved a high visibility Morgan horse rustling ring which spread from Texas to his county in Oklahoma a year ago and knew some of these men.

"We have had some serious cattle theft in the county. It's up to the Association to do the heavy lifting on the investigations. Which is why, as you know, we are allowed a good allotment of Special Texas Rangers. Almost all of our investigators are ranchers themselves. It has not become as much a full-time job in this part of the West as other places.

"Our investigator here worked with you and speaks highly of you. So does the most famous ranger in Texas right now, Lt. Bodeway over there."

Jack noticed Zack watching and recognized the

almost hidden smile under his mustache. *He's in on this!* Jack realized.

"So, we know you have a lot of work to do here, but keeping in mind this rustling might affect you, we wonder if you would become one of our Special Texas Rangers?"

"I don't speak for my husband," the beautiful redhead began, "but I would like to say something before he answers. This is the best damn idea I have heard in a long time! He can do his duty with the ranch and keep his real love, bringing in bad guys both!" She turned to her husband and smiled the smile to which he nor anyone else could ever turn down.

"I would be honored to try it on a trial basis, gentlemen. I don't fully know the time commitment doing it or running the ranch, but I sure would like to give my utmost to doing both," Jack said.

He noticed his friend Zack sidling over, his smile more apparent. His Uncle Bud, Georgia and Rich were behind him. His mother had her Bible.

"Am I the only person unaware of this, Jesse?" Jack asked.

"Pretty much. I hate to be turned down, so I got some important buy-ins first."

"Jesse? You got the badge?" Zack asked his old friend.

"I do, Zack."

"Miss Georgia, I see you have a Bible," the ranger said.

"If you'd like to make this official Jack, the Chief empowered me to swear you in," he said.

Still shocked, Jack nodded.

"Miss Georgia and Ranger Carey, I'd like y'all to both hold the bible Jack's going to put his right hand on. Jesse, give Miss Lily the badge to pin on the boy."

Zack swore Jack in as a Special Texas Ranger and Jesse left him with the letter naming him special agent for the association. Paperwork and equipment was promised to follow.

Later, Helen left with Rich and Tac and his wife left in the van. The mourners, other than Zack and Ann Ross and Cindy and Julie were gone. These four had accepted rooms for the night in the spacious old ranch house.

Everyone was too full for dinner, but no one turned down pie. As they sat and chatted over coffee, the large fireplace was roaring.

"So you had no idea you were going to be asked to be a special Texas ranger today?" Cindy asked.

"No idea at all. My friend and his Marshal confidant are pretty darn good at playing it close to the vest."

"Jack, so much has happened so quickly. Have you given much thought to the Doolin's Cave Ranch?"

"No, other than to sell it and the quarter section it's on as soon as I can," he responded.

"Cindy, Rich and I formulated a plan on the drive over. By the way, Lily, we all loved your car!" Lily smiled. The "Teutonic Hot Rod," as Jack called it was her pet.

"And, pray tell what was the plan?" Jack asked bringing the conversation back on track.

"Well," Julie began, "you have met my former husband and my divorce attorney sitting across from you. The latter, and the guilt of the former, afforded me a quite generous settlement at our parting. Cindy has a growing law practice. I, however, am bored to tears just playing with my Morgans.

"We thought about buying your ranch and turning it into a dude ranch. I would run it with a manager and staff. We'd build five or six cabins and turn the bunkhouse into several rooms with shared baths. We would build a separate new building for cooking and food storage. It would also have a family-type dining room. It may be in the new building. We have not quite formulated everything yet."

"Sounds pretty optimistic!" Lily said.

"It is. We would get a bit of an infusion of cash, we don't know how much yet, from Sheriff Ammon. He would buy the thirty acres or so near the river and particularly the cave and swimming hole. We might be able to build the kitchen, storage and dining cabin with his check," Cindy said.

"Would you be interested in buying a gynecologist practice?" Lily asked.

"Um, no. However, you do have a great real estate attorney to handle the transaction," Cindy said. "And, I have a friend in Oklahoma City who is a realtor who does nothing but sell businesses. I'd highly recommend her."

"Please text me her contact information. And, feel free to call her."

"Better yet, the three of us can meet for lunch in OKC and talk. You have to come back soon and move out of the ranch, move your horses and so forth."

"Yes, we do. We have to figure out how to get three horses four hours down to Texas," Jack said, totally forgetting such a trailer behind his barn at Cinco Peso.

"No. you really don't. You have a friend with a four-horse trailer and a Diesel dually pickup to pull it! I love horsey road trips! And, I'll stay over a few days and work the horses and check out your remuda," Julie said.

"And, you, Sheriff Ammon, what are you going to do? Pitch a tent and wait for summer to invite skinny dipping girls to the swimming hole?" Jack asked Rich.

"Close! But I was thinking a log cabin instead of a tent. The girls…well, yes!"

"Okay, now. This is more than an old man can hear," Uncle Bud said, not meaning a word of it.

"Friend Zack. You have been full of surprise secrets today. Is there anything else you have held back to shock us?" Jack asked.

"There is something, actually. Ann, why don't you share it?"

"Jack, and all of you present, will you be able to come to Zack's ranch on the first of December?"

"I'm sure we can make it to whatever shindig you and Zack have planned," Jack said.

"Good! Zack wants you to be best man at our wedding."

For once in his life, Jack Landers was stunned speechless. His uncle spoke first.

"I'll be damned! It's about time you made this beautiful badge-toting woman honest, Zack. We've all been waiting. I was getting ready to have a fatherly talk with you, boy," the old ranger said.

"I held back, Bud. I knew she was too good for me and was afraid she'd turn me down," Zack said.

"I seem to remember you on the cover of the expensive Texas magazine. What did it say? Oh, I remember 'Texas Ranger Zack Bodeway, the Lone Star State's Most Eligible Bachelor!'," Jack said.

"December 1st will be a day of mourning for women throughout the Southwest!" Rich added.

"I don't know about day of mourning. I do know I will wear Kevlar and want two of you lawmen beside me and the younger one positioned on a rooftop with his rifle. I remember the last time one of us got married!"

"Aw, Zack. It didn't count when Jack got shot at his wedding. It was just a twenty-two," Uncle Bud said.

"Now, wait a minute Uncle Bud, it did sting some."

"Two inches further over and it would have done more than sting," Lily said.

"I remember I was so mad when Tac and the little girl who had the crush on you shot the would-be assassin before I could," Georgia Landers surprised everyone with her vehemence.

"Don't be making Texas girls mad," Uncle Bud said.

"I remember a North Carolina redhead who scared the devil out of a bar full of drunk bikers with a snub nose .38, too," Jack added.

Lily patted the inner side of her left cowboy boot and smiled. Everyone got the point.

"Is there anyone in this room who is unarmed?" Zack said in jest.

The occupants looked around at each other and did a collective shrug, but Georgia admitted "mine is in the kitchen."

And, so went the banter without any more shocking news until people started to drift off to bedrooms.

The next day, Jack called Cy Cozart, the local agent for the Livestock Association.

"Cy, It's your new associate, Jack Landers."

"Jack, you are my path to my long-awaited retirement. Again, I'm real sorry about your dad. He was a fine man," Special Texas Ranger Cyrus L. Cozart said.

"Thanks, Cy. It was a surprise for us all. He was not yet sixty and had been keeping degenerative heart disease a secret."

"Are you in town long enough to take a ride out and look at the site of the last cattle robbery?"

"I'll make time, Cy. When do you want to do it?" Jack asked.

"I'm good after two today, if it's not too soon."

"Where do you want to meet?"

"There's a burger joint at the intersection of County Road 4 and Bowie Highway. How about there for a late lunch? They serve all day."

"I'll see you about two. It will be great seeing you again, Cy. We didn't get much chance to visit at the funeral," Jack said before ringing off.

He walked back into the main room where the guests were sitting and talking.

"Rich and ladies, when are y'all heading back? I'm not trying to get rid of you, but I have got to go look at a crime scene. I don't want to come back and find I have missed you without expressing my gratitude. You know you can stay another night."

"We will be going in an hour or so. Rich is aching to sit behind the big desk. Plus, your lovely wife wants to ride back with us. We have scheduled a meeting with my friend who sells businesses in the Stockyards City area of OKC. It will be over lunch tomorrow. My friend, Julia, has several doctors wanting to expand practices into the counties outlying OKC. One is a gynecologist. Julia thinks she could put together a fast sale," Cindy said.

"And we both want to get back and study your ranch and buildings. I have asked an appraiser friend to do some comps on it so we can figure out what to offer you," Julie said.

"You know what scares me? This is all coming together too smoothly. Life is just not usually this easy," Jack said.

"Maybe good things happen to good people," Julie suggested.

Rich loaded the carry-on bags for the three ladies and his small flat dark earth duffle into his former F-150 to return it and them to McKenzie.

"Rich, take some money for the gas. I didn't get a chance to fill it up with all the excitement," Jack offered.

"No need. As far as the world knows, I drove it here. Besides, you are still an employee of Warrior County Sheriff's Office. Maybe Sheriff Emeritus or something," he grinned at his mentor. Uncle Bud came up, pushing his walker.

"I'm gonna miss you two. Don't be surprised if I call and pester you about a variety of situational matters."

"Any time, sonny boy! My boy and I are always here for you!"

"Thanks, Uncle Bud. I see you returned your old piece to Jack. What an heirloom."

"You turn your matching copy into an heirloom, too, ya hear?" Jack suggested.

"Any future Mrs. Ammon's on the horizon?" Uncle Bud asked.

"Not yet. I helped out an Oklahoma City ER nurse who got mugged a few months ago. We are dating some. Isabella has gone totally work-oriented in Wichita. Her older sister calls and propositions me periodically."

"What do you hear from Polly Antrim?" Jack asked.

"Spoke with her a couple days ago. We have some openings and I might hire her."

"I was almost sure she'd show up here," Jack said.

"Got your six, boss!"

"Did you tell..." Jack began. He did not need for finish his question, reading the grin on his former chief deputy's face told him all he needed to know.

The three women came out. Georgia accompanied

them with a highway lunch better than they could have found en route.

Goodbyes were said and Rich pulled the powerful pursuit truck off. The two Landers and the old ranger stood watching.

"Best damn people ever," Bud Carey said. His grand-nephew could not agree more.

———

RICH MADE excellent time to Oklahoma City and into Stockyards City and its plethora of good eateries. Lily and Cindy got off at the agreed upon restaurant and Rich and Julie parked.

"Base, this is Warrior-1, do you read?"

"Warrior-1, base. I have you broken and barely read-able. Will you switch to cell phone?"

Rich clicked the mic twice to signify "yes," and called Tac.

"Hey, buddy, I am back in the area. Getting lunch in OKC and back in the office by maybe four. Anything hopping?"

"No, boss. All quiet on the Western Front."

"Keep it quiet. I'll see you soon."

They walked to a restaurant across the street and went in. The early forties Julie turned heads as she walked by.

"How do you feel about having such an effect on men, Julie?"

"It's quite flattering for a forty-year old. If they only knew, huh?"

"I'm not sure it would make any difference at all," Rich said.

"What are you going to get?"

"My preferred lunch. A salad and a half and half."

"A what?" she asked.

"Half sweet tea and half unsweetened. Gotta keep my trim and girlish figure right?"

"And a salad for lunch and ice tea does it?" she asked.

"An hour daily on my Peloton helps."

"Indeed."

"Don't you love 'indeed?' It commits to nothing and makes you look wise at the same time!"

"You know, Rich. It does. I never thought about it."

They ordered.

"What kind of cabin are you thinking about?" Julie asked.

"Fairly small. Square logs. Metal roof. Stone chimney and fireplace with a heat distribution fan. Bath and a half. Matching outbuilding."

"Sounds quaint. We'll be neighbors. Not just the dude ranch, but my spread, too. You will have to be a frequent dinner guest."

"Only if you reciprocate and you and Cindy let me cook at the cabin."

"So. You can cook?" she asked.

"Indeed," he gave her the grin.

"That works on women almost all of the time, doesn't it?"

"Indeed."

"Cut it out! Lunch is here. I am famished. I don't know why. I ate most of a side of beef at the after-funeral barbecue," she said.

"You wear it well."

"Indeed," she smiled back. Hers was not superhero. It was, Rich thought, smokingly hot. He thought about this flirtatious woman only ten or twelve years older than he. He wish he had met her when she was still dating men.

Of course then, he realized, he might have just been a teenager.

"What are you thinking about so deeply over your salad, Sheriff"

"You, actually. Before you...you know...ugh"

"Changed sides?" she prompted.

"Yes. I am not versed in how to talk about things like this," he said.

"Well, to confuse you further, that ship hasn't sailed. It's still puttering around the harbor. With Cindy, too. And, don't say 'indeed,' damn it!" she grinned mischievously.

"How did you know what was on the tip of my tongue?"

"You might be a tough ass army ranger and lawman, but I can read you like a book," she said convincingly.

"That scares me."

"But, you like it," she said.

"How's your lunch?" Rich asked, changing the subject deliberately.

"Delicious! How's your rabbit food?"

"Not bad. I may sneak a rare hamburger and beer when you are out of sight."

"In," she started but he held up a finger and wagged it. She did not finish saying "indeed."

They had fun talking and subsequently Cindy texted and said they were ready to be picked up and to resume the trip back to Warrior County.

Rich checked in at the office by late afternoon. Tac, who was getting ready to go off-shift, reassured him everything was quiet. He looked at a couple day's mail. The fact he was gone over a weekend had no effect on the work. Crime does not keep nine to five hours.

WHILE RICH WAS DRIVING the ladies back from Oklahoma City, Jack was meeting with Cy. The owner of the ranch adjacent to the Cinco Peso, William Stackpole, was present. He had purchased the ranch five years ago and the first time Jack had met him was at the funeral yesterday.

"It happened right here. Last night. One of my boys rode out this morning to find fifty cows gone and these tractor trailer prints on the little trail beside the pasture. This is about a mile from the main house and bunkhouse, so nobody heard squat. I been here for nigh on to five years. Never had a single beef stolen, nor a horse either. We never mounted a guard. But one or two are going to be riding herd starting tonight," Bill Stackpole said.

"What size herds to you have in other pastures?" Jack asked.

"I got me two more herds. The farthest pasture has five hundred. I don't think they could get big trucks up there. Have to rustle the old way by horse. The other two stretch out to the one I just mentioned." He pointed out towards the west. "One's about five miles out. There's a little path. Maybe you could get trucks out there. You'd need a bunch to get them all. I got two hundred-fifty there. The farthest one is six miles beyond with the five hundred head. No road to it, just a riding trail. I have two cowboys watching them. They stay at a cabin out there the whole time the big herd is in the far pasture."

"Bill, are they armed?" Cy asked.

"They have two handguns, a shotgun and a twenty-two rifle for shooting squirrels and rabbits," he said.

"So, basically they are not armed for a professional rustler gang?" Cy asked.

"No, I guess not. I have a Marlin in .35 Remington. Maybe they ought to have it up there, huh?"

"Yeah, Bill, I think so," Cy said.

"Cy, it sounds like it's about eleven or so miles out. How'd you feel about us riding out and checking on the two cowboys and taking the lever gun to them?" Jack asked.

"I am up for a ride. Bill, could you point us to some horses and saddles? We could saddle them while you fetch the Marlin and plenty of shells for it," Cy said.

"Better yet, I'll have one of the hands here get the horses ready and look for a couple of scabbards to put on them."

"Three scabbards if you have them. They will need one when they ride back in with the rifle," Jack reminded him.

"Y'all come on back to the ranch house. I'll get the missus to get you some bottles of water and a Thermos of fresh coffee."

Ten minutes later, the newest Special Texas Ranger and one of the oldest still on duty were riding towards the two herds. Jack had grabbed his go-bag from the ranch house before he left. He was using his father's truck, a five-year old but perfect Chevy 2500 with a Detroit Diesel. He retrieved the bag and moved everything into the saddlebags he had borrowed from Bill Stackpole.

"Going camping?" Cy asked him as they mounted up. Jack nodded.

"Bill, if you don't object, I might camp by the nearest herd, where the road ends. These fellas might not be aware you know about the others missing yet. With the trail out there, it would be easy pickings for them if they let lightning strike twice in the same place," he said.

"You got enough gear for me?" Cy asked.

"No, not for as cold as it's going to be tonight I suspect. I like you a lot. Always have, but this sharing a blanket thing might be sudden!"

Both the other two stockmen broke out laughing.

"Jack, give me a second to run back in. I saw you put some jerky and some energy bars in those saddlebags. Let Hazel make you a sandwich, bag up some donuts for desert and breakfast and add a second thermos of coffee. You don't want to be setting up housekeeping by cooking out there in the hills," Cy offered.

Jack thanked him. They were riding, Jack's saddle-bags a bit heavier, a few minutes later.

"Jack, I read about you going up in the hills after a bunch of escaped convicts last year. You took them all out but a boy. You brought him back okay.

"Do you suspect you will do the same tonight?" Cy asked.

"No, for a couple reasons. First, them even appearing is pretty improbable. I knew those guys were loose and where they were probably going. Second, they were escaped convicts. At least one was a cop killer. I knew if they split, we would suffer a bunch of home invasions, car thefts and the like. I'm figuring I can get some tag numbers. If it's a few, I might try to get the drop on them or call the cavalry. If not, maybe one shot from a high-powered rifle will make them take off and at least save Bill from losing more cattle."

"All makes sense. You kinda like to work alone like Heck Thomas, Bass Reeves and some of those guys don't you?"

"Not really, Cy. I like you and me riding out to check

on these two. It's good to have backup. For all we, or Bill, know, they might be involved. Until we know for sure, it might be prudent to have one of us present himself and the other cover his back from behind them. Couldn't do it with just one of us."

They rode to within a mile of the second or middle herd and Jack suggested they get off the trail the robber's trucks may use later. No need in having prints as they get closer and more suspicious.

They circled around and came in on the second herd from the side opposite the trail. It also gave Jack a good place to look for his camping and surveillance spot. He knew what he was looking for and found it.

"I was hoping it would look like this. Open around the herd all the way to where the trucks would congregate. But here, on the far side of the herd, a small rise with a dished out area behind it and a few trees. I can set up camp in the dish, dig a fire pit with a secondary air hole to make the fire hot and efficient and cut down on smoke. I should be able to get enough downed wood from the trees for fuel. From the camp, I should be able to hear the trucks and crawl up the rise to spy on them," Jack said.

"Okay, Jack. A couple of questions. Is the fire only for warmth? You have hot coffee and no cook gear I saw, so you won't be cooking on it, right?" Cy asked.

"Right."

"Okay, again about the fire. The rustlers will be parking maybe one hundred fifty yards away. Might they not smell the fire? Or even see it?"

"Good questions, Cy! The way I will build in a pit and block it will make it difficult to see. The smell maybe problematic. Maybe I will burn it until eight-thirty or so and let it die out. If they don't show and I am not a popsicle by one or two, I will figure they aren't coming tonight and relight it. It's gonna be pretty damn cold to be sleeping out with just a foil rescue blanket and a little bivvy sack."

"Jack, I have heard the term, but never saw a bivvy sack," Cy said.

Jack dismounted and began to dig through the contents he had placed in the saddle bags. When he came to a draw-string bag three or four inches in diameter and six inches high, he removed it and withdrew an orange bag from it and unfolded it. It was an insulated orange bag one could crawl into and pull it up over his head and stay dry and reasonably warm in most types of weather.

"What a great emergency item to carry!" Cy said

"And, I have this Mylar and aluminum foil blanket which also gives some insulation. I will probably wrap it around me and cover my head inside the bivvy."

"Beats the old days on the trail with wool blankets and tarps to sleep in and under," the older investigator said.

"Uncle Bud taught me a lot about living out, tracking, keeping aware of my surroundings and threats. He taught me the old foods and how to make them. Jerky, pemmican, trail coffee, and fry bread. I have added the new technology over time," Jack said.

"Jack I heard you mention a pit fire. I have built hundreds of campfires to brew coffee, roast a rabbit or heat a branding iron. But always on the surface of the ground.

"Let me show you on the way back. We still have six miles to ride and deliver a rifle I hope those two punchers don't need," Jack said and they remounted.

About forty minutes later, they saw smoke spiraling up from the chimney of a line shack. The large herd was still and there was one cowboy sitting on a log bench outside the shack smoking a cigarette.

"You want to be the greeter or the one circling around behind?" Jack asked.

"I'll greet him. He may know me anyway." He pinned his badge prominently on the left breast of his coat. The sun was still high and he was riding towards it, so the badge should glint in the sun.

Jack circled around behind the building and rode in silently to within fifty feet of where the man was sitting, but out of his line of sight.

"Hello, the cabin! This is Cy Cozart, agent for the live-stock association," he called out in a deep commanding voice which could not be missed or misinterpreted.

The man rose and waved him in. "C'mon in, Cy. My pard is brewing up a pot of coffee. Get yourself down and have some!"

At this point the man inside walked through the door empty-handed and Jack rode around the side towards him. His rifle was already sheathed.

"We got something for you from Bill Stackpole," Cy said, now close enough to speak in a conversational term.

"Them Russian dancing girls?" the man asked with a grin.

"Naw. They hadn't arrived yet. A Marlin rifle. The first herd by the ranch was all rustled last night. We don't think they can get the big trucks out here, but they could come the old way by horse. Bill figured you needed one more decent long gun. The .22 is not enough and the shotgun won't shoot far off.

"My pard is coming around the side. He's a new agent for the association. Former sheriff out of Oklahoma."

"You're the fella they made that movie about!" the man blurted out.

"Yeah! Landers," the man in the doorway said.

"Afraid so," Jack said as he got down off the buckskin Stackpole had loaned him.

"Cy has a .35 caliber Marlin and some cartridges. Y'all familiar with lever guns?"

"Only from watching John Wayne."

Jack gave them a quick lesson in loading and particularly lowering a cocked hammer. Cy then gave them some boxes of rifled slugs for their twelve gauge shotgun.

"It will raise your effective range from twenty-five yards to maybe one hundred. One seventy-two caliber slug instead of pellets," Cy told them. He untied a large bag from his saddle horn and gave it to the two. It was a couple dozen homemade donuts from Hazel Stackpole. The two appreciated those more than the rifle.

"I doubt they will come here by horseback to steal the herd. They'd have to herd them down to the second herd which is about as far as they could get the big trucks. Then they would have to load them in. Such an operation takes time, which is a major risk for robbers. They want to get in and out quickly," Jack said.

The stayed and visited about half an hour then wished the two their best and retraced their hoofprints back to the far side of the second herd.

As promised, Jack showed Cy how to make a fire pit and lit it briefly with twigs to illustrate how it worked. He had an eight inch diameter hole to suck in air. It was connected by a hand dug tunnel to a twenty inch hole. The larger hole was deeper. The end of the tunnel from the small hole was at half the depth. He used a small trowel he carried in his bug-out bag along with a toma-hawk for gathering wood.

Jack showed how the small hole sucked in air and sent it superheated through the tunnel to ignite the wood in the larger pit and keep them burning at their hottest. The efficiency of the burn eliminated a lot of the smoke usually associated with campfires.

"Thanks for sharing it, Jack. I wish I had known how to do it years ago. My trail camping days are about over. My RV camping days are about to start. Now you are here I can finally retire in good conscience.

"I better be heading back to get to the Stackpole place and return this mount before dark. Be safe out here, okay?"

"You are a good man to ride with, Cy. I thank you. I suspect this will just be another cold camp. Let's get together in a day or two and figure our investigative plan. These fellas did not leave much in the way of clues, did they?" Jack asked.

"Nary a one, Jack. Well, I'll be riding. You should be in cell phone distance. I will call the sheriff on the way back to Bill's and let him know you are out here and to jump if you call 911 with gunfire in the background."

Jack grinned at him.

"I'd appreciate it, Cy. Have a good ride in and we'll talk soon."

Jack watched his soon-to-retire associate ride off. He called the ranch and said he was riding on the Stackpole ranch and would camp in a nice spot for the night and see his mother and Uncle Bud tomorrow. He called Lily. She had a successful meeting with the business realtor and was picking up some needed grocery items in his little step side Chevy pickup.

He gathered loose branches and larger wood for a fire, accumulating a night's supply.

His bivvy sack laid out and emergency blanket ready, Jack dug into the food bag Hazel Stackpole had sent. There was a roast beef sandwich, an apple and some donuts. Enough donuts for dessert and breakfast.

Before eating, he took his knife and made a fuzz stick from a broken off branch of dry wood. He struck his ferrocerrium rod with the top edge of his small seven inch blade Bowie knife and showered sparks on the fuzz stick. It caught and soon he had a hot little low-smoke fire.

Jack took the bigger pieces of wood he had gathered and made a reflector. It was tall enough to block the flames from distant view. He dug into the sandwich, apple and two donuts. Half a bottle of water later, he unscrewed the lid of the Thermos and had some hot coffee.

So far a good night. And, good to be camping alone on the trail. It had been a while. He enjoyed the wind, the stars becoming visible, the smells and particularly the solitude. He would not have minded sharing the solitude with a certain redhead though.

Jack looked at the luminous face of his watch. It was already nine o'clock. Time to let the fire die down to make him invisible to anyone driving up on the track to the opposite side of the herd.

He reckoned a pickup or SUV would arrive first to reconnoiter, slowly and carefully scouting the area for guards. They would give an all-clear and the big trucks would move in. Jack thought there would be several horses for wranglers to use moving the cattle aboard the trailers.

The horsemen would be his biggest threat. They

would be fast and mobile. Their probable lack of experience riding and shooting at the same time would mitigate in his favor.

He moved the bivvy sack and his Winchester to the edge of the rise and got in. He was asleep shortly.

Jack was awakened around midnight by a motor sound. He crawled out of the bivvy sack and peered over the rise towards the herd. A full-size pickup truck was stopping directly across from him. The herd was between him and the truck a hundred fifty yards away. He aimed the small Steiner binoculars but could not see the license tags because of angle and darkness.

A couple men got out. He saw one held a long gun, either rifle or shotgun. He might have guessed rifle had he seen a scope. But, absent a scope, it could have been either. The other began scanning the area with a powerful, high lumen light.

Jack ducked down as the shaft of light moved horizontally in his direction. It kept on going. He stayed down in case it scanned back over where he was hidden. The man made the mistake of not looking closely enough. Instead, he used the light to signal vehicles or horsemen as yet unseen.

Soon, a dually pickup with a multi-horse trailer pulled up, followed by three semi-trucks pulling large cattle hauler trailers.

He wanted to act before the horses were unloaded. Jack took a couple of twenty round boxes of Hornady .30-30 rounds out of his pocket and set them on the ground. He levered the model 94 and stood.

"You men! Livestock association rangers. Put down your weapons and raise your hands!" *Sometimes a bluff worked. Sometimes it doesn't. But I have to start somewhere,* he thought.

It didn't work. Not at all. The man with the long gun shouldered and fired in his direction. Rather professionally. The bullet zipped by at over two thousand feet per second. It was a rifle, not a shotgun.

Jack dropped him with a shot to the center of mass. He could sure use former sniper Ammon about now.

Several of the cowboys by the horse trailer fired handguns in his direction as one tried to open the gate of the trailer to get some horses into the fray.

Jack fired carefully aimed shots at them. One dropped hard. The man at the gate of the trailer fell and was screaming. The others sought cover. Apparently only some were armed.

Jack called 911 and identified himself as a special ranger in a firefight. He gave the location and description of the vehicles and approximate number of adversaries.

The dispatcher rolled several sheriff's patrol vehicles and several DPS troopers towards the Stackpole ranch.

Intermittent shots were also still coming his way.

Jack concentrated on disabling vehicles. He did not want the horse trailer to get out of range and deploy horsemen to his location. So, he shot the front tires out on the truck hitched to it.

Jack focused on the front tires of the several tractors hitched to the cattle haulers. He did not care if the men got away. He would have vehicles with registrations and fingerprints everywhere. The registrations would lead to the owners. It was the bosses he really wanted.

The vehicles, except for the first scout truck which Jack hoped would be used for their getaway, were all crippled. Four men were down. He felt one or two were dead, the rest in various wounded conditions.

As he had hoped, several with pistols put up covering

fire as more helped the wounded into the bed of the truck. Jack held his fire. He had accomplished his goal.

The big pickup spun around and headed back to the way from which it had come.

Someone riding in the front passenger seat fired a handgun in his direction.

Jack did fire back at him and the man would never fire a gun at a lawman again. Nor, would he ever take another breath.

Jack reloaded and surveyed the scene. He called 911 again and gave a status report, requesting an ambulance. Wishing he had a tag number, he described the retreating truck. A shot up truck with a dead man and several wounded in the bed should be easy pickings for responding peace officers.

Unless the truck took off across country, they had to run into the police vehicles somewhere around the Stackpole ranch house. Jack called Bill Stackpole and warned him.

"I'll alert the boys. I don't know how them trucks got past here coming up to you. I hope my wranglers are better shooters than they are watchers!"

Five minutes later, Stackpole called back.

"They came roaring by. No sheriff cars yet. My boys shot at them and might have hit a couple. If nothing else, they marked up the truck something fierce!"

"Bill, call 911 and tell them what you just told me. I am going to walk over and take a body count and check out the trucks still here. All the shooting made your herd move off, which is a good thing. No cattle were injured in our little action here."

"Well, sounds like you saved my herd. I surely appreciate it, Jack. You are a one-man SWAT team. Let me run and call 911 back now," he said as he rung off.

Loaded and with his .45 as a dependable backup, he began to cross the field in front of him. He watched the trucks and the two men on the ground.

The first, who had been the rifle shooter, was hit in the upper center chest. He had bled out and died. Very fast, no doubt.

The second was the man by the back of the horse trailer. Jack had hit him in the femoral artery. He was dead also. Jack could hear sirens in the distance. He quickly wrote down license plate number and collected registrations from the glove compartments. He wore purple nitrile gloves from his pocket to protect the paperwork for prints. Jack put all of them into a zip-lock plastic bag. He took his iPhone and photographed every aspect of the scene, including a long shot of his firing position across the field. He was continually amazed at the photos his new phone could take at night with using the flash.

The ambulance and a sheriff's Tahoe pulled up.

"The shooters are beyond help," he said as the EMT's began to unload trauma kits. One checked the bodies and nodded for the other to replace the kits.

Jack identified himself by Special Texas Ranger badge to the deputy, a sergeant.

"Do you have paper credentials, Ranger?" he asked.

"No, I am new and they are being prepared. Do you know Cy Cozart, the area cattle association agent?"

"I do and heard over the radio he is on the way here."

"He will identify me."

"I already knew who you are. I just thought it would be simpler to write down everything from your creds," the sergeant said.

"Let's walk around this thing. I want you to see freshly fired guns and cartridge casings to know I was returning fire. It was about six of them and one of me," Jack said. The sergeant had some markers in his car and dropped them by every gun and pile of empties along with taking photographs. He had a rolling traffic distance marker used for accident reports. They rolled it over to Jack's shooting position. He photographed the position and the .30-30 brass scattered around.

"I would fire and roll to another location as I had incoming rounds from them. Hence the rifle brass in small piles around the area," Jack explained.

"Okay, I think we got it.

"We may as well start with the report. How about you taking my report case and fill out what happened on the blank report on top? I suspect it won't be the first of these you have filled out."

"Not by a long shot," Jack smiled. He took the metal case and wrote out a full page report of what had happened. He showed it to the sergeant who said it was fine, then both signed and dated it.

"Is there any update on whether your guys or the DPS troopers intercepted the big pickup with the bed full of wounded? I understand Bill Stackpole's boys marked up the truck with more holes on the way by his ranch. I had given him a description."

"No, we have not got them yet. They had to have a rabbit hole they ducked into. We and the DPS have the roads cordoned off. Hell, we even have the game wardens out looking."

"Good move. Those fellas can often think like a wounded animal and come up with fugitives better than us mortal cops," Jack said and the sergeant nodded in agreement.

"I see a white pickup flying towards us. Looks like Cy," the sergeant said.

"You okay, Jack? I should have never left you out here by yourself!" Cy asked.

"He's fine. The rustlers, not so much," the sergeant said pointing to the as-yet uncovered bodies and piles of empty shell casings.

"Looks like the first Bull Run. Or, maybe the second Bull Run. I don't know. Hell, my side won both," Cy said.

"If you have access to law enforcement computers, we have a lot of fodder to chew on. I have the information on all of the trucks, including the registration papers. They may be straw companies, maybe not. But, it's a start at finding out whose behind these cattle robberies. I want to take pictures of the ID's of the deceased when the medical examiner gets here and removes their wallets. I didn't want to mess up the crime scene. I used nitrile gloves to get the motor vehicle paperwork.

"I do have a question though, Cy. Is this still going to be our case? Or does it now fall to the sheriff's office or DPS investigators or the Texas Rangers?"

"We kinda negotiate it out. They are usually glad for us to take the case and work it. I have, and you will have, easy access to the computer systems at the sheriff's office. Some of the guys use a trooper barracks because it's closer. But, you will have the assets you need to build a case. We even do the arrests, but usually take some deputies with us," Cy explained. "Because you are deputized as a ranger, one Texas Ranger needs to be in the shooting team which will assemble here tonight. I know you have been through them before. You, the first responder sergeant, and I will be questioned. The written statements and photos and site will be examined and you will be exonerated. Not to worry," Cy said.

"I'm not. It was righteous self-defense. While I cannot

prove I fired only after being fired upon, I don't think the finding will rest on it.

"Talk to me a little about our authorities as special rangers, Cy."

"First off, obtain and study Chapters 142, 143, 144, and 146 of the Texas Agricultural Code. They are the ones of primary interest to us," he said as Jack noted the legal cites in his notebook.

"Our primary time is spent investigating cattle, horse and related equipment thefts. We also go after people who commit agricultural fraud.

"Another area is identifying who owns livestock when they get free under virtually any circumstances, such as tornados, floods and the like. We also try to instruct landowners on theft prevention. Same for high school Future Farmers of America and 4H groups.

"Then, there is the big, kinda vague one which gives us the greatest authority. We are Texas peace officers.

"You can make arrests and exercise all authority given peace officers when necessary to prevent or abate an offense which regards livestock or related property. You cannot, however, arrest on a traffic offense.

"We are missing a manager in this district. We really have not needed one. It's a one-man operation. Not like he would have to supervise three or four special rangers, or agents as we are called half the time."

"Livestock agent sounds kinda like a type of extension agent to me, not peace officer," Jack said

"Yeah, me, too. I never used the agent term much," Cy said.

By the time the orientation was complete, the shooting team had assembled. They interviewed the first responding sergeant first, then Cy. Jack was last. The team took Jack's rifle and his empties and loaded cartridges. They checked his .45 and saw it was unfired. Also, there were no .45 empties on the ground. They studied the scene, the evidence, the distance between Jack's and the outlaw's shooting points and came to their decision. Jack and his employer would be advised by letter in the next few days.

Jack and Cy went to the local sheriff's substation and commandeered a desk with a computer just after daylight. They researched the ownership of the trucks and trailers. Each was owned by a series of shell companies. The ownership, while not well-defined, always came back to Austin. They checked the backgrounds of the two dead men. Both had lengthy criminal records in a county outside of Austin.

Jack decided he needed to go to Austin. He would meet with people from their county sheriff's department about the two deceased rustlers. His primary goal would be to tie them to a person or organization behind the robberies.

He would then get Zack Bodeway to refer him to someone in Ranger Headquarters to talk about criminal organizations in the area which might be involved in livestock theft.

The ranger with whom he spoke would be well aware of Jack breaking up the Morgan horse rustling ring out of Texas last year and Bodeway shooting the head of the ring at a DPS road block.

The last thing he obtained from Cy was a list of times, dates and places of livestock thefts in the counties surrounding and including his own Ranger County.

Jack planned a murder board like the one Rich had used several months ago in Warrior County. He would put pins on a map on the board and crime scene photos. Something so simple as a circle around a cluster of crimes, the middle of which is where the bad guy would be found. Even if not, it could simplify understanding the case and its breadth.

He called Lily and told her he was okay after a "little excitement" last night at the Stackpole Ranch. Jack then called Uncle Bud and told him about the interaction with the cattle rustlers and asked him to tell his mother he was on the way home.

Jack had only slept a few hours the preceding night. He took a shower and a nap which lasted until dinner. During the nap, he did not sleep either.

AFTER A NICE DINNER with his mother and great uncle, Jack retired to a spare room next to his father's former office. It was basically a junk room and he spent several hours discarding the junk and storing anything worth saving in the barn.

The next day, he set up his laptop in there and took the big Diesel pickup into town where he bought a table, a desk chair, a side chair and a second-hand wooden desk. He also bought a large corkboard and lots of colored pins. His last purchase was a small printer for his laptop and a box of printer cartridges, and office supplies.

Jack moved these items into his ranger office at the ranch and hung the board. He put information about the deceased robbers and what he had learned about the ownership of the trucks on it. He also placed every photo he had taken at the scene there. He wanted to keep the ranch office separate from the one for his livestock investigations. The murder board was up.

As he sat at the table in his new office chair and

pondered, he considered the difficulty of surveilling a large area with only himself doing the work. There had to be an easier way.

It hit him. A drone! He got on the Internet and researched commercial drones which had reasonable endurance or flight time, good altitude capability for stealth, and a decent camera to record evidence. He found several he could afford.

Next, he researched where to learn to fly the darn things. Jack found a guy in the next county who was a drone flight instructor. He called him, was told where to buy the recommended one of the several on his list and they set an appointment for two days hence.

He spent some time filling out the employment and tax paperwork with his new part-time job with the association and got a passport photo made at the local pharmacy to return with the paperwork for his ID card.

He researched the Texas statutes Cy had recommended and printed them out to carry with him. He was a bit undecided about what to drive. His hot little step side Chevy was cool, but not very official looking. The ranch truck was better. He did not need a heavy duty pickup with a Diesel, but it is what he had. The Suburban might be better, but his mother loved it. So, Silverado 2500 Diesel it was then.

He went to a police supply about fifty miles away and bought several more pairs of handcuffs, some pepper spray and, having seen Cy's ID, a leather cred holder for it and his badge. The Chevy had a black corrugated box in the back for his investigative gear and the bugout bag he had used the night before. He cleaned it out and put the gear in it. There was an old Mossberg 500 twelve gauge pump in the gun rack at the ranch. He took it and picked up an eighteen and a half inch barrel for it at a local gun shop and put it in a case in the box. His last stop was to drive seventy-five miles and buy the drone.

Jack wanted the rifle in the cab with him. He had yet to figure out how to store it for safety yet quick access without a police rack and finally decided a rack was the only option. He went back online and found one and ordered it. The ranger on the shooting team promised his Winchester back within a week.

He had spent a thousand dollars and, realized he had no idea what his salary would be. He called the Director and asked the salary and benefits question and whether they supplied any equipment.

Satisfied, he walked back into the world of his ranch and went out to meet with Jess and check on progress. He also worked with him to set up some security for the cattle and horses in view of what had happened next door. Over the next two days, up until Jack needed to leave to learn how to fly his new drone, they installed inconspicuous wildlife cameras. He would do more when there was more money. Which would be the proceeds of the sale of Doolin's Cave Ranch going into the ranch's general fund.

The next action was a call to Zack Bodeway.

"Hey, Zack. How are you?"

"I'm fine and really happy you aren't dead," the ranger said.

"Me, too."

"You have to stop this thing of taking on entire gangs alone in firefights."

"I'll work on it," Jack said without quite promising.

"I spoke with the ranger who ran the shooting review board. Be surprised when he calls you today, but it was adjudicated a clean shoot with no further action required."

"Thanks, Zack. My only worry was the guy who was trying to get the horses out. His gun was in his holster, I think unfired."

"The report stated it was, but noted he was part of an armed group firing at a Texas peace officer. He was armed himself and may or may not have just holstered long enough to try to open the gate on the horse trailer. It was unfortunate he was hit in the melee. For him."

"Glad they it's how they saw it. It's how it was."

"The other thing he told me, off the record, was the county judge called him and strongly suggested you have made a good start eradicating horse rustlers and he needs to get off his ass and help you," Zack said.

"Help is good. Pressuring a ranger is not," Jack said as he thought about the implications.

"Don't worry. The two are longtime friends. It's how they talk with each other, according to Ranger Blevins."

"Good. I need a referral. The evidence we picked up from the tractor trailers I rendered immobile suggests they are owned by a series of shell corporations. I don't know who the owners are, but whoever they are is behind this cattle stealing operation. And, it all seems to lead back to the Austin area.

"Do you have a ranger in headquarters who does intelligence and can tell me who the big players on the dark side are? I need some computer analysis help which is beyond my resources and capabilities."

"I do. He is Ranger Elliot Madison. He was in the field for years. Damn good ranger. Was in a traffic crash responding to a kidnaping a few years ago. Has to use a cane all the time, so he moved into HQ and does exactly what you need. I will call him as soon as you say 'Bye, Zack.'"

"Bye, Zack. And I do need his number." Zack gave him the HQ number and Madison's extension.

As soon as he hung up, Cy called.

"My retirement is official and I was told to pass my one-year old white F-150 to you. You can pick it up anytime. I have a new Tahoe I just bought. It's just crowding the drive."

"By drive, you mean the quarter of a mile long drive into your ranch? Ha. Thanks, Buddy. Can I come over shortly? I am going to Ranger HQ in Austin to talk with their intelligence guy. I will drive it."

"See you when you get here, then. I will give you the information on my retirement party, too," Cy said.

Jack's mother dropped him at Cy's ranch about five miles away.

"Here's two sets of keys to the Ford. There is some stuff you can use in it. Extra handi-tie cuffs, evidence gloves and bags, and some report and arrest sheets. There's an instruction manual for various computer things we use. Call the office and get them to give you a sign-on. Also, get them to send you a windbreaker with the badge logo and a more decorated up raid jacket. We just dress just like you are now with white or blue shirt, blue jeans and boots, white Stetson or similar and brown belt gear for your pistol. A lot of us carry 1911's with fancy grips like yours. So, you are pretty well set for image, in your nice chore coat over the white shirt and all," Cy said.

"Here's the invitation to my retirement party at the Cattleman's Club in town. It will be in two weeks. Maybe your wife will be back from Oklahoma in time to come. She sure caused a stir at you father's funeral, looking like a movie star and all."

"She's so perfect, Cy, I can't believe she married me.

People see the beauty. But you have to know her to realized what a kind, wonderful human being she is, too," Jack said.

"I will keep you advised on how this case goes. Just between you and me, I picked up a drone for surveillance. I have lessons on how to fly it tomorrow."

On the way back, Jack called Texas Ranger Elliot Madison.

"Ranger, this is Jack Landers. Zack Bodeway referred me to you."

"Yeah, Jack. He called earlier and filled me in on you and what help you were looking for. And, call me Elliot. We're all driving the same herd here. Congratulations on living through some late night fireworks," Madison said.

"Thanks, it was pretty low risk, even with all the shots which were fired.

"I'd sure appreciate driving over and buying you lunch to pick your brain. It looks like I have a pretty determined corporate cattle theft ring hitting the state. It seems to be coming out of somewhere near Austin. The trucks are registered with a series of cut-out shell companies. I could also use some technical help on tracking them down," Jack said.

"I have some ideas about possible suspects in this part of the state. I also have a computer guru who might be able to make sense of those shell corporations. Especially since we have a short list of names. When do you want to come over?"

"I'm tied up tomorrow. Are you available from mid-morning on the next day?"

"I am. Let's make it around noon and I will take you up on lunch. And, maybe bring the guru along. Meet me at Maria's Grill. We are on Lamar Boulevard. The Grill is a block away. I will make sure we have a private room.

See you then. Do you look like the guy who played you in the movie?"

"Haha, no. He's better looking. I do look like Bodeway's younger brother though," Jack said.

"Okay. I'll watch for a horde of screaming groupies. See you around noon on Friday."

The F-150 was a V8 and nicely, but not heavily equipped. It had a flip-down alternating red and blue LED light on the passenger sun visor and a basic siren. Unlike his past positions, he would not be doing any traffic stops. So this equipment should be sufficient for rare high speed runs to crime scenes. It had three hundred ninety-five horsepower and would be more than sufficient for his type police work and towing horse trailers and the like. The handiest thing, he suspected, would be the Motorola radio with the sheriff net channel and the DPS channel.

Cy had the tank filled, the mark of a lawman. Jack did a thorough mechanical and fluids run through back at the ranch. The truck was spotless and did not even need a hose down.

It was ready to go droning, then on to Austin to meet with Madison the next day.

From the new ranger office at his ranch, he called his headquarters and ordered a windbreaker with the badge imprinted, a raid jacket, and several patches to have sewn on a winter coat.

Jack was pleased so many of the special rangers wore the Western brown belts and some pretty fancy 1911's. His research even showed photos of Colts with engraved sterling silver Tiffany-style grips. His .45, passed down from Uncle Bud, with its custom lock work by 1911 maestro Smith with its stag grips would continue to serve him with pride.

The next morning, Jack drove to the drone trainer's home. He trained out of his parent's small ranch *which gave lots of open spaces to crash drones*, Jack thought as he pulled in.

He knocked on the door. The instructor was a nineteen year old with acne. He ended up to be far better than the initial impression he gave.

He and Jack unloaded the drone from the truck and assembled it. The first time took a little while. Subsequently, Jack would be able to assemble it and get it into action quickly under any conditions. The instructor, Jason Everett, checked the battery, the blades and the camera turret. Everything was in order.

They left the drone by the house and went in to Jason's office, which looked like a nineteen year old computer geek's workspace. Jason opened a simulation program for Jack's drone model and showed him how to fly it. After some pretty erudite directions, Jack took over the controller. He crashed it three times until something clicked and he got the feel for it. He learned how to take off, land, hover, climb and descend and soar in a straight line. He learned to stay away from towers, cell sites, powerlines and trees.

Jack suspected he would not encounter many of those obstructions. Jason told him his biggest enemy would be wind. Jack learned to deal with wind and ground effects.

After an hour, they went live. The drone Jason had recommended had optical avoidance, which helped. He also had purchased an emergency kit with extra blades. He ended up needing one replacement blade before he was comfortably taking off and flying and landing.

Jason asked if Jack bought it for recreational use. Jack, who had left his badge and gunbelt in the plain white truck explained who he was and how he planned to use the drone. He was not sure how Jason would take this revelation. He was enthralled with the use and offered several additional quick lessons to help surveil covertly.

The several hours were well worth the money and Jack left confident he could use the drone effectively with a little more practice.

He set it up at home and gave his mother and great uncle a demonstration. His mother was still on autopilot from his father's death. Uncle Bud immediately became enamored of the new technology for law enforcement use.

"Uncle Bud, once Rich started talking about his experiences in Afghanistan and other places he was vague about, he talked a lot about the use of big military drones and how efficiently deadly they were. All I want this to do is silently search areas that would take me days to search on foot or by vehicle. It's going to take more practice, but my first place to look will be the woods down the road from Bill Stackpole's ranch. The pickup with the fleeing outlaws disappeared there somewhere. There were sheriff and DPS roadblocks just beyond and they never made them to them. They launched a helicopter, but the FLIR or forward looking imaging radar was inoperable and they could not pick up an image or heat signal," Jack said.

"Do you think you ought to go there first thing in the morning and search?" Uncle Bud asked.

"Normally, yes. But, by this time they have gone. I suspect they left or killed their wounded. I expect to find them and more evidence at the scene when I locate it. Just not the people. I think they split and left through the woods before daylight. They probably walked to where some of the survivors had parked and left from there."

"Did the roadblocks pick up anybody suspicious?" the old ranger asked.

"Not a single one, according to what I have learned. Not a one. Strange. It's like the earth swallowed them up."

Georgia had left to do something which normalized her life. She began supper. It was the manager, Jack, Bud and her. She had stopped setting five plates only yesterday.

"Is Mom going to be alright?" Jack asked his great uncle.

"Yes, son. She is. The Carey women are some of the toughest Texas ever bred. They began protecting this ranch against raiders with muskets, then black powder cartridge rifles and shotguns, and finally smokeless powder guns. They shot and killed invaders including Yankee marauders with cold efficiency. It will take her a time. I don't know how long. But, she will come out of it. As I reminded you when you were in the coma, some little grandchildren would be the best cure in the world for her."

Jack smiled at the old man.

"I'm afraid she is going to have to do with a little black and white cat for a while, Uncle Bud."

"Well, little Jasmine sure does love her and vice versa. Every time Georgia sits down, she jumps right up on her lap and goes to sleep purring," Uncle Bud admitted.

———

JACK GOT UP EARLY and took his time. The drive to Austin from the ranch was only an hour and a half. As he was prone to do, he arrived early and parked. He found a coffee shop across from the restaurant and ordered a cup and sat watching out the window.

Just before noon, he saw a tall man who was dressed, armed and badged like a Texas Ranger. He was probably early fifties, with a craggy, handsome face under the shade of a white Stetson. What gave him away as probably being Elliot Madison was the cane he was using and a limp as he made good time down the sidewalk. He was accompanied by a black female in her late twenties or early thirties. From the outfit and gun belt, she was clearly a Texas Ranger, too. The guru to which Madison referred, no doubt.

Having already paid, Jack laid a dollar tip on the table and arose. He walked across the street and met them before they got to the grill.

"Elliot? Jack Landers," Jack greeted, sure of his identification.

"Hi, Jack. Say hello to Mary Brown. She has the bad luck of being assigned to me for a year before going back into a district."

"Hey, Mary. Good to meet you."

"You do look like the guy who played you in the movie after all," she noted. "And like Lt. Bodeway, too."

"Makes it hard to sneak up on people, huh?" he asked.

They went into the grill and were obviously expected. The hostess led them to a small private room with a table which would barely seat four.

"Good arrangement. I feel like we should sweep the room!" Jack said in jest.

"Probably not necessary here. We in the Rangers are about the only ones who use this room. A retired ranger runs the restaurant."

They ordered, chatted about events in their world,

then ate. Once the plates were cleared, they got down to the real reason for the lunch meeting.

"I made copies of my research on the two decedents and the vehicles I managed to disable the other night. The vehicles are registered to a shell corporation which is owned by another, then another. As I mentioned to you on the phone, everything seems to point back towards this part of the state," Jack said.

Mary immediately started to study the paperwork.

"Jack, there are a couple or three organized crime figures here who come to mind. I suspect when Mary has finished her research, one of their names will be sitting on the table in front of us. You might note Smith, Gonzales, or Heinrich. All have their own mobs and all have included ag crimes with a variety of other crimes. All can afford a fleet of tractor trailers and have connections to resell the stolen livestock quietly and at a good price. The presence of brands or tattoos does not phase them at all," Elliot said.

"I need to do a lot more work. But one of the shell corporation names rings a faint bell. I am mentally associating it with someone on Elliot's list he just mentioned. I just don't know who yet. Give me a couple of days," Mary said.

"I appreciate anything y'all can do," Jack said.

"When you have a case, we will help you get a warrant. It will be your bust, but we will send in a lot of cavalry. Forget the one riot, one ranger deal with these guys. We'd back you up heavy. Watch your back when you start rattling cages. Any of the three of these guys would hire a hitman in a New York minute."

"Sounds good to me. I've spent most of my career tracking bad people alone. Sometimes a party is more fun," Jack said. "I'll watch my back and those of my family members. I have a wife, mother and my great uncle with me now. Which is only a few year's new after being on my own all my life. I'd have had confidence in my great uncle taking on anybody a few years ago. Now, not so much. Age impacts everybody, even a superman.

"I included info on the two guys who died in the fire-fight. Another one might have died shooting at me out of the truck as they fled. Nothing on the truck or wounded in the bed.

"The two I included have ties to a county adjacent to Austin. I figured I should go by the sheriff's office over there and ask some questions."

"You can if you want, but we can probably save you the trip," Mary said. I will include data on them, including prison associates in the package I will put together for you."

"You are a lifesaver. You're allowing me to get back to Cinco Peso Ranch and protect my own cattle and horses today," Jack said.

"Jack, how did the ranch get the name?" Elliot asked.

"My five times great grandfather bought it with a bunch of wooden buckets of Mexican cinco peso coins in the early 1850's. His name was Helmonius "Hellraising" Carey.

"Any kin to Texas Ranger Bud Carey?" Mary asked.

"Three or four times great grandfather. Bud Carey is the great uncle who now lives with me. I owe everything I am to him. He taught me how to ride, shoot, track and think."

"Amazing! How old is he now?" she asked.

"A slower but still very deadly eighty four. I was shot by an assassin at my wedding. While I was staggering over towards the shooter with my backup gun, Bud was shuffling along ahead of me with a Colt snub nose ready to fight. It was just a year and a half ago."

"What happened to the shooter?" Elliot asked.

"My dispatcher and a young woman I recovered from a kidnapper in the woods, both shot him. Every one of their shots would have killed him. My successor, Sheriff Rich Ammon, is getting ready to hire her as a deputy this month."

"How did she deal with taking a life? And how old was she at the time?" Mary asked.

"She was nineteen. I spoke with her about it and she was tough and logical. She took it fine. No PTSD or nightmares I know off. Just more conviction to get her criminal justice degree."

"Jack what ever happened to the female serial killer in your movie?" Elliot asked.

"She escaped from a psychiatric hospital and died. She was a sad case," Jack shared without hinting what he had never told a soul. The truth. She had gotten plastic surgery with money from her trust fund and became his girlfriend without him having a clue. She did die. After coordinating her hated father, a serial bank robber, to shoot it out with Jack. The father lost in the middle of Main Street. And, before she and Jack could marry, she bumped into and confronted the woman who had sexually assaulted her in a teen jail and messed up her mind for the rest of her life. The doctor who tried to save her on a bloody café floor was Lily Laughton. Now, Jack's wife. It was a part of his history. He, probably illegally, destroyed any proof of her identity and buried the story with her cremated remains. The "rest of the story" was not an epilogue in the movie or book. Nobody in the entire world but Jack knew it. And it would go to his grave with him.

"Were you relieved she died?" Mary asked.

"No. Not at all. She had been a bright person, ruined by a gang rape in a prison she was wrongly in. It scarred her and she was denied help by a father who thought it would ruin his career. She was a sad case. A heart-breaking case," he answered.

His quiet seriousness put an end to the personal questions.

Their food came and the conversation became lighter as they ate.

Jack reached for the check when the server dropped it on the table, but Elliot insisted on letting the Texas Rangers pay for it.

"This is a meeting and your badge says you're one of our own from out of town," he said.

"Uncle Bud and Zack Bodeway, who I met in college, both wanted me to be a ranger. It was the eight or so years as a trooper part just to get a competitive shot which kept me from trying."

"You've got the image and a legend in your bloodline. With the support of Bodeway, a legend himself, you would have cinched it after the requisite years with the DPS troopers."

"Thanks for your confidence, Elliot. I never second guess myself. Me being a ranger was Bud's dream. Me being a rancher was my dad's dream. Maybe finally I have come close to satisfying both. Unfortunately my dad died a few weeks ago and I resigned as Sheriff of Warrior County, Oklahoma to come be a rancher in his place. He never knew."

"I bet he's up there smiling," Mary said.

"I hope so. Thanks again for the lunch, the help and the friendship. All are highly appreciated," Jack said as they rose to leave with exchanged cards in hand.

He got back in the white Ford pickup and drove home, getting back in time to check on the horses. He hoped Remington, his troubled horse, was doing okay back at Doolin's Cave Ranch. He would take the horse trailer down and pick him and the two mares up this weekend, barring a cattle theft or other ag crime.

Jack strongly suspected Remington had been abused as a colt. When he first got the young horse, he had to be wary of a surprise bite or kick. He had gotten much better.

During a ride on the ranch with Lily, a rattler had spooked Remington on the side of a rise. He had reared up on his hind legs. Jack drew the frontier sixgun he often wore around the ranch and shot the snake while the spooked horse was on two legs.

Remington fell over and Jack jumped clear, hitting his head on a rock. He was lucky his wife was a cool-headed physician and his young deputy, Rich Ammon, was willing to destroy a hemi-powered Charger police vehicle to get to him fast.

Days later when he came out of his coma, he had asked about Remington with great apprehension. He remembered the horse falling and no more.

Lily told him the horse was fine and even came over to him while he was lying unconscious and she was calling for help and nuzzled him with concern. The man and the horse had a strong bond. Even stronger than Jack had known.

He immediately called Rich, who was looking after him and inquired.

"He's fine. Has some winter coat and a bit of fat. Sure would not hurt him for you to ride him some in Texas," Rich said.

"One of the reasons for my call! I am going to try to

pick him up this weekend. The mares okay, too?" Jack asked.

"They are good. Same for them. They need to be ridden."

"How are you? And the sheriffing business?" Jack asked.

"I am good. Seeing the nurse pretty frequently. Isabella not at all. Our relationship is now pure business associates, but with a past. I like it like it is.

"Nurse Jenny is not only an absolute doll, she gets this whole thing of working strange hours and getting called out. We are taking it slowly, but there could be something there," Rich said.

"I hope so, buddy."

"Sounds good. Oh, and don't be jealous, but Cindy and Julie have adopted me in your place."

"Haha. I won't be. And, you don't be convinced they are what they seem, because I don't think they are," Jack said.

"If they are lovers, it's okay with me. But I think they are roomies and best friends and it ends there. I don't care either way though. They are super people and great neighbors to you and soon to me."

"How's the thirty acres on the river acquisition going?"

"We haven't closed yet, but within days, I suspect. I have a contractor who will build the cabin I want and a matching storage building and stall combined. He will do it within the approved loan amount for the whole deal at the bank.

"Don't forget to share all the outlaw hideout history about the cave you researched, okay?" Rich asked.

"I will. Fantastic plans for your new place, Rich. You will have modern conveniences like wiring, heat, flush toilets and all built in. I had to work around the historic ranch house I had. Which had virtually no post-home-steading conveniences other than rudimentary electricity and water.

"You are going to love it there, Rich. You might have to throw some gravel on the dirt road leading down there. Don't forget to get a permanent egress and exit written into the deed."

"Got it covered. I am looking forward to it. The cabin and outbuilding are both in kit form. The contractor can put them up quickly, even in the winter. Unless it snows, of course."

"Snow is a very real possibility. Maybe the first effort should be gravel on the dirt road," Jack said.

"No *problema*! I have a great four-wheel drive with aggressive tires my former boss left for me."

"Yep. He's a helluva guy," Jack kidded.

"Don't tell him, but I agree wholeheartedly," Rich said.

"You used up a Dodge Charger and a .30-30 slug to keep him around and kicking. I will call on the way, assuming I come over this weekend."

They rung off and Jack continued to drive through the hill country afternoon.

CHAPTER SEVEN

JACK CHECKED the cattle on horseback with manager Jess Noland. He noticed Jess had put a rifle scabbard on his horse. Jess had shot with Uncle Bud and Jack when Jack was in high school. He knew his manager was a capable shot. A fact which may become very important in the current rustling environment.

Jack rode a horse he had broken himself during one of his last visits to Cinco Peso. He remembered his father's pride he still retained the skill to ride and break a bronco.

His father and Jess had continued to work with the horse, but Jack felt it was imprinted to him just as Remington was. He wondered how the two would get along. Perhaps not well. The barn was large enough to put them in stalls at opposite ends of the stall line.

They rode around the herd. It was in the first pasture near the ranch house. With the newly installed cameras and alarms, they should have some notice of rustlers. If nothing else, they should hear the large trucks. The cameras would be twenty four-seven. They would set the alarms each night, since there was virtually someone at the ranch every day.

The cattle looked good. Jack instructed Jess to choose a cowboy candidate for a fulltime addition to the ranch. They would both interview him. Just a little more expansion and they would need two ranch hands to help Jess with the stock.

He told Jess to get a couple of temp wranglers to help put out the winter bales and salt. If needed they could use the Diesel he drove, now he had the association truck for most trips.

Jess would need the temporary help quickly. It was a several man job and Jack had to go to Warrior County five hours away and pick up the horses this weekend.

He had let Lily, Julie and Rich know he was coming. He decided to take the Diesel after all and haul his own horse trailer.

The drive was slower with the farm truck and towing a heavy trailer. He went to Doolin's Cave ranch first and unhooked the four-horse trailer and left it there.

The next trip was to Lily's office to pick her up for a late lunch.

"I surely have missed you, Red Rose of Texas!"

"Have I officially earned the title?" she asked.

"You have. Mom is going to sign over the deed to Cinco Peso to me via the trust next week. Which will officially make you the Red Rose. She will be kinda like queen mother. She told me she wants us to build her and Uncle Bud a duplex which matches the ranch house. She will be near enough to help him as he begins to need more help. She is old school and thinks we should have the whole ranch house. I suspect the wish for grandchildren is hidden somewhere in her musings."

"Can we afford to build a duplex?"

"We will get perhaps four or five times the cost of a duplex in a week at the closing on Doolin's Cave Ranch. So, yes, we can. It appears I own two ranches free and clear at the moment. As we discussed several times, we need to make Cinco Peso more than just self-sustaining. We need to make it a profit generator. Putting all the money from our ranch into Cinco Peso improvements will go a long way towards the goal.

"I have Jess looking for another full-time cowboy and he managed to hire two casual ones for while I'm up here picking up our horses. They will be putting down winter supplemental feed bales and salt. We seem to have enough vehicles and equipment. I've checked and it's all in good shape. Jess has done a stellar job on maintenance. We need to give him either a raise or a big Christmas bonus. As you might suspect, I got along better with him than dad as a boy. He's like family to us.

"How is the sale of the practice going?"

"Real well, honey. Julia, the business broker, has found a buyer. She is another GYN, practicing in Norman. I gather, while successful, her partner is a jerk. She cannot get out of there fast enough.

"My deal with her is to maintain the practice by seeing patients every Thursday and Friday for a month. After a month she will take over. She is keeping my nurse and receptionist.

She has offered two hundred fifty thousand, lock stock and barrel, and five percent of her gross profits for five years. How does it sound to you?" Lily asked.

"Not being up on sales of professional businesses, it sounds fine. Will it give you everything you need to get started here? And, where?" he asked.

"It should, plus five year's increasing income, hopefully. I will be totally out of the ownership picture for liability purposes.

"I am thinking Lampasas. It has over seven thousand people in town and more in the surrounding area. A half hour commute from the ranch. A small hospital there and another in nearby Killeen. I should be able get privileges at both."

"Makes perfect sense. Have you looked into office space in case in Lampasas?"

"A cursory look so far. I don't think it would be a problem. It may be cheaper to set up the way I want it than to pay to take over a practice with a variety of patients. I want to continue in GYN and not ease over to family practice, geriatrics, or something else. I worked hard to get my board certs and want to keep them."

"You are the very best at what you do, darling. No need to change. It's bad enough our lives have been turned topsy-turvy. But we'll get past it and make a glorious success of whatever we do together."

"Have I mentioned adoring you, my long tall cowboy cop?"

"Perhaps, but it always bears repetition."

"How about I come back to Cinco Peso with you and the horses and stay a couple days?" she asked.

"You have a deal! Fly back to OKC for Thursday and rent a car?"

"Just what I was thinking," she said. "Going over to Will Rogers Airport in OKC to leave your little hot pickup takes us out of the way."

"We should have room for the three horses and all the saddles and tack. We can leave the food for Julie's horses. We have plenty at Cinco Peso. If you are going to rent a car on your trips over, do you want to follow me back in the little Chevy? We have to move it to Texas some time. Now's as good as any," Jack suggested.

"Sure. I will drive the small one. You pull the horses in this behemoth. Did you let Julie and Cindy know you are here?"

"Only told them and Rich I was coming. Why don't you call them now and bring them up to date? I promised to call Rich, too."

Lily called and they said they had some plans to discuss and wanted them to spend the night with them instead of at the ranch. They agreed.

JACK AND LILY arrived with two pickups, one small and the other large.

Dinner was waiting. Jack knew both women were superb cooks but could never tell them apart as to which one cooked.

"Lily, why don't you stay here in one of our spare bedrooms, both tonight and when you come back for your Thursday and Friday visits? We would love to have you."

"That's so nice. It got pretty lonesome out there for the past few days. I didn't even have little Jazz to keep me company, much less this big bruiser to look after me."

"As the attorney of the house, I have to make a statement of intent here," Cindy said.

"We'd like to start some renovation and construction on the place. With you not staying there, we could start before it got really cold and the ground was frozen. You know we'd still love to have you here, the construction notwithstanding."

"I know. And, it makes sense. I will be glad to stay.

The only livestock you will have to worry about are the bison. Jack, aren't they pretty much okay on their own?"

"They are. I have a vet take a look at them periodically. They have been grazing on their own for eons. They might need a bale of hay if they stay in one pasture and eat all the graze in it. You certainly don't have to worry about them in the weather. There's a reason why both Indians and mountain men cherished buffalo coats. They are impervious to cold, bad weather," Jack said.

"You have a five hour drive. Maybe six pulling a loaded horse trailer. When do you want to head over to the ranch to start loading up?" Cindy asked.

"Probably as close to six in the morning as possible," Jack said.

"Cindy, if you will do one of your fantastic breakfasts, I will go over and help Lily and Jack load the horses in and get them settled. I think Remington even likes me!" Julie suggested.

"You got it! Maybe I'll make my signature French toast with lots of Applewood-cured bacon pre-soaked in jalapeño juice."

Jack like the sound of this plan. Especially the bacon part.

The French toast was really good the next morning. The bacon was great as expected.

Remington was glad to see Jack and the mares to see Lily. Julie brought carrots with her and they were chomped up quickly by all three horses.

They put the two mares in, then Remington. He had not ridden in a trailer for five years and was somewhat skittish. The caravan of three trucks and one trailer left, stopped at Julie's ranch as she turned off, then two proceeded to Texas.

The trip was without issues and they pulled under the arched entry of Cinco Peso Ranch at one-fifteen.

Jack could see Jeff and two hands distributing the bales and setting out salt blocks as he rode in. He opened the barn and led Remington to the stall which would be his new home. Once he was settled, Jack got the two mares and put them in adjacent stalls.

He noticed Remington eyeing the stallion at the other end and vice versa. Only time would tell how much of a problem this might be.

With all the newly added horses fed and watered, Jack took the trailer around back and removed it from the truck. He locked the hitch with one of the common-keyed padlocks they used around the ranch. This was new to the area. However, things like the Stackpole Ranch cattle theft changed a lot. People were now even locking their doors and not leaving keys in the switches of trucks in the yard.

He went in and checked the game cameras on his computer. No sign of anything worth noting. Jack returned to the barn and saddled Remington. He slipped the old .38-40 lever action carbine from his youth into its scabbard on the saddle and rode out to see Jess and meet his new temporary hands.

"Hi, Jess. Everything good?" he greeted the ranch manager.

"So far, so good. Boys, meet the boss. This is Jack Landers. He owns this ranch which has been in his family well over a hundred fifty years. Jack, this is Chet," pointing to a stocky guy on a horse, "and, Beau. They will be here for a couple more days."

"Howdy, men. Thanks for coming over and helping out. Has my ma been feeding you okay?" he said, like in his favorite kind of interview, already aware of the answer.

"Yessir, Mr. Landers. We've been eating real well."

"Good! Let me let y'all continue and I'll exercise Remington a little" Jack said.

Jess had heard of the horse and his issues, but never seen him. *One powerful piece of horseflesh*, he thought.

Jack rode of at a canter and followed the fence line looking for truck tracks. There were none. He checked the cattle with their "$5P" brands, derived from Mexican use of the $ mark for pesos.

"You're feeling frisky getting out in the cool air and trotting around. Maybe we'll do a little gallop when you are ready, huh?" he asked the horse.

They reached a wide expanse of grass with some little hills in this, the northeastern edge of the part of Texas known as Hill Country. Jack let Remington run free and was, once again, intrigued by the speed and power this horse possessed. He had an even run. Jack could hardly feel the saddle hitting his butt as they flew across this meadow at speed.

He felt, rather than heard, his iPhone ring in his buttoned jacket pocket. He slowed the big horse and checked the screen. Mark Baxter. The district supervisor for the district northwest of Jack's. He knew him from the Morgan rustling case a year ago.

"Hi, Mark. What's up?" Jack answered.

"You are working a case with rustling by tractor trailer. I think you missed disabling a couple. We just had two trailers involved in a robbery up here. It just happened. Broad daylight! You want to come up and see the crime scene and compare notes?" Mark said.

"You bet I do! I am riding some fence. I will immediately head to the barn and trade this horse for four hundred horses. Will you text the address to this number while I am on the way so I can put the location into the Nav app on my phone?" Jack said.

"You bet. Do you know Keith Broughton? He's the agent for this district. We will both be waiting for you."

Jack took Remington up to a healthy trot. He did not want to run the unexercised animal too much all at once.

At the ranch, he changed into a white shirt with the badge, strapped on his gunbelt, and donned the coat with the badge and title embroidered on the chest. He fired up the Ford and took off. His rifle was not back from the rangers, so he put the shotgun in the cab of the truck.

Jack had Mark text the location and put it into his phone. He then hooked the charging cord into the truck's system. Apple Play navigation directed him verbally on the truck radio and visually on the touch screen. Even pushing hard, it took him an hour to reach the ranch where the robbery had occurred. He saw a couple of white Ford F-150's and parked next to them.

"Hey, Mark and Keith. What happened?" he asked, getting down to business right off.

"Special Ranger Jack Landers, this is Rod Grubinger. He owns the Flying G ranch. Let's get him to tell you what he told us," Keith said.

"The missus and I were over at the co-op getting some groceries. We came back and saw two trailers full of cattle coming towards us on the main road here. I thought it was a little odd. Where did those cattle come from?

"As soon as we pulled in here, we knew where. Right damn here! They stole our small herd up by the house. Got fifty beeves, near as I can tell!"

"Rod, were they branded or tattooed or what?" Jack asked.

"Branded. Every damn one of them! My wing in front of a G tattoo. My boy and I did it before he left on deployment."

"Rod, tell Jack about the trucks like you did us," Mark said.

"There were two semi tractors pulling livestock trailers. They were both Volvo. I noticed it because we don't see them much around here. One was blue, the other maroon. The trucks looked brand new. Coulda been rentals. The trailers were old. Some rust showing. Didn't match up with the trucks at all," Rod said.

Jack turned to the two other livestock investigators.

"Do y'all know of any Volvo heavy truck dealers or rentals around here?" They did not.

"Since it looks like these guys have some connection to the Austin area, I will start snooping for the trucks there. The tractors used the other night were left there and the registrations were cloudy. Went through several shell corporations. A ranger who is an analyst in Austin is trying to ferret through them now. This may make it easier," Jack said.

Jack looked at the feet of the two investigators and the rancher. Like him, all wore cowboy boots.

"Wait here a moment please," he said as he walked over to where the soil was soft and imprinted with hoof marks. There were some boot prints where the other three and possibly rustlers had walked. There were also prints from athletic shoes and what was probably work boots with Vibram and similar imprint soles.

Jack took closeup photos of each different print. He then walked down the dirt road upon which the stolen cattle were loaded onto the trailers. He went far enough away from the group to avoid where they might have walked. He studied the tire tracks, particularly the new ones of the Volvo semi-trucks. He took photos for file, then found what he was looking for.

One truck tire had a cut in an outside lug or cleat. It had apparently been driven over something sharp enough to cut the tread, but insufficient to flatten the tire or cause a blowout. He took several photos of it.

"So, what do you have, Jack?" Keith asked.

"Just some prints. I eliminated our and any rustlers wearing cowboy boots and got some good, possibly identifiable athletic shoes and one probable work boot prints. I also found a distinctive cut in the tread of one of the Volvo tires. Whether it would stand up in court is doubtful. Maybe as circumstantial evidence. The more important thing is if we find the Volvo tractors, whether on a rental lot or in a warehouse, it will support the probability we have at least one of the right ones for this robbery," Jack said.

"I have begun a murder board for the robbery in my district and will start a second one beside it for this one. It looks like they are connected. The two boards full of photos, people and other facts may help prove they are connected," he said. He also made a mental note to buy a second board on the way back to Cinco Peso Ranch.

The men all shook and agreed to stay in touch. Owner Rod Grubinger took one of Jack's and the other investigators' cards and promised to call if he remembered something else or saw something new.

Jack purchased and hung another murder board. *Those British DCI's on tv are on to something*, he thought. He printed the photos from his phone and posted them, as well as location, *modus operandi*, date, fifty head, and ranch owner.

He sat there a while waiting for the clues to speak to him. They did not. At least not now.

Jack got up and walked into the kitchen. It smelled great. His mother, always a great cook, was attempting to quench her sorrow with cooking. All three of them had better be careful. Even in his eighties, Uncle Bud was trim and healthy. His mother was remarkable for a woman who just turning sixty. The three were not working cowboys who needed to burn several thousand calories a day. He would try to tactfully speak to her. Steaks and potatoes and large multi-meat breakfasts could become their ruin.

Tonight's chicken fricassee over wild rice might be a bit of an improvement. Especially if he did not eat as much as he was tempted.

After dinner, Jack dug out running shoes and sweats. He found a butt-pack, which he always thought signaled "gun here." But he was on his own property and if he wanted to carry a small Glock 43, it was nobody's business. He put the Glock, a high-lumen headlamp, a spare magazine and a Benchmade automatic knife in it for a planned, pre-daylight run.

He eschewed the office tonight, spent time with his mother and great uncle and called Lily, who was at Julie's ranch. They spoke until both were dozing off. All was well with the sale of her practice. She would be flying in to Austin for five days at Cinco Peso and gave him the particulars of her flight. She hoped to settle on an agreement with the new possible partner.

Jack awoke at his usual pre-dawn hour and put on the sweat suit, running shoes, a stocking cap with the headlamp to energize if needed and the butt pack.

He had not run in a while but was generally fit. He ran what he thought was about three miles. Since it was around the perimeter, he could measure it on one of the trucks' odometer.

He came back, fixed himself a quick breakfast, showered, and dressed,

Jack spent the next hour and a half searching the Internet for Volvo big truck sellers, renters and leasers in the general Austin area. He came up with a larger list than he expected. It would take several hours unless he hit pay dirt early.

He told Uncle Bud his plans as he poured him coffee from the pot he made over an hour ago and got into the white F-150 and headed to the Austin area.

Jack worked the list geographically instead of by type. The first hour was not productive. Well into the second hour, he found a leasing company which had leased two Volvo VNR model regional trucks. They had been leased a day after he had shot up and thereby confiscated the older trucks on the Stackpole Ranch.

He verified with the company they would be sufficient to haul cattle loaded into the largest cattle trailer available.

"Who rented these two trucks? They are part of an on-going investigation."

"We treat our client's privacy very seriously. Information about them would have to be either approved by them or obtained by warrant."

"I see. I will rush a warrant. You need to understand this is a serious set of felonies including attempted murder of a peace officer. If you in any way warn the lessor's, you will be complicit in those felonies. I am assuming you do not wish a long stint in the Texas penal system?" Jack asked.

Several shades of color drained from the leasing manager's face and he gulped.

"I don't. But I still need a warrant to give you the information," the man said, holding his ground.

"I will get the process started. Remember, you really don't want to give the renters or lessees, or whatever you call them, any hint about this investigation," Jack reminded him.

"I understand. I don't want to go to prison. I have heard what happens to even hardline criminals there. Guys like me would not last. Not at all!" Jack nodded soberly.

Jack stepped over to the corner of the office and called Elliot Madison. He was not in, so Ranger Mary Brown picked up

"Lieutenant Madison's office, Ranger Brown speaking."

"Mary, it's Jack Landers. How are you?"

"Great, Jack. I still have not finished diving through those shell corporations though," she said.

"We may be getting close. There was a fifty cow theft yesterday in a county adjacent to my district. The district supervisor called me and I went up. The rancher was returning and saw the trucks coming towards him before he reached his turnoff. I got some tire print photos. One truck had a distinctive cut in the tread on a front tire. They were new, blue and red Volvo tractors.

"I have been in your area tracking down Volvo truck dealers and people who rent or lease them around Austin. I am at a leasing company which leased two trucks matching their description the day after I shot up the old trucks. Pretty strong coincidence, I'd say!"

"I would, too. Who leased them?"

"Therein lies the rub. The manager will not release the information without a warrant."

"And, you leaned on him hard?" she asked.

"Oh, yeah."

She smiled at the thought of the big tough lawman and how scary he probably was.

"Elliott is just in a brief meeting. I will explain what is going on and we will walk over and request a search warrant immediately. Are you still there?"

"Yes."

"Where are you?" she asked.

"I'm in a mall in Kyle," he said.

"We can be there. In a half hour the way most people drive. I can do it in less than twenty minutes. I know. I live in Kyle. With the research I have done and what you just told me, I believe Judge Simmons will issue a warrant we can get to you this afternoon. Grab some lunch and Elliott or I will call you back with an update."

"Thanks, Mary. See you soon." Jack hung up and turned to the manager.

"I will be back with several Texas Rangers in an hour or two. They will have your warrant with them," Jack said.

"My warrant? They will have a warrant for me?" he exclaimed.

"Should they have a warrant for you? Are you involved in this?"

"No! I'm not! But you said 'your warrant'" he said.

"Yes. The warrant you demanded in order for us to see the leasing contract. I am being a gentleman here. I could interview you about what these guys look like and their names without a warrant."

"All I will say now is these guys are scary. Neo-Nazis or something. Nobody I want mad with me."

"Young or older?" Jack asked. He may as well probe while the guy was talking.

"Young. My age. Late twenties. Tattoos."

"What type tattoos? Badly done prison tatts?"

"Not at all. German stuff. Swastikas. German words. Daggers."

"While we are waiting, Peter, why don't you take a blank piece of copy paper and draw them from memory? You don't have to sign it. Nobody will know where I got the tattoo pictures."

"Okay. I guess I can do some sketches."

"And, Peter, the question I have not even gotten to yet is whether you have security cameras out back by your yard. I don't see any inside, nor did I see any in the front," Jack asked.

"Yes. We have them in the yard. There is a high chain link fence and heavy gate, but the trucks, like the VNR Series of regional semis run around a hundred fifty thousand each. Six or seven of them out there and you are talking a cool million. Or more, say some of the number are more expensive. It goes up fast."

"Okay. Let's look at the tape for when you leased the two. I assume we will see you and at least two of the people who leased them and drove them off, right?" Jack asked. Peter nodded his head. He looked like he was going to throw up.

They went into a back office. Peter still had the tape from the beginning of the week in. He looked at one of the leases he would not show Jack without the warrant and noted the date/time stamp. He rolled through the film, then stopped. He motioned Jack over. Jack bent his long form down close to the screen as Peter ran it in slow motion.

He recognized Peter in the black and white film. He saw two guys. Both had jackets, so he could not see tatts. Both had clean shaven heads. He could see from consistent dark shadow neither were actually bald.

Skinheads. He agreed with Peter's Neo-Nazi assessment.

Jack's iPhone buzzed in his pocket and he glanced at the screen. Elliott Madison.

"Hey, Elliott. We have good film of the two guys who rented the trucks I think were used in the last robbery."

"Excellent! Mary and I are close and have the warrant. She drives damn near like Bodeway!"

"A complaint?" Jack asked.

"More like pride. See you in about fifteen or twenty minutes."

"Peter, the call was from the Texas Ranger and Ranger Lieutenant bringing the warrant. They will be here soon. Let's leave the tape where it is so they can view it. We'll go to your files and you should pull out everything you have on those two trucks. Every person who leased one, when, their names, companies, addresses, miles put on the odometer.

"Oh! Do the trucks have GPS recorders. I know many companies put them on."

"They do. We don't care where they use them legitimately. But it is not unheard of for one of these buck fifty trucks to be stolen. Then, we do want to know their location."

"So you have a way the rangers could access a site and show where each truck was and when it was there?"

"Yep. Would it help?"

"Hell yes. It would place the two trucks at the ranch at the time of the robbery. Pretty solid evidence!"

Jack wrote something on his notepad and ripped off the page, handing it to Peter.

"Find out where each was during this period of time on this day. Both trucks should have identical reading. Then do a screen shot. Then track them to somewhere they stay an hour or two and do a screen shot of the location. Then track them to somewhere they stop and remain for a long time. Maybe they are there now," Jack said, seeing his case solution materialize as he spoke.

By the time Peter finished, Elliott and Mary walked in and served the warrant on Peter. He was visibly relieved to see the company name was on it and his did not appear anywhere.

"Now you have the warrant, I want you to share the video with these rangers first. Then, we will come back in and go over the locations of the trucks from the time they left here to wherever they are parked right now.

"While he is reviewing with you, I will call Rod Grubinger, the rancher who described the trucks. I will get his GPS coordinates."

He stepped outside and looked up the number in his notebook. He dialed Grubinger.

"Rod, this is Special Ranger Jack Landers from yesterday. I have located the red or maroon one and the blue one's GPS. So we know where they were and when. I need the GPS reading for your pasture to make sure these were the trucks which drove off with your fifty head."

"Jack, I don't even know what GPS is," Rod said.

"I can walk you through it. You might have to go in where you have Wi-fi to download a new app if you don't have what you need on your phone. But let's check first. Do you have Google Maps? You do? Great. Click on it.

"Now on the blank line type in 'my location right now.' Give it a second to load up. Scan down and look for a series of numbers in parentheses. Got them?

"Please read them to me. Thanks, Rod. I will let you know what we find. And, keep those numbers. They are the exact location of your ranch for a rescue helicopter or whatever. Good information to have in your phone! Bye."

He went back and handed the Lat and Lon numbers to Peter who showed the rangers the two trucks were at the location for about thirty minutes yesterday. The time of the cattle theft.

The lease was with one of the shell corporations associated with the trucks Jack disabled.

The went outside to talk away from Peter's hearing.

"These guys must be pretty confident of the invisibility of their series of cut-outs," Jack said.

"Either they are, or they panicked when you disabled their fleet. The next thing is to find out where they got more cattle trailers so fast," Jack said. "I will check with one of my opposite numbers from this area to see if he knows."

"We can poke around some, too," Elliott said.

"One of those renters with the skinhead looked familiar to me," Mary Brown said.

"Elliott, you know the whole Nazi and skinhead thing kinda tips the balance towards Heinrich," she said.

"Because of his German name?" Jack asked.

"More because of his known Neo-Nazi sympathies," Elliott said.

"Really?"

"Really. We have suspected him to have ties to the movement for years but cannot seem to pin it on him. We have thought some of his criminal enterprises—and he has diversified all over the map—were to fund the movement."

"How about Klan?" Jack asked. "Any suspicions there?"

"None we have found out about," Mary answered.

"Have you done an ancestry rundown on him? Not just his criminal record here, but to see if his father or grandfather was a Nazi?" Jack asked.

"Not really. Just the normal criminal ones during his own lifetime," Mary said.

"Might be interesting to see where his forebears were in the 1930's and 40's," Jack suggested.

"I am more worried about the socialist influence in government right now, but the Nazi's tend to be organized and often well-armed. I will say the guys I took on only had one rifle and some handguns. I considered them minimally armed, though they threw a lot of lead my way for a long few minutes."

"The final report said you had twenty .30-30 cases in a ten foot square area. They had about ninety 9mm and .45 ACP cases and one .270 Winchester case."

"I took out the rifleman early on. The others were doing some good Tennessee elevation on me from a hundred yards with handguns. Bullets were buzzing all around my head," Jack admitted.

"I will check my sources in the domestic violent extremist squads and pass around the picture of the guy I think I've seen before. Actually, I will pass both around and see if anything pops up," Mary said.

They went back in and reviewed the materials there. The leasing operation made its money on a relatively small number of trucks compared to a car rental company. The records were appreciably less. Mary downloaded everything of interest on the computer onto one flash drive. She did not see the need to deprive the business of its sole computer. Trained in IT forensics, she was able to tell there was nothing else hidden on the computer. She had a non-Internet computer at the office she could run foreign data on without infecting everything in the office. She would download on it, check for viruses, and study the leasing company records in her office.

Jack called and found the name of the livestock agent for the area around Austin. He arranged to meet with him once they departed the leasing company. Elliott and Mary said they had a meeting back at Ranger headquarters. Jack felt it would have added some impetus to the case to have had them stay engaged at this point.

He met with the agent, Roy Herring, and asked where someone might get several fifty-cow trailers quickly in his area. He said "Nowhere I know of in this immediate area. About fifty miles west, there's a place on the side of the highway. Middle of highway. It's called Melvin's Used Ranch and Farm Equipment. Last time I was by there, they had four or five old cattle trailers in the back. It's just a shacky office and a bunch of junk sitting out rusting. But it if you need something cheap and it doesn't need a motor to start anytime soon, Melvin is your man."

"Can I find it on the Internet to put into my Nav app?" Jack asked.

"Oh, yeah. It's a pretty well-known spot."

"Thanks! I will check it out on the way back to my district. This gang has a couple of new leased semis but no trailers. We have their trailers and the old trucks. Or at least, the rangers do after we presented them with two rigs."

"And, a couple of bodies I heard?"

"Well, they were shooting at me," Jack responded matter of factly.

"Good luck. These sound like bad dudes. They have not hit here yet. I guess we are too close to home."

Jack nodded and got back into his truck. He looked

Melvin's up on the Internet and found an address he would never find in a couple lifetimes. The map app found it immediately.

He started towards Melvin's, some fifty miles distant.

"Yep, Ranger. I sold two cattle haulers to a couple of guys two days ago. Shifty looking guys all right. Shaved heads. Maybe thirty. Had something I don't see much of. Cash. Three thousand five hundred for the two haulers. Fast deal."

"Do you happen to have security cameras in your yard?" Jack asked.

"Nope. No cameras. Most of this stuff is kinda junky. Not worth the effort."

"Did they take them with them when they bought them?" Jack asked.

"Nope. Drove in with a couple of new Volvo semis a bit later in the day. Hooked 'em up and took off," Melvin said.

"Are these the guys, Melvin?" Jack asked, showing surveillance photos from the leasing office.

"Same two. I deal with all sorts. I ain't scared here after twenty-five years of this. I got a Rottweiler and a twelve gauge. But these fellas gave me the willies. I'd just as soon not bump into either or both ever again."

"I understand. I plan on finding them and putting cuffs on them as soon as I can," Jack said.

Melvin looked at the lawman's size then down at the cocked and locked .45 on his hip.

"I'm thinking it will take everything you got, son."

"So be it. Thanks for talking with me. You've been a big help," Jack said and left for the Cinco Peso Ranch.

He called Lieutenant Elliott Madison.

"This is Jack. I have a positive ID on our two who

rented the Volvo semis. They paid thirty-five hundred cash the next day for two old, rusty cattle trailers."

"Good addition to the list of evidence. Mary has searched back through the shell corporations and has ended with one owned by none other than our alleged Neo-Nazi friend, Frank Heinrich. I have spoken with the ADA for the county where the first robbery occurred. He said his judge would surely issue an arrest warrant for Heinrich and the two skinheads once we get their names. Mary is working on it right now. She's pretty sure she can ID them.

"Given this, I will reach out to the ADA in the county where the second robbery occurred for a similar warrant. The first ADA said we could have conspiracy and attempted murder of a Texas Peace Officer as backup teasers. I will mention this to the second ADA.

"Jack, this is your case. If you want to talk to the county ADA for the Grubinger Flying G robbery, go ahead. I just thought packaging them as a state case might fly faster," Elliott said.

"I agree. I am from Texas, but my lawman days were in Florida and Oklahoma. You know best here. Sounds like we are at a standstill until the two younger guys are identified. I sure wish I could have placed them at the firefight at the first robbery, the Bill Stackpole ranch next to mine. But, it was too dark and I was too busy ducking rounds."

"There's not a cow ever created which was worth dying for, Jack. We'll get them and you will serve the warrant as a special ranger. Mary or I will call you once we have the two names and the two warrants.

"I admit, I have been after Frank Heinrich for a long time. You arrest him, but I'd like the honor of placing the nippers on his bony ass," Elliott said.

"You have it my friend! I look forward to hearing from you or Mary as soon as the ID is made and the warrants are signed."

They broke the connection and Jack drove to the Austin-Bergstrom Airport to wait for Lily's flight to come in. Her plane was due in several hours. In his uniform of white Stetson, white shirt with badge pinned on and gunbelt, he walked right in. The first stop was the news stand for a magazine. The second was for a large black coffee. He settled in the waiting area. Texans nodded at him as they walked by. Tourists stared. One wanted a photo. He complied.

Time passes slowly when you are waiting for the world's most beautiful woman, he thought to himself. *But the wait is worth it. Every single second.*

A redhead who many might legitimately consider one of the most beautiful women anywhere came walking towards the waiting area. People were trying to figure out who she was, dragging her wheeled carryon by the handle. They saw her go from pleasant to excited. Then her pace sped up.

She almost ran into the arms of a big, handsome lawman with a Texas-sized hat and gun.

Hollywood could not have cast or directed the scene better. An embrace. A long kiss and they walked off hand in hand. However, the big lawman's gun hand stayed free. Always.

———

"THIS IS the first time I have ridden in the white truck. It's not a super truck like your Sheriff one was, is it?"

"No. Sure isn't. But, it will allow me to run on an emergency. I won't be making any traffic stops either unless it's to stop a fugitive I am after. It still has around four hundred horsepower. Just not the thousands of dollars' worth of lights and sound equipment. It also does not scream 'police' which is not a bad thing for a guy who is purely an investigator now."

"How is your rustling case going?" she asked.

"It's cases now. Related cases. It appears to be organized crime. Maybe a Neo-Nazi connection," he said.

"Those guys are still around?"

"Seems so. I have no idea why. People are just nuts."

"Do you miss being the sheriff?"

"I only miss us living five hours apart for a while. I got really spoiled listening to you sleep every night."

"Do I snore?" Lily said with some alarm.

"No, the snoring is Jazz. Just don't tell her!"

The doctor giggled at his quick save.

"I am kind of liking being a rancher and lawman. Both are challenging. The only thing worrying me is this organized crime angle. This guy is a longtime hood with a lot of money and influence. Remember how the guy in Texas was in prison, but still engineered the death of the judge who put him there and the son-in-law who figured out the car wreck was a hit?

"This guy is richer and smarter than the man in prison. The man whose son was the murderer Rich had to kill to save Zack Bodeway. There is no end to the inconvenience he could engineer.

"I am a bit worried about you, Mom, and yes, Uncle Bud. I believe he'd take the first attacker down. I am not so confident over his ability at neutralizing subsequent ones. It's hard for me to read Mom's strength now. Would she fight back when she seems to have given up on everything else? I just don't know, honey."

"And me, darling?" she asked softly.

"I believe you have the skill and the willpower to fight back. But, against several trained and better armed killers? Ones you don't know who they are there until the shooting starts? Bad odds, Lily. Bad odds."

"Is my little snubbie revolver enough?"

"For a normal walk. For a trip to pick up a quart of milk? Sure. To hold off a group of well-trained, well-aimed attackers? No, I don't think so. I think we need to re-evaluate the protection of the ranch and our procedures. Now. Not later."

"You sound pretty serious, cowboy," she said.

"I am very serious. I am worried. After I got here, I called the Ranger lieutenant I have been working with. His name is Elliott Madison. He gave me a full run-down on the prime suspect.

"If his goons came after me, you and the rest would be targets of opportunity. They would hit hard and fast.

"They would have to die the same way," he said.

"What should we do?" she asked.

"I know what we should do. But I want to ask Uncle Bud out of respect for him and his history. After, this is what we *are* going to do. I am going to pick up several AR-15 rifles or newly manufactured M1 carbines which have a simpler manual of arms. Both rifles are light, low recoil and easy to operate. I might integrate a couple short Shockwave shotguns into the mix. I would load them with about ten of the little inch and three quarters buckshot shells.

"That is the house armory. Jess is adequately equipped as is.

"The big change is hopefully temporary. The long guns will be secreted throughout the ranch house. Especially near doors. When you and Mom go out to sit on the porch, you each should have one nearby."

"How about pistols?" Lily asked.

"They are for two things: carrying all the time; and using to fight your way to a long gun. But the procedures trump the guns. And, part of the procedures will be almost paranoid awareness of everybody who comes near you as a threat. We'll have the same talk with Mom and Uncle Bud nearby."

"It all sounds easy and logical to me, honeybun," Lily said.

"It all may be for naught. Or not. Either way being aware of your surroundings and having a plan to defend yourself is important for everybody."

Before dinner, Jack sat on the front porch in one of the six rockers. Uncle Bud was in the one next to him. He outlined the fears he had as to threats on the ranch and its people and said he had thoughts on how to mitigate the threats but wanted to hear Bud's ideas first.

"Sonny boy, this ranch has been defended by its owners, their wives, their children and their ranch hands through four Indian attacks, two Yankee raids, several rustler attacks and one renegade rebel attack. There may have been more, but those ten or so are all I can call up right now. We sustained losses and we gave our attackers bigger losses. The first was when the initial owner Helmonius Carey got tired of fighting Comanches from inside and went out and greeted them close up. He walked back in with some arrows stuck in him and a pile of dead warriors behind him.

"I trust you even better than me to set up defenses. Rangers had to worry about personal attacks at home by the moonshiner's, Klan and others. Billy Tilghman at age seventy was murdered in a gangland hit back in '24 in Cromwell, Oklahoma. This is nothing new.

"You get the extra firepower and we'll place it strategically. I'll be the eyes while the women or just Georgia, if it's when Lily is doctoring and Georgia's here doing homemaker things."

Jack and Uncle Bud discussed the possible threats and remedies in a family meeting at the table after dinner and all were on board. There had not been a serious crime so near Cinco Peso during Georgia's sixty years there, so she realized the proximity of the recent crimes and also bought into her son's concerns about organized crime's retribution.

The next morning Jack picked up three Mossberg twelve gauge Shockwave shotguns, boxes of the short buckshot, and three M1 carbines which were new replicas of the WWII and Korea military rifle. His former deputies would have pushed him towards AR-15's but he thought he could teach his family how to use the carbines faster.

They adjourned to a remote pasture and Jack set up targets. Even Uncle Bud practiced with two guns he had not used in the past. Jack liked the new little Mossberg pump as a truck gun. This time, however, he loaded it with full length and full power buckshot.

He had already spent almost six hours during which he felt he should be investigating.

Jack called Elliott just after lunch. Mary got on the line with them. She had identified the two skinheads and obtained addresses. Jack called Mark Baxter, the district chief in the livestock district where the Flying G was located.

"Mark, we are pretty much sure who the two guys with the new Volvos and some old cattle carriers are. And, thanks to some great work by Texas Ranger intelligence, we are sure enough we're going to get a warrant for them and the head of a criminal enterprise funding the operation. He is a Frank Heinrich. Heinrich is an Austin area longtime crime boss. He's never been arrested for even a parking ticket. This could be big.

"The rangers say this is our case and we can serve the warrants with their Special Response Team support. First, we need to surveil the company Heinrich runs near Austin and see if the two drivers go there often.

"I was wondering if since your and my areas were hit, if you and area special ranger Keith Broughton, and Austin special ranger Roy Herring and I could do the surveillance? I am new enough with the livestock association I am not sure how we work on multi-jurisdictional cases."

"We work just like you laid it out, Jack. Let me earn my supervisory pay and set it up. You text or email me the names of the skinheads, their addresses, and this guy Heinrich's full name and company info including address. I will share what we are doing with HQ. They will like the fact it's our agent's initiative and the Texas Rangers are doing some serious backup on it!

"Good work, man! The boss is going to be tickled."

"Thanks, Mark. It's a team effort for sure. I will send you the information today. We can decide when to commence the surveillance operation and where. The Texas Rangers want Heinrich. I want to stop the cattle thefts. While they think we should concentrate on Heinrich's business address, I am thinking we have enough guys to watch both him and the two flunkies where they have the trucks. We have the truck location information from their lessors' GPS right now. I thought about just monitoring the GPS information real time now. We obtained the rights to do it in the warrant. I just fear if we don't have eyes on them, they could pull a fast one. If we see the trucks moving, how are we going to lose those monsters? I am getting ready to run Google Earth on it and see what type place this is—a rural field or warehouse area in town, or what. Then, we might be able to follow them to a cattle theft attempt and arrest them red-handed," Jack said. "He can be picked up for conspiracy and so forth afterwards."

"I love it! I'll tell the boss and you tell me when to start. I will alert the others to pack some clean shirts and drawers and a lot of extra ammo." They said goodbye and both rung off to await the information to begin their parts of the plan.

Jack ran the latitude and longitude for the trucks. It looked like a warehouse yard in a seedy area. There appeared to be some places to set up surveillance. He would go by there and check it out.

Unless they planned to break custom and drive a long way to the next robbery, the trucks should be there until the next robbery. Late afternoon would be the earliest he could imagine.

It was now primarily a waiting game. Jack decided to take advantage of the gift of time to work on the ranch for most of the day. He had mentioned the possibility of a threat to manager Jess Noland, but wanted to pre-plan how Jeff, outside, would respond to an attack. The defense had to be coordinated.

Jack knew the threat was far from probable. His approach had always been to begin his planning with the worst scenario and hope it did not happen. Paranoid? No. Prepared. Especially when the only three people he loved in the entire world were the potential targets. Him being a target? Well, no matter. He had spent most of his career being one. It was what he did.

It was no longer what his aging great uncle did and was never what his wife and mother did.

Jack and Jeff spoke about the situation in much more detail riding fence along the perimeter where the largest herd was grazing.

This was their most vulnerable point for theft at the Cinco Peso, though unlike the others hit so far, the Cinco Peso main herd did not have a road beside the fence. Any rustlers would have to take their trucks off road across hilly prairie or use horses. Not the *modus operandi* used by this group of rustlers yet.

Cindy Bouvier called him later in the day,

"Hi, Jack. Julie has moved some assets around and is ready to close on the sale of Doolin's Cave Ranch. It will be a simple closing. Your ranch's deed is clear from where you used the movie money to pay it off several years ago. She will be using existing assets and not getting a loan. Rich will buy his thirty acres from her later in a separate closing. There are no real estate commissions, just the normal filings, deed search and so forth. The latter has already been done.

"Do you want to come to MacKenzie for the closing or do it remotely?" she asked.

"I have to do it remotely, Cindy. I have a really big case getting ready to break here in Texas. What's involved in a remote closing?"

"There are several ways to do it. Since there is no major sense of urgency of which I am aware, I can overnight you some paperwork to sign in front of a notary and return the same way. We can have the closing over Zoom. Send me a direct message over the encrypted Secret Messenger, or Signal—I have both— with your account number and we will deposit funds in the one you send me. I doubt the Zoom will take more than thirty minutes since you will already have signed a plethora of paper. Not all have to be notarized. I will mark those which do."

"Sounds good, Cindy. I'll turn the notarized and signed paperwork around as soon as I get it and await your time for the closing. Love to you both."

One more thing off my to-do list. I will send the ranch's account number and have the money deposited where it will do us the most good, he thought.

Jess had said they needed more salt blocks for the winter. Jack said he would pick them up at Tractor Supply. They both agreed having Jess and the hands working as normal and being the outside eyes was a logical approach.

He fired up the big Diesel and drove over. The ten additional salt blocks were fifty pounders and the big truck's bed swallowed them up with room to spare.

Jess hopped into the cab of the truck when Jack returned to the ranch and they drove across the grassland as Jess pointed out places to stop and unload a block. Jess was a fit, lifetime cowboy. He was in his sixties and Jack wanted some exercise, so he hopped out at each point and unloaded the salt blocks.

The other benefit of this exercise was giving the longtime ranch manager a chance to look carefully at virtually each head of stock and check for any issues.

The got back by lunch and Jess joined the family, something he was always welcome to do and did about half the time.

"Jess and I spoke about the new security plan. He's going to stay strapped and keep his rifle in a scabbard on his horse when he is riding. Jess is essentially your outside eyes. The first sound of a shot, dial 911, okay?" Jack asked.

"What about the new hand?" Georgia asked.

"I'm still watching him, Miss Georgia. He seems good, but I want to know more about him before I turn him loose on the ranch with a gun. A lot of us grew up with them. Most of the new generation did not and their knowledge comes from computer games. Those things look realistic. But, the action is far from realistic," Jess noted.

After lunch, Uncle Bud followed Jack back into his office. Jack added a photo and information on Frank Heinrich to the first and second murder board, only because he did not have a large enough board to add him by each robbery and connect with a line.

He stood and studied the twin murder boards. Finally, he spoke.

"Sonny, explain these to me."

"You know how Lily and I enjoy those British, Scottish and French mysteries? This is what they use. Maybe other big US police agencies do, too. I never worked for one, so I don't really know.

"What you do is put pictures, evidence and so forth on the board. I have two. One for each robbery. Now it looks like they are related, so one big board would be better.

"Anyway, I'll connect bits of evidence and people. And stare at it. Hopefully the connections will show me something I might miss in all the piles of information," Jack said.

"So, it's kinda like tracks on a trail. Some prints veer off. Others join. This makes you see the sense of what really happened," the old ranger said, verbalizing his thoughts.

"A real good way to put it, Uncle Bud. Every mystery case involves tracking. When you find out whose tracks, you tie the people together. You want to see who did what and who the head of the gang is. This helps me do it."

"It ain't as simple as it used to be," Bud Carey said.

"It's more similar than you might think. Murders are murders. Cattle rustling is about the same, except for guys on horses, most of the time now it's guys in trucks. Either way, they'll shoot you if they get a chance."

"Boy, I'm going to leave you to stare at it. When you get some sort of epiphany, you call me back in and tell me how you came to it, okay?"

"You will be the first to know. I'll probably be like old Archimedes and run out yelling "Eureka! I found it!" Jack said.

"Damn good thing you don't have some bathtub in here. There's ladies about!"

Jack grinned at his great uncle, the man who taught him how to grin. *How did he know about Archimedes figuring out his principle about his body displacing like amounts of water in the tub and running naked through the streets? They didn't teach it in the schools he went to. Or, did they?* He thought, shaking his head to himself as the old man pushed his walker ahead of him out the door.

At three PM, he kissed Lily and told her he would likely be back very late. He was going to drive to the Volvo truck location outside of Austin and look around.

Jack drove fast to the turnoff for the warehouse area where the trucks were stored. He wanted a quick look at the front tires to assure one had the cut he photographed at the robbery site. He realized the tire might be sitting on the cut anyway. It the way was clear, he still wanted to chance it.

The warehouse area was seedy, as he suspected from the Google Earth view. He rode over towards the trucks' location and the amount of activity diminished more each yard he walked. He saw the trucks, but there were no cars or pickups parked nearby. His truck was ubiquitous and he parked around the corner beside an abandoned warehouse. Jack walked over, taking his flashlight as it was darkening quickly. He squatted by the front tire tread on the first truck. Nothing. He hit pay dirt on the second one and took a phone photo of the cut in the tread. This was the truck at the Flying G Ranch cattle theft for sure. The two rusty cattle haulers were backed into the rear of the lot, ready to be hitched to the semis.

He walked back to his truck, knowing to sneak around furtively would attract attention. Uncle Bud had once told him "a confident man with a clipboard can go anywhere."

His best bet was to stay out of sight for a few hours and see if the two drivers and perhaps others showed up.

Things can happen fast, so he called Ranger Lieutenant Elliott Madison and told him where he was and what he had found.

"So you are tucked in and waiting for a few hours in case they have another robbery tonight?"

"I am. I am positive these are the two right Volvos. Right for the ones leased to the skinheads because the GPS put them right here. Right for the Flying G robbery because of the matching cut in the front tread of one of them," Jack said to the senior Texas Ranger.

"I like the idea of letting them commence a robbery before serving a warrant. Red-handed is always best. We will begin some surveillance on the Heinrich building with our guys. If you want, you can have the ones on your team who were going to do some surveillance reach out to me. However, I think Heinrich isn't going anywhere. He sees himself as some sort of commander who sits on his ass and directs his troops," Elliott said.

"I suspect you are dead-on about him. With the hauter you have said he has, I bet he is going to have one shocked look when we walk in with warrants and put the cuffs on him," Jack said.

"You bet he is! I have been after him for a while with absolutely no joy whatsoever. This will be a big day for me."

"Elliott, you have to be the one to serve the warrant!" Jack said.

"It's your case, Jack."

"No, my friend, it's our case. You do the warrant on the big day," Jack said with finality.

"We'll see. Listen: if they show up tonight and you are still there, and alone, let them head out. Call me when it's safe and I will get a bird up. Ours or any agency bird available to track them.

"Once you give me a direction of travel and a major route, I will deploy our Special Response Team or SRT. You are gonna love these guys! Along the way, you can give a heads-up to your Livestock special rangers who you have on stand-by. We don't want anybody to miss the party, Jack!"

"You got it. If you don't hear from me, assume nothing happened. No need waking you up to say 'go back to sleep.'"

Jack had prepared with a takeout cardboard jug of Dunkin Donuts black coffee and a small bag with a toasted bagel with cream cheese and two donuts. Cop health food.

The warehouse yard had a fence and a gate with a lock. Jack had parked adjacent to another, unrelated warehouse outside the fence and walked inside to inspect the two Volvo semis.

209

He watched as someone locked the gate, then drove off. Coffee time.

JACK HAD COMMENCED his surveillance at around seven, just after dark.

So far, by ten, he had knocked off the bagel and both donuts and two cups of coffee. He called Lily and told her where he was and asked her to text instead of calling if she needed anything. He made sure the ringer on his iPhone was in the silent, vibrate mode.

Cy had done what virtually all cops do. He had turned off the feature on the F-150 which illuminated the inside of the cab when a door was opened.

Since it was late fall, he kept the two front windows slightly down to hear better. He had to turn up the collar of his jacket against the cold.

The hip carry for his .45 was awkward for drawing under duress in a vehicle. Especially under a coat and with a seat belt and shoulder harness on when driving.

The Mossberg 509S Shockwave shotgun readily solved the quick access firearm issue. Barely over two feet in length, it lay on the truck seat in patrol mode. Fully loaded with an empty chamber which just took a quick pump of the handle to load and make ready to fire. He had nine rounds in it. Four were buckshot. Five were rifled slugs. The little inch and three-quarters slugs had approximately the same power as the black powder .45-70 Sharps his forebears used against buffalo. *Probably enough for these guys*, he thought.

Solo surveillance is not ideal. Just sometimes necessary. Jack was awakened by a metallic noise. It was someone opening the gate. Once open, the man, almost impossible to see in the dark, flashed a light several times in succession. It was not a high lumen light. It was yellow and weaker like a drug store flashlight with a couple of D batteries.

Several cars and pickups pulled into sight. Two cars drove through the gate toward where the Volvo semis were parked.

In the dark, Jack bent over and cupping his iPhone, read the time. Just before midnight. He had already created a text group with the SRT commander, Elliott, Mary, and all of the livestock investigators committed to the case. Jack put his Stetson over the phone to further keep the light from giving him away in the total darkness.

He sent his message: *It's going down. Midnight. Several vehicles. Two went in for the trucks. Will advise direction of travel ASAP. Jack Landers.*

Jack set the Stetson over the phone. He would answer texts once they left and it was safe to do so without giving himself away. There was time. They were in a rough part on the edge of the city. There were no ranches around. It would take some driving time to get to anywhere to rob. Time, for once, was in his favor.

Ten minutes later, the two Volvos with the cattle trailers behind, pulled out. As they passed he noted something. Several cars and pickups remained parked outside the gate. One large pickup like the getaway vehicle he spared for his own safety at the Flying G, did a U-turn and followed. The men from the vehicles left behind were likely inside the large pickup. A horse trailer was missing this time. Would it meet them? Or would the men load the cattle on foot?

Jack could see them pull onto a westbound highway and texted the group.

Elliott texted and said an Austin PD helicopter was up and heading his way. The commander of the SRT said his team was mounted up and running to the area.

Jack sent he was following and could only answer emergency messages. The other guys with the Livestock Association would have to operate only with the information they currently had for a few minutes.

Jack was still driving without his lights on. He waited until the three vehicles had pulled onto the main road and were half a mile in front of him, then turned his headlights on and accelerated after them. He stayed in the light traffic several hundred yards back.

A text came in from the SRT commander saying they were underway and all units involved should switch to sheriffs net tac 2 on their radios. All did.

"SRT 1, this is livestock agent Landers on tac 2. I am several hundred yards behind the two Volvo semis with empty cattle hauler trailers. We are still westbound at sixty miles per hour."

"SRT 1 copies, Agent Landers. You have the eye," which told everyone Jack had the lead position and would call the pursuit, such as it was.

They proceeded farther west and the speed picked up to seventy. Austin PD Air 1 called in on scene. They began a play-by-play. Jack was not sure if he had lost the "eye" or not, but decided it really did not matter. He felt comfortable with the helo up and dropped back a bit. He still was able to watch the three trucks.

The police helicopter certainly eased the situation. Jack and any involved vehicles which subsequently moved up behind him could hang back with less chance of being made.

The growing procession continued unabated for another forty-five minutes until the three targets pulled off on a farm road. Once they stopped and got out of their trucks the helicopter would have to back off and probably return to base.

Its noise and lights would be too noticeable on a quiet Texas night. A small fixed wing aircraft with FLIR would have been a perfect handoff, but none was available.

For its final call, the helo reported two dirt roads coming in from the right. One was a half mile ahead, the other a mile.

Jack accelerated and came up to within several hundred yards of the last semi and trailer. He gave an obvious right turn signal and turned into the first dirt road. He drove down far enough for trees to hide his actions. He switched his headlights off, did a Y-turn and proceed back in the direction of the farm road with no lights on.

He turned right on the farm road and saw the lights of the rear vehicle. He pulled in a quarter mile behind and reported his action and location over the net.

Austin area livestock agent Roy Herring reported he thought he was several hundred yards behind Jack, running black.

Jack hit his brake lights twice in quick succession.

"Gotcha, Jack," Roy said over the radio.

Elliott, as a lieutenant, was the senior Texas Ranger on scene. He broadcast for Jack to wait until the rustlers were actually loading cattle into the trailers, then advise. SRT could come in hot in a shock and awe mode, followed by the rest of the livestock agents and him and Ranger Brown.

Jack spoke up. "SRT 1, Agent Herring and I are dismounted and are behind a slight barrier. We both have rifles. How about we cover you guys until you are dismounted and moving. Then, we'll stand down until time to come forward?"

"Glad to have you watching our sixes. Dismounting is our most vulnerable time. Somebody gets violent, neutralize the threat. We'll take it once we are boots on the ground." Jack acknowledged with a double click of the mic.

Jack looked at Roy and they nodded at each other. Neither chambered. Despite doors closing and cattle noise, they did not want the metallic sound of a high powered rifle bullet being chambered in the otherwise quiet night.

It was not how loud it was, but how different.

Jack watched Roy slip five cigar-sized .444 Marlin cartridges into a spare ammo sleeve on his lever gun's buttstock. Roy was clearly sincere about winning any gunfight which happened in his general area.

The rangers, both full and specially appointed, eased their vehicles to within fifty yards. Their lights were off and the braying of cattle with men on foot trying to herd them into the trailers provided the lawmen with some noise cover.

The SRT commander observed radio silence this close. He used Jack's group text to ask if Jack and Roy were ready to provide fire support. All of the participants read Jack's response.

"Go"

Truck engines wound up as the police trucks ran silently towards the trucks, men, and cattle. Within a hundred feet, SRT lit up the target group of shocked and off-guard criminals.

Jack and Roy watched in the headlights as one of the two skinheads grabbed a rifle and aimed it at the oncoming SRT truck. Before his own, Jack heard Roy lever the Marlin.

He was temporarily deafened as the big .444 round went off and hit the man with the rifle. It was a center of mass hit. The best for the dark circumstances and melee. The man went down.

The excitement stampeded the cattle which trampled one rustler standing in the wrong place at the wrong time.

Before the SRT operators dismounted, another man aimed a heavy semiautomatic pistol at the oncoming vehicles. Jack dropped him. Another center of mass hit for the special rangers of the livestock association. He was using his late father's deer rifle until he got his Winchester back.

A team of SRT operators bailed out and began taking prisoners. All were told to lie face down on the ground, feet and arms apart.

The SRT operator behind the wheel of their special-ized heavy vehicle doused the arrest scene with a flood light. Night became day. Cattle were still running away as fast and far as they could. In effect, they were just moving to another adjoining pasture. No problem for the rancher or the lawmen.

The criminals were thoroughly patted down and hand-cuffed from behind. The two on the ground were checked for life signs. None were present. All the weapons of the cattle rustlers were picked up with nitrile-gloved hands and locked in the bed of Elliott Madison's truck. Mary Brown was taking names of the arrestees, now standing in a straight line, guarded by the livestock agents as the Texas Rangers photographed and collected evidence.

The ranch owner showed up, albeit timidly because

of the shots he had heard and the collection of people—good and bad—he faced.

Elliott Identified himself and explained who the guys with badges were and how they were being trailed until stopping at his ranch at the last minute.

"By the time we knew where the cattle robbery was going down, we had to act to prevent your cattle from being stolen. Preventing the crime became a higher priority than calling you. We figured you'd appreciate the approach?" Elliott said.

"I surely do, Ranger. I surely do. Any of my cattle hurt or killed?" the owner asked.

"Not any I know of. One might have twisted his ankle trampling a rustler over there," pointing where an SRT operator was draping a plastic blanket over the body of the man who stood in front of the herd as they began to stampede.

"If you want to stand by and watch for a while, we'll finish up our work and want to take a report from you about how many cattle in this herd, their approximate value and all," Elliott said.

The man nodded, still amazed at the action and follow-up activity on his ranch tonight.

Elliott called his dispatch and requested the presence of the county sheriff or his chief deputy or undersheriff, and a couple of sergeant or above DPS troopers for a shooting board.

He then walked over to the line of prisoners where Ranger Brown and Jack were taking names.

He heard Mary.

"You would be Terrence O'Hara. Odd name for a Nazi," she said.

His response was a short sentence. Five words which

incorporated both a racial and gender slur aimed at Mary Brown.

Jack saw his new friend Elliott almost imperceptively nod at the female ranger.

Mary gave O'Hara a front snap kick in the groin. He bit his lip to keep from giving a mere female and black one at that the pleasure of seeing his pain.

But he could not help doubling over and beginning to black out. Jack caught him before he hit the ground.

"Mister, if you are going to be a cattle rustler in Texas, where they still hang rustlers," he lied "you sure better learn to walk on prairie land without falling over," Jack said.

"Will I be fired or censored for my action?" Mary whispered to her lieutenant.

"Damn fast action against a man you thought was going to head butt you," he said, looking at Jack.

"I sure thought so, too," Jack said. "She reacted fast. I saw what was happening and went to subdue him, but he was already heading for the ground."

"I'd like a written report to that effect from both of you by tomorrow," Elliott ordered. He walked away smiling in the dark.

CHAPTER EIGHT

By five in the morning, the scene had been documented and prisoners in the back of trucks to be transported to Ranger Headquarters. The shooting team had met and declared both shootings to be self-defense of a fellow peace officer. The death by cattle trampling was just a police report one of the responding deputy sheriffs wrote. It was a death by misadventure. The unfortunate death arising from a risk the decedent took voluntarily. For example, choosing to rustle cattle.

The same team of rangers and special rangers left before daylight for the headquarters of Heinrich's company with felony conspiracy warrants for him and his corporate officers as starters.

Ranger Mary Brown led the questioning of the suspects in custody while the others were en route to the Heinrich offices.

According to the sign on the door, the business hours commenced at 9:00 AM.

Neither the rangers stationed in the rear nor the ones in front to breach the door saw or heard any activity at nine. They knocked and yelled "Open up! Texas Rangers! Search warrant!" getting no response.

An SRT operator employed a ram for a dynamic entry. Three swings and the door was able to be kicked out of the way. A "stick" of operators went in preceded by a flashbang grenade.

After several minutes, Jack, Elliott and the other peace officers outside heard the "Clear!" yell from an operator inside. They went in.

It did not appear the office had been in business and quickly deserted this morning. It appeared neat and normal, nothing strewn about, no file drawers left open or safes insecure.

"Either Heinrich and his lieutenants felt something was in the wind and cleaned the place out much earlier than we would have guessed, or he heard, did not come in, and every bit of evidence we need is here untouched," Elliott said.

He sent left several rangers to guard the facility and wait for a forensic team to arrive. Elliott, Jack, two Texas Rangers, SRT, and several livestock investigators left in a hurry for Heinrich's home on a small ranch ten miles from their current location.

They ran lights and sirens, hoping to get there before the apparently warned Heinrich could escape.

A mile out, they cut the sirens. A half mile out, the doused the red and blue lights and slowed down to a bit faster than the traffic they encountered.

Via radio coordination, Elliott pulled over and SRT took the lead. The hastily agreed plan was for SRT to hit the house fast and hard with the remaining vehicles pulling in as soon as SRT deployed to provide perimeter security on all four corners.

Jack and Roy partnered again and headed for the

right rear. Neither carried rifles this time, but Jack had the Shockwave shotgun in hand.

SRT breached the door. Heinrich had grandchildren, so no flashbangs were used in case they were in the house. The operators quickly cleared the house and Jack and Elliott went in while the others maintained outside security. Too many feet would hamper the crucial work of the forensic team.

"It appears the house, unlike the office, was abandoned in a rush. Everything's a mess," Elliott said as he and Jack walked through, touching nothing, even with nitrile gloves on.

Jack went straight to the large Liberty gun safe.

Jack motioned Elliott over.

"The long gun and handgun racks are empty. There is a file box, also empty. There is a small safe within the safe. It's doors are open," Jack pointed out.

He took his small, high-lumen tactical flash and shown moved the beam around inside. On the floor of the larger safe, he spotted a coin.

Jack bent over and put the light on it.

"It's a Kruegerrand."

Elliott fingered something into his phone,

"Worth about eighteen hundred thirty-four dollars in today's market," he said.

"There's room in this sub-vault for a bunch of them, literally hundreds," Jack said.

"Looks like he has plenty of traveling money. Unless he has a private plane chartered, he probably is running for Mexico. He sure wouldn't go through a CBP entry point with guns and gold," Elliott said. He cleared his phone and called dispatch. Reading information from notes, he put out a BOLO on a maroon late model

CINCO PESO

Suburban. He made sure it included "possibly armed and dangerous."

"Well, damn, Jack. We did so much right, then we let the big fish swim away."

Jack nodded and walked to the kitchen. He thought there might be a clue there he could use without touching it. There was.

He bent over the kitchen table and sniffed a small pitcher of coffee cream. He guessed half and half. It smelled like what it was. It had not spoiled.

"What are you doing?" Elliott asked.

"Cuttin' sign! This half and half creamer is not spoiled!" He quickly Googled and said "They have not been gone more than three hours." He checked something else.

"It's a four hour drive. He won't speed for fear of a traffic stop. If the border is his destination, he's still in Texas," Jack said.

Elliott called dispatch back and added the updated information his BOLO.

His next call was to Mary. It took several minutes and he asked a lot of questions.

"She got some respect from the Irish heritage guy who thinks he's a Nazi. He's singing his head off. The big thing for your group, Jack, is he told where the stolen cattle are. They are in holding pens ready to be trucked to Mexico under an illegal sale scheme. The best part is they are still in Texas. It's a small ranch just off I-35 South not far north of Laredo. If you want to pass on making the actual arrests of those guys Mary is interviewing, you might just be able to hold the cattle for owner pickup."

"Elliott, getting credit for big arrests was important as a sheriff who ran for reelection. Looking after the members of the livestock group for whom I work is my main mission now. If you will arrest the robbers, I will gladly stand beside you at the press conference and grin a lot. But, I will call some of the livestock agents and start putting together a recovery plan. Did Mary say how many actually made it to Laredo?" Jack asked.

"In fact, she did. Two hundred fifty are there now, according to the driver. The number is an aggregation of the ones y'all were investigating and some from some smaller robberies which went unnoticed. The guy said there are three armed guards watching them, so be careful," Elliott said.

"You should be able to arrest the three for harboring stolen cattle and maybe some gun violations, especially if they are felons. Let the BATFE have them after us for some mandatory sentences. I think you can do all of this without a specific warrant," he added.

"I will. Not to worry.

"We should be able to identify the ones from unknown robberies from brands or tattoos. There was one decent sized robbery before I started.

"I want to go down and inspect them first and see how many have brands and the like. Then, I will call back about who should come down and pick up how many cattle.

"You might warn the DPS guys on I-35 I'll be coming through at a good clip!" Jack said.

"Will do. I will have some Laredo area rangers standing by. I will get their lieutenant to call you. His name is Boyd Asher. He's a good man."

"The only Texas Ranger I ever met who wasn't a good man is a great woman, Mary Brown," Jack said.

"Surely true, my friend. I'll tell her what you said. She will appreciate it. Be safe!" Elliott said.

Jack called Mark Baxter, supervisor from the district near his. He reckoned most of these beefs had come from one or the other of the two districts. Mark confirmed it, saying an earlier robbery had been investigated by Jack's predecessor, Cy, a year ago with no resolution. It had a bit over seventy-five stolen. He was not sure the exact count. Mark added he heard some talk about a few cows here and there missing, but nobody actually reported a cattle robbery.

"Well, we have about two hundred fifty being watched north of Laredo by three armed men. I suspect the Flying G brand will be there and who knows what else. You want to grab your guys and call the Laredo agent and we'll meet the Texas Rangers down there?" Jack asked.

"You bet I do. Give me a call when you get the exact directions and have a meeting place in mind," Mark said.

"I will know a little more when the Texas Ranger lieutenant from the area calls me while I am driving down. When I know something, you will know it."

———

RANGER LIEUTENANT BOYD ASHER called an hour and a half later. Jack answered and they spoke through the truck's audio system as Jack drove very fast.

A meeting place was arranged and Jack passed it along to Mark and his associates.

They met several hours later. While the others waited, Jack and Boyd Asher drove in Jack's truck to near the cattle site.

Jack quickly readied the drone and they flew it over the cattle and guards at high altitude.

They did not see any alarm expressed by the three

223

men. They were sitting under a canvas shade stretched off one of two pickups. Jack and Boyd could see them drinking beer and several long guns propped against the truck through the video lens.

"It's about three hours until darkness sets in. If we want to assess whose cattle are there, we need to take them pretty soon," Boyd said.

"Or, we could let them drink some more beer and impair their aim!" Jack noted. "A couple of us can watch the cattle overnight afterwards and determine brands in the morning," he added.

"I think you have a valid point. We only have one way in. Even if a couple trucks tried to circle around them off-road with four wheel drive, the land is so open they'd be seen by the three for sure. What if you put the drone back up and watched as we approach in our trucks via the dirt road? If you see they made us, let us know over the radio and we'll pick up our speed and hit them fast."

"Sounds like a plan, Boyd. How about I stay here? This is close enough I can fly the drone and still get there quickly once y'all make the actual contact," Jack suggested and the senior ranger nodded affirmatively. He went back to the rally point in Jack's truck.

Fifteen minutes later, Jack heard a single click on the ranger frequency handheld radio Boyd left with him. They were coming.

Jack turned slightly and saw the first ranger truck of four. He turned his attention back to the video feed from the drone. No change in the men yet.

The trucks got within several hundred yards and one man looked up and spread the alarm to the other two.

"They are on to you. Go!" Jack radioed and he heard the sound of four high horsepower pickups accelerating full out.

"Careful, they are grabbing rifles! I will create a diversion!" Jack said into the radio.

He dropped the drone down to seven feet off the ground and buzzed the makeshift shelter. One man saw it coming, raised his rifle and decided discretion was the better part of valor and ducked instead of shooting. The other two turned towards the drone as Jack swerved it around for another close pass.

The drone clearly threw them off kilter and drew their attention to it instead of the four pickups nearing at speed.

Jack returned the drone to his position and landed it handily. He arose and began the hundred yard walk to the site, ready to drop at any time should they fire at him. He held his and formerly Uncle Bud's, proven stag-gripped .45 Commander in his hand. His trigger finger rested straight out along the frame under the slide.

Rangers were behind trucks, rifles aimed at the three befuddled men, who still seemed to be looking skyward for their former menace. Jack grinned at their antics, too dumb to realize their real threat had been the rangers roaring towards them in trucks.

They were arrested red-handed for possession of stolen goods, *to wit* approximately two hundred fifty stolen cattle.

Disarmed, checked, handcuffed, they were put in the Texas Ranger trucks and taken to jail for interviews.

The livestock agents began to document brands and tattoos on notebook computers. At the end of the process, they all sent results to Mark's computer and he combined them for a final tally.

There were fifty Flying G brands, one hundred seventy-five tattoo numbers to research. Of those, there were four sets of numbers indicating robberies from four different ranches. There were twenty-five unbranded nor tattooed cattle. One of the agents had a chip reader and noted five sets of chip numbers to research.

After some hours of work at the local agent's home office, Mark had a list of seven ranchers to deliver good news to about their stolen cattle being recovered. Of the seven, one was the victim of the robbery Cy was unable to solve in what was now Jack's district.

"Jack, it's a good day! We are making seven ranchers very happy. Men who never expected to see their cattle again. At a rough conservative price of a thousand dollars each, we recovered a quarter of a million dollars' worth of stolen cattle today. Probably closer to a third of a million.

"We did what the members are paying us to do and not a single person, especially one of us, was injured," Mark said.

"Yep. A week or so well spent," Jack responded. "How long before the last cow is picked up by the owner?" he asked.

"Probably three days. So we have to watch them in the meantime. Are you good for a couple days, Jack?

"I am, Mark. I just have to call my wife and let her know what's going on."

"You have enough gear?" Mark asked.

"I sure do. I keep a bug-out bag in the truck. I may need to slip into town while someone else is here with the cattle to pick up some groceries more satisfying than my jerky, but I have everything else. I don't see much fallen wood around, so I might pick up a couple of fire-place wood bundles, too," Jack said.

While a couple of the other livestock agents were finishing with the cattle, Jack slipped into town and picked up two bundles of fireplace wood and to-go meal, a six-pack of water bottles, another big cardboard container of strong coffee, and something for breakfast.

He viewed the outlaw's tarp strung from the no-confiscated truck as a shelter he could use. Jack knew he could find some branches for two supports and some tent stakes. There was no wood sufficient for firewood, just saplings he could cut and trim with the tomahawk or Bowie knife in his bug-out bag.

Before dark, Jack moved away from the truck and the outlaw camp and picked a rise with a good vantage point.

Within a very few minutes, he had a lean-to set up with the tarp and a fire pit dug with the trowel from his bag. The firewood was stacked and he was ready for the evening. He ate dinner with a bottle of water then poured some coffee.

Jack took a photo of his almost dark camp, again surprised at the clear photos modern smart phones could take in the dark. He sent it to Lily, who was still at Cinco Peso. He said in the text he would call her before bedtime. Jack knew Lily would share the photo with Georgia and Uncle Bud. He knew Uncle Bud loved his days camping on the trail, in pursuit of bad guys.

Jack liked it, too. The wind, the smell of the campfire were balms to his soul. The fact it was late fall in Texas and going to be cold as all get out tonight did not faze him at all.

He had his bivvy sack and an emergency blanket as used a few days ago. He had a fire pit and would be warm and cozy. Again, he wished his redhead with there with him.

Growing up in Tennessee with an outdoor family, she was used to primitive camping, shooting, riding and all the things he loved. He felt blessed. A dark qualm passed over his being as he thought of the dead girlfriend Lily had tried to save on the café floor several years ago. They had loved each other, too. But, her love, though genuine, was based on a horrible truth. A truth he had buried with her ashes. The cremation had assured she could never be exhumed and identified. She took her secret to her grave. He would take it to his also. There was no question about it.

SHERIFF RICH AMMON was winding his day down also. He wondered how Jack was faring with his big case.

Rich had his own plate overflowing. The crime situation in Warrior County had taken a temporary vacation. The personal situation of the County's sheriff had not.

Isabella was calling him again, suggesting meeting on the weekend. Her sister, Myra, was calling suggesting more prurient endeavors than dates.

He was trying to solidify his relationship with the nurse who lived and worked between MacKenzie and Oklahoma City. Jenny O'Neill struck him as perfect. She was sweet, beautiful, caring, funny, and he believed she was in love with him. He thought she might be the one.

Of course he had thought someone else was the one. Another nurse. One who took a job on the other side of the state with no notice to him or her employer, Lily Landers, MD.

Rich was excited but busy with the thirty acre parcel he was buying from Julie Moran. It had been Jack's favorite part of his ranch except for the historical old homesteader house.

The part along the Cimarron River. The swimming

hole where members of the Doolin Gang has lived in a cave and Bitter Creek Newcomb had swum with his outlaw girlfriend. Was she the legendary Rose of the Cimarron? Maybe.

Jenny would like swimming there. They had already spoken about it.

The thirty acres had been appraised a couple of days ago. The county verified his new salary. One much higher than the previous one as a sergeant. The mortgage loan company representative thought the loan was a sure thing. And, it included construction of his cabin and an outbuilding.

The encroaching winter was not the best time to build anything. The cabin would have its pieces brought in on a flat bed and assembled on the spot he selected.

The digging of a well and a septic system would be the challenge if not done quickly. The cabin would have piers to support it several feet off the ground and gravel underneath. He was pretty excited about it, with its solar panels unseen from the front. But they would be facing the midday sun on the rear of the roof. The solar panels would provide most of his electricity with an outside generator providing any additional needs.

He had given a lot of thought to his Saleen Mustang. It was a collector's item and proceeds from selling it would buy a virtually new SUV. His sheriff's truck would handle the dirt road into the small ranch just fine. But he needed something he could use to pick up building materials. Rich was looking at a several year old three quarter ton four wheel drive pickup and would probably sell the Mustang and buy it.

The piece of land was somewhat remote from the office, but Jack made the commute and did emergency responses from there for a number of years. He could also.

His phone rang. He looked at the face with apprehensions. It was okay.

"Hi!" Jenny said.

THE WIND PICKED up on the big pasture north of Laredo. Jack had just put several big pieces on the fire and was deep in the bivvy sack. The only thing he wished for was a stocking cap. He knew from his man overboard days in the Coast Guard much of a person's heat loss was through the top of his head. He took his ever-present bandana from his right rear jeans pocket and fashioned a hat. Not much. But better than nothing.

He found himself humming Marty Robbin's iconic The Streets of Laredo. About the cowboy who helped a dying cowboy on the town's streets. Jack thought he liked Robbin's song El Paso best, with the wicked Felina. He was about asleep at ten when Lily called him to wish him goodnight. Their talk was short. She could tell he was barely awake.

He tried to keep the conversation with his Red Rose of Texas going, but the hours put in during the past few days won out and he drifted off, leaving her smiling. Her cowboy. Nobody could have done better than she.

Jack awoke once to put the rest of the logs on the fire. It was three AM and they would suffice until daylight. The cattle were quiet. The burst of heat helped him go back to sleep immediately.

FUGITIVE FRANK HEINRICH was not heading for the Mexican border. He was holed up with his family in his off-grid cabin fifty miles from Austin. Like the trucks, it had been bought with a series of cut-out shell corporations. Different ones from those he used for his corrupt business practices.

Heinrich admitted to himself he was a "convenient Nazi." He was, without a doubt, a racist. Anyone who did not possess his Aryan good looks was a lesser person and undoubtedly had a lesser intellect.

A large part of the convenience factor was his ability to attract and hire people who were Nazi sympathizers and wanted to follow him and gave extraordinary loyalty for a minimal amount of money on his part.

Basically, Henrich was a user of people. He used them how he wanted in order to steal what he deemed valuable at the moment. Cattle prices were up, so cattle were his primary target now. He had avoided the Texas Rangers for some years by staying under their radar.

Now, this damn livestock agent, the one who had been a sheriff, had a movie made about him and was almost nationally famous as a modern day gunfighter. This Landers person. He had to stick his nose in Heinrich's business.

Heinrich would see to him. In his own good time. He had his family here, his transportable wealth. Food, water, power. All off-grid. He felt he could hold off an army, even with no storm troopers aboard.

He had listened to the DPS frequency. They were all looking for him. At exactly where he was not. Dumbasses!

Heinrich poured a glass of eighteen year old Scotch whisky. It was real Scotch. He would have written "whisky" properly without the "e."

Little things were important. They were the difference between people like him and the rest of the horde.

He took a sip and let it burn all the way down. It was late. The family was asleep. He leaned back in the chair. He might fall asleep soon himself. It would be okay. He was safe where he was and could strike out at his targets at will and retreat back here. Then, when they were not looking for him, he would fly his family to the Caribbean and come into Mexico the back way.

Heinrich knew people there. People had bought from him. People who would take his money and look the other way. Soon, perhaps. But there was still work to be done here.

CHAPTER NINE

JACK WOKE up and crawled out of the bivvy sack. Frost covered the ground. The cattle were still quiet as they had been all night.

He stirred the fire. There was no more wood. He ate one of the cold donuts he had saved for breakfast. The bottled water was virtually ice water, but he was thirsty.

He got in his truck and started it, putting the heater on high.

A fast run at dawn to a drive through donut shop yielded a toasted everything bagel with cream cheese and a giant coffee.

He sipped the latter on the way back to the herd.

By the time he had finished his breakfast and broken camp, the first couple of livestock agents returned.

They advised about talking with the owners who would be down later in the day. They would have cattle trucks to begin to take their property back home. Since none of them had semi-trucks and large trailers available at short notice, most would have to make several trips.

Luckily for the agents, one of the ranchers had a

small motor home. He would stay with a couple of his cowboys to guard the dwindling herd until every cow had been transported home.

Jack received a call from Elliott at nine.

"Hey, where are you?" the Ranger lieutenant asked.

"Still at the storage pasture for the stolen cattle north of Laredo."

"Can you be up here with the head of your association and the Director of the Rangers at one for a formal press conference where the recovery and return of two hundred fifty stolen cattle and arrest of many of the rustlers is announced?" Elliott asked.

"I'm about three hours, maybe more. I have to stop at a truck stop and take a shower and shave. I have a clean white shirt and pressed jeans with me. I'll have to clean my boots after walking in a cow pasture. It's going to be close."

"Do your best and I will delay as much as possible. You are going to be credited with a lot of the success of this operation. I am just sorry Heinrich is not in cuffs, but we all did pretty well anyway," Elliott said.

"I will haul freight getting there. I really need to clean the boots. You can imagine what they smell like."

"Yep. I grew up on a ranch, too."

Jack took off. He found a truck stop with a shower and cleaned himself and wiped down his boots. He decided to skip shaving in the interest of time.

By pushing hard, he made it to the HQ at twelve forty-five and parked out front with his visor lights blinking.

He ran inside and the association president who had hired him at his dad's funeral grabbed his hand and congratulated him. A lot of white shirts, brown pistol belts, and white Stetsons were gathered. The Texas

Rangers all wore neckties, whereas the livestock agent special rangers generally did not. The president of the livestock association and the Attorney General, a surprise to Jack, wore suits.

There was a gaggle of media and camera operators.

The Attorney General spoke first and the livestock president next. The final speaker was the director of the rangers who listed the contributions of Jack and his associates, Elliott and Mary, and the SRT. Each was asked to identify himself or herself by stepping forward and touching their hat brim. Jack was the first to do so.

When they broke up, Jack spent a few minutes with his employer then sought Elliott and Mary.

"Anything on Heinrich's whereabouts?" he asked.

"Not a thing. He seems to have fallen off the edge of the world," Elliott said grimly.

"We have alerted everybody. If he went to Mexico, he swam the Rio Grande the wrong way from everybody else," Mary said.

"So, he's in a hidey-hole, planning his next action, which may be retribution against any or all of the three of us," Jack said.

"Yes. Mary and I spoke about it yesterday and think it's a very real possibility. It fits the personality profile of the man I have tried to get evidence on for the past five or six years. He is vituperative and easily moved to violence. None of his victims have lived to testify.

"I have taken a close look at my personal and family security precautions and ramped them up," Elliott said.

"I live alone. My cat does not shoot. But, I do. I have added one more seven round mag to my gunbelt and a now-constant backup in an ankle holster inside my boot," Mary said.

"Cinco Peso has been attacked a number of times in

the past hundred and seventy years. Comanches were the first and where the original owner, Helmonius "Hell Raising" Carey killed a bunch single-handed. Some were reputedly in hand-to-hand combat. Then came other war parties over the years. The Union army. Rag-tags from the Confederate army. Rustlers.

"Uncle Bud always carries his Colt Cobra snub nose .38. The ladies are carrying their usual revolvers. I have stashed short Shockwave shotguns with nine rounds of mixed slugs and buckshot, and a number of M1carbines at every door and inside selectively. I have had all practice," Jack said.

"M1 carbines instead of AR's?" Mary asked.

"Yep. One, I personally like them better and two, they have a simpler manual of arms."

"I cannot comment, being unfamiliar with them. They were used before I was born."

"Before I was, also. But I became a fan early on," Jack said.

"Actually, I am a big fan, too. Did you get war surplus ones?" Elliott asked.

"No, I bought some Auto Ordinances by Kahr. They and the Inland ones are new and good. The ladies love them and at five and a half pounds, they are handy for Uncle Bud. He's tough as nails, but in his eighties, is not as strong as he was as a Texas Ranger."

"He's already earned legend status as a ranger, Jack. Anything he does now it just icing on the cake," Elliott said.

"As an old line ranger, how do you think he'd accept me? I may look a little different from the rangers he was used to," Mary asked.

"Bud and I know each other better than either of us

knows anybody else, Mary. He'd base his assessment of you on your toughness, your devotion to being a ranger, and your class. Class for a ranger is paramount to him. As to whether you fit a historical composite of what a ranger looks like? He would not bat an eye. I promise you."

She just smiled, thinking she'd love to meet the iconic old Texas Ranger.

"Well, I think I am going to head back to the Cinco Peso and shave. You two looked the part with your crisp shirts and clean boots. I looked on TV like a guy who slept in the open in a cow pasture last night. Which, of course, I did!" Jack shook with both and headed out. His truck was still there and sans any traffic tickets. He turned the red and blue LEDs off and started home. Home. It had a good ring. Just like it did when he was a kid. Now, maybe even better. All the people he loved were there with him.

———

JACK ARRIVED at the Cinco Peso just as his family finished watching him on the news.

"I looked pretty bad, huh?" he asked rhetorically.

"Not at all. The five o'clock shadow did not show. You looked just like the others, except you weren't wearing a tie. Where did you get the crisp shirt and creased jeans?" Georgia asked.

"I always carry a change in the truck. I've done it for years."

"No need to ask where you learned to carry a change," she said, looking at her uncle.

"Nope. No need at all," Jack said winking at the old ranger, who nodded and grinned.

"Does this mean we can ease off some of the security concerns?" Lily asked.

"I'm afraid not. I met with the senior ranger on the case. The suspected kingpin, a crook named Heinrich, is missing. Both of the rangers on the case are apprehensive and tightening their personal security.

"If anything, we need to ramp ours up for a while," Jack said.

"Honey, it does not seem normal. I admit somebody shot you at our wedding, but you have arrested people for years," Lily said.

"The way to assess a threat from a person is to look at their history, intent and capability. When Lieutenant Elliott Madison did it for Heinrich, he came up with over the top figures in all three categories. Heinrich is a Neo-Nazi and is as cold as can be. We cost him a very large, profitable criminal enterprise. Elliott believes he's not going to let it go without getting even."

"This sort of thing happens. Maybe the greatest Texas Ranger of all after the West was won was Frank Hamer. Before my time, but he still used automobiles more than horses. He is most remembered for what he did after his ranger days. He tracked down Bonnie and Clyde and led the posse which killed them.

"While he was a ranger, he was coming back from testifying. Hamer had his pregnant wife, his brother and another fella with him in the car. While they were getting a tire fixed in Sweetwater, an ex-ranger and another fellow opened up on him. Frank caught two .45 ACP rounds. One in the shoulder and one in the leg, but he kept on fighting. When a second fella ran towards him, his wife Gladys emptied her Colt .32 pocket automatic at him. She missed and he shot for Hamer's head, missing his head but tearing up his Stetson. He went down for a minute, but came back up and killed the ex-ranger with one shot from his .44 Special revolver.

"I have two points with the story. People come after you for revenge. This was 1917. And, you have to keep fighting during a fight, even if hit. You fight until you just can't fight any more," Uncle Bud said.

"Frank Hamer was living proof of what I'm trying to illustrate. He was in around fifty gunfights in his career and was wounded almost half the time. He just was a man who never gave up and it worked in his favor. He died at home with his boots off."

"Careys never gave up either, did they Uncle Bud?" Georgia asked.

"I never heard of one who did," he said.

"How about my commute?" Lily asked.

"Your commute to the airport is worrisome. Departures, arrivals, and transportation are primary times for assassins to target someone," Jack said. "Whenever possible, I will try to take you and pick you up. Once you have a practice here in this area, we will make adjustments."

They changed the subject and had a light dinner.

BACK IN MACKENZIE, Rich Ammon still had one deputy position to fill. He had hired the former MP he met at Walmart when he also met Jenny O'Neill. He was almost through this riding with a field training officer, or FTO. So far, he had lived up to the high expectations Rich had for him.

Which left Polly Antrim. Would she really be happy as a deputy there without Jack? There was only one way to find out. He walked over to the county personnel office and spoke with the personnel director. He asked her to send an offer letter to Polly. Polly had been in frequent contact with her, too.

Polly called him three days later.

"I accepted! My next to last semester in Criminal justice will be over in a week. I will finish online in the spring and graduate *in absencia*! I am so excited, Rich!" she said.

"Did you two work out a start date?"

"January second. I wanted to start the day after Christmas, but my action is not popular at home, so I figured I better go home and play the somewhat less recalcitrant daughter," Polly said.

"Still pushback at home on your career choice?" Rich asked.

"Yes. Some. It may be getting better. Knowing Jack is gone helps convince them I am serious about the job, not just who I would have been working with. My folks never blamed him. It was always me. He was always professional in their eyes. Mine, too, of course."

"Well, all of those days have past, Polly. It is time to test your mettle from a commitment standpoint. I have always had faith in you to be a great deputy. I'm convinced you won't disappoint me," Rich said.

"I won't. I promise! Oh! Will I be able to carry my 1911?" she asked.

"Assuming you pass your qualification with it, yes," he responded.

"Who will qualify me?"

"I will."

"I will pass with flying colors!"

"I don't doubt it. I saw the result of your performance under stress at Jack and Lily's wedding. I know which hits were yours and which were Tac's. Both were terminal, just a different approach to aiming."

"Where should I live?" she asked.

"We have about three weeks. I bought the thirty acres of Jack's old ranch which are on the Cimarron River. The area with Doolin's Cave on it. My cabin won't be ready for another several months so I have borrowed a friend's camper trailer. I am going to move into it as soon as my lease expires in a week.

"The point of all of this personal stuff is I am vacating one of the few apartments which will be available in MacKenzie. Perhaps you should call the rental agent and put in for it," he suggested, giving her the contact phone number.

"Because there is no state academy starting in time, you will be sworn in and ride with a field training officer, per standards, until you head off to the academy. I went through it and it's fun. I found it to be the practical application of what I learned in my Criminal Justice degree program.

"Lastly, I have a note from Helen Adams to get some sizes from you for uniforms. We can get them pretty quickly. I will send you her email. The sizes are waist for duty belt, button up uniform blouses, golf shirts, coat, trouser size for utility field gear, and chest for Kevlar duty vest. We wear jeans. I am not sure we did when you were in the office last," Rich said. She promised to immediately text him the requested sizes.

"Mrs. Adams was really kind to me during the time when I had to have the medical exam and answer the questions after Jack recovered me from the kidnaper."

"Good then. Please report to me first thing in the morning on January second. And have a Merry Christmas and Happy New Year," Rich said.

"Oh, I will. You just guaranteed it! Bye!" and she hung up. Rich thought about her for a moment or two after the call. He had first seen her when Jack had carried her off the helicopter after rescuing her from a misguided, but not ill-intentioned kidnaper. She was just a pretty teenager. Several years later, he had interviewed her after she and Tac both killed the ex-con who shot Jack at his wedding. He thought she had matured remarkably in the short interval. He suspected her maturation was continuing. *A few years on the road should speed it along*, he thought.

His intensive final week before Rose leaving as chief deputy and almost immediate departure of Jack as sheriff left Rich having to train on the job with relatively little experience about personnel matters, decisions regarding impoundments, and the boring things which never make it onto television shows or into movies.

He would have to research, call other sheriff's or Clive, a former chief deputy, or just decide by the seat of his pants. His intelligence and judgement pulled him through without too many mess ups. All the way to the countdown before Christmas.

Rich had closed on the land along the Cimarron but moving into a cabin there appeared to be not in the cards until mid-spring at the earliest. The travel trailer was better than camping. It was warm enough and the bed was good. The portable sanitary unit would have been a distinct inconvenience. In view of it, the septic system was in, as was a well with a pump. Electricity had been run all the way in from the county road, albeit at more expense than he had envisioned. The combination of utilities gave him the opportunity to convert a home supply store shed to a bath facility with a sink, commode and shower. Lines for water, electricity and sewage would be run to the cabin from there. In the meantime, Rich had most of the conveniences of a house. They were just a short walk away. Perhaps a short walk in rain or snow, but at least they were available.

He left the office around seven and drove to the camper in the dark. He saw his personal vehicle there and smiled.

The several year old Saleen Mustang had brought more at a Ford dealer in Oklahoma City than he expected. He was able to replace it with a Jeep Gladiator pickup. It was the Rubicon model, set up for serious off-road use. Just what he would have loved to have had when he trashed his Charger sheriff's car rushing across rough terrain to get to Lily and Jack when his friend and boss was injured almost two years ago.

The Gladiator was two years old, but he walked away with a bit of much-needed cash to put into cabin improvements once he moved in. And, he had a personal pickup to haul items in. Anywhere.

Rich settled into one of the two chairs and looked at his two foot high Christmas tree. It had tiny balls on it and the red and green lights were twinkling. He had seen some mistletoe in his woods and shot it from high in the tree with his .22 Marlin 39 lever gun.

It was hanging over the camper door. Where Jenny could not miss it.

He called her.

"Hi! We have talked about spending Christmas together and I really want to do it. What would you think about out here? It's out of the weather, so you could consider it glamping instead of camping," he said.

"So, glamping, huh? Sounds pretty luxurious. What are the bathroom facilities like?" she asked.

"Superb! Commode, sink with small counter and mirror and a shower. All heated. And, are you ready? Only a hundred yard walk from the trailer!"

"I guess, then, at three in the morning, I should plan way ahead, put on the appropriate covering for rain, sleet or snow, and have you with gun and light walk me over?"

"Yes! Exciting, huh? And, what an expression of caring from the county sheriff!"

"Expression of caring sounds like walking your dog. Isn't there something more personal you could add, in view of months of dating?"

"Hmmm. I put mistletoe over the trailer door. How about I tell you something really personal and romantic when we stand under it and kiss?"

"Better, I guess. How romantic, Sheriff?"

"Very romantic."

"And, followed by a gourmet turkey dinner with everything?"

"Absolutely!"

"You will slave over a Bunsen burner in the camper trailer cooking it?" she asked.

"Of course not. Cindy and Julie have invited us to dinner at their ranch on Christmas Eve. We need to be there around seven."

"You just have all the t's crossed don't you?"

"I do."

"I like the choice of words. They seemed to flow easily from your lips. Will you say them again, just to please me?"

"I do."

"Okay. Good. Keep practicing. Dinner with your lovely neighbors sounds great. I'm betting one or both are fantastic cooks. What can I bring?" she asked.

"I have no idea what to get them for Christmas. They sold me a prime part of Jack's ranch for far less than it is worth. They have looked out for me with meals and calls. They are great neighbors and friends and will be for you, too," he said.

"Let me think about it. Certainly a bottle of wine for the dinner, but also a very unusual and personal gift. I will go to some of the upmarket department stores on OKC and see what I can find. If you will just trust me, I will get it wrapped and it will surprise you also."

"That's great of you, Jenny! I will reimburse you immediately."

"You have a lot of money flooding out, building and all. Let me do this!" she said.

"No. Actually, I sold the hot rod Mustang for much more than I thought. I bought a couple year old Jeep pickup for less and have some Christmas cash. I am flush for now, so we should take advantage of it," he said.

"Okay. I will find something nice for Cindy and Julie. When do you want me to come?"

"Since I don't have any family, I have assigned myself for patrol on Christmas Eve up until about four. If you want to come early, you can be a ride along."

"Will we get back in time for me to shower and put on a cocktail dress for dinner?"

"Barring something bad, yes. In this business there are few certainties," he said.

"Sounds like fun! How about I come around noon? Can I park in a secure lot?"

"Yes to both. Call me when you are near and I will meet you at the office. We will lock your car in the entry-controlled lot, then go down the street for a quick lunch."

"Donuts and coffee?" she asked teasingly.

"If you want. I usually have a Cobb salad and half and half tea."

"Did you put your Peloton in the trailer?" she asked.

"Unfortunately not enough room. It is in storage until the cabin is ready."

"Makes sense. Anything special I should bring besides the bottle of wine and gift for the ladies?"

"Yep. A toothbrush. I have toothpaste. Maybe a heavy coat for late night trips to my deluxe bath facility."

"Sounds like I can put the cocktail dress on a hanger and my high heels in a bag hung from it. The toothbrush can go in my pocket."

"I believe you have it all covered," Rich said.

"Do you wish it was Christmas Eve already?" she asked.

"I do." There was no reply.

"I was just set up, wasn't I?" Rich asked.

"Maybe. See you day after tomorrow at the Sheriff's Office just before noon. I will call you from about twenty minutes out."

"Be safe. You are pretty important to me you know," he said.

"I know. I will, Rich. You, too! By the way, I will also call you before day after tomorrow."

"I hope so."

After the call, Rich thought about he had not seen Cindy and Julie dressed up in anything other than mini skirt and cowboy boots or Cindy in business attire at her lawyer's office.

He called the ranch.

"Hiya, Sheriff!" Julie answered.

"Hiya, horse and dude rancher! I have a quick question."

"Yes, we have room at the table for you tonight if you are hungry," Julie said.

"Thanks, I am more tired. I will take a rain check

until Jenny and I see you on Christmas Eve. Which is what my question is about."

"Fire away."

"She is bringing a cocktail dress and high heels. Should I tell her Western ware and boots, instead?"

"Heavens no. You have not seen her in full war paint yet, have you?"

"I have not."

"She has probably picked this occasion to knock your socks off. This will be fun! Cindy and I both look for reasons to wear the closet full of dresses and shoes hidden within. We will wear cocktail dresses, too. You wear a suit with your boots, cowboy!

"Oh. I wanted to ask you something. I never heard you talk about horses or rodeos or such," Julie said.

"I was raised on a small ranch in West Texas. I did some cowboying once upon a time."

"Are your folks still on it?" she asked.

"No. They died in a fire at the house. I was away talking to an army recruiter in El Paso," he said.

"I am so sorry, honey! What did you do?"

"I was eighteen. No other kin. I had our attorney put the ranch and herd on the market and joined the army just after the funeral. It sold just after I started ranger school. He put the money into a trust we had established. I left for the Middle East. Then...other places. The money just sat, invested. I had most of my salary and combat pay added to it over the years."

"Smart! Which is how you got approved for the loan to us so fast?"

"I guess."

"What have you gotten for Jenny? A diamond?"

"You mean like in engagement ring?"

"Exactly," Julie said.

"No, we are certainly heading along those lines. I suspect by New Year's we will know. Any ideas in the meantime?"

"Maybe...what color are her eyes?" Julie asked.

"As blue as the sky on a clear day."

"Oh, you are smitten aren't you? Well, I have the solution. Can you go fifteen hundred?"

"I can. She's really special as you will see on Christmas Eve. You've only seen her in passing up until now," he said.

"I was in Buehler's Jewelry earlier today. I was looking at a beautiful diamond and sapphire necklace. It should match her eyes. I bet she'd love it. Either Cindy or I sure would."

"Do you mind calling them as soon as they open and telling them which one to hold for me? I will be there and get them to wrap it shortly after they talk with you," Rich said.

"You just let your Aunt Julie take care of it!"

"Aunt? You are hardly ten years older than me, if that!"

"Okay, how about your older, but really hot sister?"

"You could be my hardly older really hot sister! Cindy could, too. Thanks, Julie! I hope Jenny will be pleased."

"You can bet on it! See you at dinner!"

Rich smiled with a feeling he had not had for a very long time. He had gone from no family to having an Uncle Bud, and now having two beautiful sisters. And, Jenny. He had a title in mind for her but was not going to say it aloud quite yet.

The next morning, Rich was at the café by six-thirty. He missed his breakfast sessions with Jack and Rose. He had coffee, and egg white omelet and wheat toast and was at the office twenty minutes later. Tac had arranged for grants for systems in the police vehicles which allowed reports to be immediately typed into the on-board computer. The sheriff or chief deputy no longer had to wait for deputies to hand write reports in the office at the end of watch. They were immediately available and legible. He went over the previous night's reports. They were few and simple. People were getting ready for Christmas. Maybe some drunk driving or the odd domestic, but usually nothing major.

Rich remembered from the army how depressed soldiers got during the holidays, especially on deployment away from loved ones. Depression was something he would warn his deputies to watch for at role call at seven-thirty.

"Okay, guys. This is the thirty minutes a week when the county is the most uncovered. We have some important things to go over and have to do it quickly so you can get back on the road.

"First off, thank you third shift deputies for coming in when you should be asleep. Looking out at the group I see some of you still are." This caused some guffaws and guys punching each other.

He introduced two new deputies who had finished their field training and were patrolling on their own. Each had met deputies from two shifts and had missed one.

"These are fine deputies. One came with local police experience and one was an MP. We are lucky to have them. We are getting to a point where the illusive thing some departments call "backup" will be true in Warrior County, too.

"There is one other bit of staffing news. Some of you remember Polly Antrim, the kidnap victim a couple years ago. She is finishing a Criminal Justice degree and reports for duty early in January. When the next academy convenes she will go. In the meantime, per state regs she will be a sworn deputy here in the office or will ride along with one of you. You want to know how cool she is under fire, ask Tac. He will tell you. And, as you know, he's cool under fire. Actually, Tac is just generally cool!

"One thing we have to be aware of on major holidays is depression. People get sad. Sometimes they want to do something hurtful. Be fair and kind. But, also don't let your guard down, okay?

"Everybody grab an envelope out of the door," Rich said. "And, be safe out there!" Inside, Rich had included personally purchased twenty-five dollar gift certificates to Nix' Barbecue, the town's most popular restaurant.

Rich looked at his dive watch. He had fifteen minutes before Buehler's Jewelry opened. He verbally marked out with Tac and walked down the street. He was standing there when Mr. Buehler opened the door at nine-oh-five.

"Well, Sheriff. I was late because I was on a call being told you were going to come and buy a Christmas present!"

"Yessir. I hope it's still here," Rich said.

"Come on in. It's here and I will show it to you."

Rich noted his counter displays were empty for the night. He was already aware of the window security mesh Buehler had already raised before Rich arrived. He watched as the jeweler walked to a safe in a back room. His security precautions seemed excellent.

The jeweler returned with a velvet box and opened it on a glass countertop. The necklace was gold with a small diamond in a heart-shaped cluster of sapphires the color of Jenny's eyes.

"Perfect! I will take it," Rich said handing Buehler his credit card.

"I will have it wrapped for you. My wife is running late and she is the better wrapper. Can you pick it up around ten?"

"Unless you hear me go by with a siren on, yes," Rich said. He took his receipt and left smiling.

The morning flew by quickly with lots of citizens dropping by and giving holiday wishes. They depended on their sheriff's office and were proud of it.

At ten-thirty, Rich walked down to Buehler's Jewelry and picked up the nicely wrapped gift for Jenny. The office used Carhart coats with patches and a badge embroidered on as winter coats. He stuck the gift in one of the big pockets and hurried back smiling.

He was not sure he had ever bought a gift for a female before. As a high school kid, his idea of a gift was a milkshake. Then, the army. College was a blur with a few dates, but mainly studying to get through. Afterwards, the police academy to meet Oklahoma standards. Then, he joined the Warrior Sheriff's Office as a road deputy. It had been a blur ever since.

Rich had given Jenny a lot of thought. He could not help contrasting her with the two sisters in Wichita Falls. The sisters each caused questions and an underlying discomfort, no matter their looks and appeal.

Jenny was more beautiful, but in a quiet, refined way. Like him, she did not talk about family much. She became radiant though each time her niece came up. She adored the toddler who was in the stroller at Walmart the night they met.

She made him feel happy. She gave him purpose. Eleanor was fading from his consciousness quickly. After dating him for several years, she up and moved across the state to take a new job with no notice. She had made him happy also. Then, she was gone. Which was now okay as far as Rich was concerned.

Their relationship had been comfortable, but not exciting. Rich got more excited as time went on with Jenny. He was starting to think about a life together each time he thought of her. He believed she felt the same way and had a feeling he would know before the Christmas weekend was over.

The day was amazingly quiet, even for a rural Sheriff's office. He actually marked out at six and went back to what he was calling his ranch and began cleaning the camper for his guest. He then went out and placed clean towels, new soap and shampoo in the shower and toilet outbuilding. He had installed a motion detector light which lit the path all the way from the trailer to the small outbuilding.

Bears once roamed freely in Oklahoma. Now, sightings are extremely rare for them as they were for mountain lions. Nonetheless, he kept late hours and did not want for him, or Jenny in the future, walking in the remote woods in the dark.

Rich had heard Julie and Cindy remark about Jack's outdoor shower enough to want one for his house as part of the final installation work. Even with the small electric water heater, it was far too cold out to even spend much time thinking about it now.

Once the cabin was built, his plan was to have the current shower stall, sink and toilet put into the bathroom and move the outbuilding behind the new larger one which matched the cabin. It would become the backup storage shed where he would keep and use his Peloton.

The pump for his artesian well would remain where

it currently was. A new hookup to the septic tank would be made at the new cabin.

Rich's apartment had been a fully furnished rental. He would have to furnish the cabin almost from scratch. Again, his mind drifted to Jenny, who he hoped would help with the decorating.

He arrived at work early and eagerly on Christmas Eve. Eleven forty-five finally came and he saw Jenny's black Subaru Outback all-wheel drive pull up out front. He walked out and directed her into the locked area were police, and impounded vehicles were parked.

Though Jack had motion detector lights and a surveillance camera to the dispatcher desk installed, he greeted her with a long embrace and kiss. Rich reckoned he would see the video at unexpected times. *But, hey. It's Christmas after all!* he said to himself as he walked Jenny O'Neill into the building, introduced her to the skeleton crew, and took her to his office.

"Okay, I know you are very special and I am the sheriff, but I still need you to sign this hold harmless before you can ride along," he told her. She did without hesitation.

"Where will we go today, Sheriff?" she asked.

"I thought we would stop a Nix' Barbecue for lunch, then head over to Quanah," he said.

"I've never been there. This will be fun!"

"I hope so. Things can get kinda crazy on the road sometimes, so if I ask you to stay in the truck, please do it without response, okay?"

"Okay."

They got into his marked white F-150 Responder. It was the one which had been Jack's for a matter of a month or so. It still only had less than two thousand miles on the odometer.

It appeared Nix' was hosting a number of store and business Christmas parties. Nix led them to a corner table and Jack seated Jennie on the side and took the seat with his back to the wall and his front facing the door.

"Honey, when we are out and I say 'under the table,' please do so. It means I have seen something I need to worry about," he asked.

"Just when you are in uniform?" she asked.

"Then, especially, but really anytime," he responded. "It's the way of the world now. And definitely the way for those of us who wear a badge."

"I know, my dear Rich. As an RN who works the ER, I see the results of needless violence every day."

"I am sure you do! Also, I have a tourniquet, Quik-Clot, and an Israeli bandage in my Kevlar tactical vest. This pocket," he pointed to her.

"You are a regular walking trauma center. How about surgical gloves?" she asked.

"This pocket for the gloves. I use them more for evidence than first aid, thank goodness," Rich said.

They chatted and had a great lunch. Neither had much to catch up on, since they spoke nightly.

Jenny told him what she had gotten for Julie and Cindy and he paid her over her protests. He was sure they would they would like it.

"Do you think I will be overdressed?" she asked.

"No. I called them and told them you were wearing a cocktail dress and Julie was excited. She said 'It gives us a chance to wear ours we leave in the closet way too much,' or something similar.

"It just means I will be having dinner with the three most gorgeous women in Oklahoma tonight!" he added.

"And, they are partners?" she asked.

"They are, but I think the actual relationship may be

more like roommates. I can't tell for sure. Either way, they have quickly become like the sisters I never had. I think they were for Jack also."

"Should I be jealous?" she asked cautiously.

"Darling Jenny, there is not a single person in the world you need to be jealous about. You have my full attention and I don't ever see any changes there."

"Ever? You really mean 'ever?'"

"I do." Her favorite words in his response engendered a radiant smile. A smile to die for.

They finished and got into the Responder. Rich checked back in service on the radio and they pulled out onto the main state highway to Quanah.

After about twenty-five minutes, the radio sounded.

"Warrior-1, are you near Quanah?"

"This is Warrior-1. I am about fifteen minutes out at normal speed."

"Warrior-1, there is a white male suicide jumper in the steeple of the First Presbyterian Church. Handle Code-3,"

"Warrior-1. Code-3" Rich said as he hit the LED light around the truck and the siren.

"Hold on, honey. We have to run fast on this one. I just hope we make it in time." She patted him on the leg of his jeans.

"Go for it. I'm ready."

Traffic was light on the four lane road. Rich accelerated up to triple digits. When he got behind a vehicle, he slowed somewhat, hit the high-pitched alert, then the air horn and usually the person moved over. Either way, he was in the passing lane and blasting past.

The two lanes in their direction were blocked ahead for another church.

Rich pulled onto the left shoulder and pressed the

alert on constant as he and Jenny bumped by at about sixty. Once past the church traffic, he doused the siren and accelerated up to over a hundred again.

"Warrior-1. Are you close? The minister thinks the white male subject is going to jump soon. Quanah Pumper-1 is on scene. They do not have inflatable landing cushions. They are just standing by."

"Radio, mark Warrior-1 on scene in two mikes. Out" Rich indicated his arrival on scene in two minutes in advance, so he could bail out and make contact with the jumper.

Rich and Jenny heard two clicks signifying agreement.

They sped down the street of the small town without sirens. Rich bailed out as soon as the truck stopped rolling in the church lot and ran into the church.

The minister's wife, ashen with fear, pointed to the steps up to the steeple where the bell and its controls were.

"Name?"

"I don't know," she said as he bounded up the steps.

When Rich got to the top, the first thing he saw was the minister. He was a thin man with a long face and a fastened, but loose collar. He nodded to an open tall window.

Rich walked past the bell mechanism to the window. There was a young looking man, at least from behind, straddling the railing which ran around the point of the steeple spire.

He eased out of the door as the man watched him.

"You are going to just have to shoot me!" the guy screamed in a nervous, screech.

"Nope. Not gonna do it. Unless of course you come over here and attack me. I might have to then," Rich said, thinking he could take the guy if both were away from the railing.

"If you think it's going to happen, why isn't your gun out?" the man, who Rich now determined to be early thirties like him, asked.

"I can draw and fire pretty fast. I had to do it a few months ago at a truck stop. But, I'd really like to talk first.

"I'm Rich. What's your name?"

"What difference does it make?"

"It will really simplify all the paperwork if I have to kill you. Or even if I miss a little and you are crippled in horrible pain for life. So, tell me. What's your name?"

"Brian."

"Hi, Brian. It's nice to meet you. I have to ask, it seems like you have been drinking a little bit of Christmas cheer. Am I right?"

"Ha! No cheer here, Rich! Sorrow," Brian said, giving Rich a glint of hope when Brian personalized the conversation by using his name.

"You know, we seem to be about the same age. Probably have the same types of problems, Brian. Tell me about yours. I will match you I bet," Rich said.

"It's my girlfriend. She dumped me this morning. On Christmas Eve of all times!"

"Man, Brian. On the surface, it really sucks! But, let's talk about it. What did she say?"

"She said I was boring and not so good in the sack."

"What a lousy thing to say! What are your interests? You don't seem boring," Rich said.

"Just work. And, my truck," Brian said.

"Truck? Now you're talking my language! What kind of truck?"

"It's a ten year old GMC with a Diesel. I'm fixing it up nice."

"You have the Duramax Diesel and an Allison transmission in it, right?"

He could see Brian perk up.

"Brian, you have a bullet proof engine and tranny in a great truck You get one of those fixed up and every woman in Oklahoma will want to go out with you! I think you are being real premature with this jump off the steeple crap," Rich said.

"Ya think?" Brian asked.

"Darn tootin'! As a matter of fact, my girlfriend was with me when I got the call. See the pretty blonde down there? No, don't crane your neck! Anyway, she has a girlfriend, Eva, who loves guys with big manly trucks. Diesels only. I know she could arrange a date with you guys. Interested?"

"Ya think?" Brian asked again and Rich nodded excitedly.

Brian swung his outside leg over the rail and staggered drunkenly toward Rich. Rich turned so his non-gun side would be away from Brian and put his arm around his shoulders. They passed the minister and walked down the steep steps talking about trucks.

Rich really wanted to use handcuffs, but it was not time. He thought he had Brian under control, but acknowledged it was a gamble.

One of his three Quanah district deputies was standing by his SUV next to Rich's truck.

"Hey, Steve, you still got the F-250 with the Powerstroke Diesel? Great! You and my new friend Brian need to discuss Diesel stories on the way to the regional hospital for the evaluation.

"Brian, here's how this has to go down: whenever

anybody is suicidal, the law requires we take them to a hospital for an evaluation. In my experience, when liquor is involved, they let the person sober up and return home in a couple hours, okay?

"You are not being arrested. Understand? But you have to sit in the back of the sheriff's vehicle in cuffs. I don't care who you are, it's mandatory procedure. I'm the sheriff, but my mama would even have to sit back there. You understand I'm sure. It's for your safety if you get sick after so much drink in your system. You don't want to hit your head or anything."

"Sure, Rich. Don't forget about Eva now. Okay?" Brian said.

"Okay, buddy. Steve is going to check you for weapons. Another standard thing. Then, he will cuff you and put you in his Tahoe. You guys can talk trucks all the way to the hospital. Play your cards right and you might get a turkey dinner for Christmas there!

"Is there anybody I need to call and tell you are okay and where to pick you up?" Rich asked.

"Yeah, my folks." He gave Rich the number, was patted down, cuffed and put in the prisoner compartment of the Tahoe.

"Hey, Brian. Merry Christmas, buddy. You, too, Steve!" And, the Tahoe pulled off for a forty-five minute drive.

Rich winked at Jenny and then walked over to the assistant fire chief for the Quanah station.

"You guys can get back to the turkey. Brian will get his at the Regional, then probably get released once he's sober. Tomorrow, I hope he comes back here to get his truck and looks up at the tower and says, "I almost did *what?*"

Rich walked back to where Jenny was.

"Ten more minutes to get some names and times for the report. Your friend Eva saved the day."

"What friend Eva? What on earth are you taking about?" Jenny asked.

"Your imaginary friend who likes suicidal drunks and Diesel pickups. She's the reason Brian did not jump sixty feet to his probable death."

"You are pretty devious aren't you? He's headed for a hospital Christmas dinner and a seventy-two hour psych evaluation hold isn't he?"

"Yep," Rich said.

"To which of the two questions, Rich?" she asked.

"Both."

"By the way, Nurse O'Neill. You are here with someone who loves you and prevented you from having to render first aid to a drunk because he went splat off a church spire," he said.

"Well, I guess you—wait a minute!—did you say someone who loves me? You never said 'love' before!"

"Don't you think it is high time I did?"

"I certainly do! And, I love you, too!"

"I am glad you do. I put mistletoe over the door of the camper. It would go to waste if we stood in the doorway and shook hands."

"And, you really love me?"

"Yes, I really love you."

They drove back towards his small ranch without talking. Rich sneaked a sideways glance at her. She was smiling.

He reached over and took her hand. He held it all the way home.

"Will you tell the story about what happened today at dinner?" she asked as they pulled into the ranch's two lane track.

"It might be better if you told the buildup to it. The hundred plus mile an hour ride and you looking up at us."

"It would, wouldn't it? Our first teamwork exercise," she said.

"Appropriate lead up to our first 'love' exercise."

"The 'love' exercise has not happened quite yet." *Quite yet...has suggestion of soon. Sounds good*, he thought.

The mistletoe worked well. The shower worked better. They were a Julie's ranch on time, presents in hand.

"Jenny, you are simply beautiful. And, in a sapphire blue dress! It matches your eyes!" Julie said, winking unseen by anyone except her target, Rich. She did a double-take on seeing Rich in a dark pinstripe suit and lace-up black shoes. He had a small sheriff star lapel pin, but nothing else to indicate who or what he was. Cindy looked at her and nodded, sharing her approval, too. Approval of the couple, not just the sheriff.

Rich gave them the wine Jenny had found and followed Cindy into the kitchen. She got four glasses while he opened it.

"Good heavens, Rich! She is a knockout with the low cut blue dress and killer heels. Where did you find her?"

"Walmart," he grinned.

"What?"

"Get her to tell the story at dinner. She also rode along with me and saw an odd police call today. She will be full of stories for you," Rich said.

"So! You are the one making last year's Oklahoma Police Officer of the Year smile all the time?" Julie was asking Jenny as the other two came in with wine and glasses.

"Jenny, how long do you think we need to let this wine breathe?" Rich asked.

"I always decided based on how thirsty everyone is," she replied.

"I'm ready!" Julie said.

"Me, too," echoed Cindy. "Let's get seated.

Jenny's wine choice was a hit. Because of his gun and badge, Rich only had one glass.

The bottle did not last long and Cindy began bringing the serving dishes out. The Christmas dinner was more stereotypical than Western, with turkey, dressing, cranberry and sauce.

Julie suggested they open the several presents afterwards. She and Cindy had already exchanged and were wearing their shoe and jewelry gifts, respectively.

They gave Jenny a gift certificate for a Stetson or Resistol at a nearby Western wear store.

Rich got a very difficult to find item in the current market. It was a beautifully wrapped box of Speer Gold Dot cartridges in the larger fifty round LE box.

"The color and size are perfect!" he told them.

Jenny gave her hosts a chef knife set in a wooden storage block from the two of them. It had six knives of various sizes.

She gave Rich a certificate to pick up a Warn winch for the front of his new Jeep, which he would find one of the most useful gifts he had ever gotten.

The final gift was the seven inch long box from Rich to Jenny.

When she saw it, tears appeared in eyes matching the sapphires in the necklace. It far exceeded anything she anticipated and caused her to get up and sit on his lap long enough for a sincere kiss.

"I absolutely love it, Rich!"

"And, I absolutely love you, Jenny!"

The evening lasted into the wee hours. Tryptophan and the accompanying carbohydrates did their work and the hosts pointed the guests to a bedroom at the far end of the hall.

"I had expected to cuddle up with you in the camper. I guess this bed with its silky sheets may be even better for first time we actually spend the night together," Jenny said.

Rich motioned her over and she rested her head on his shoulder. She tilted her head up and kissed him. And fell asleep immediately.

Rich stared at the ceiling and grinned. Not exactly how he expected the night to go. But as he smelled the sweet smell of her hair and felt her breathing against him gently, he decided it was a perfect ending to a perfect day.

He kissed her blonde locks softly and drifted off to sleep.

POLLY ANTRIM REPORTED on time just after New Year's. She actually reported early. Having moved into Rich's old apartment, she was up by six AM on report day and went to the café near the sheriffs' office. None other than the sheriff was having breakfast with a very pretty woman in her late twenties or maybe thirty.

She had long shiny natural blonde hair and a tiny waist. Polly was quick to note the woman was as buxom as she. They waved her over.

"Soon to be deputy Polly Antrim, this is Jenny O'Neill," Rich said as he motioned for Polly to sit down.

"Are you with the Sheriff's Office, Jenny?" Polly asked.

"No, I'm with the Sheriff," Jenny replied matter of factly, but in a pleasant tone.

"Oh! Sorry."

"It's fine, Polly go grab a menu unless you remember the fare from when you and your family stayed here a couple years ago. Three, I guess."

"We had lunch here and most dinners at Nix. We stayed at a bed and breakfast and dad wanted to make sure he got his full value," Polly said.

"Can't blame him. How does he feel about today?" Rich said.

"He's in a bit of a tither. He'll get over it."

"You ready to be sworn in after breakfast?" he asked.

"I sure am! And, ready to take my .45 qualification," she said.

"You have to go over to Personnel. Or, Human Resources, as they call it now. There's some paperwork to do to get on the payroll. I will swear you in before you walk over.

"When you get back, we will ride out to the ranch and I will brief you the rules for a deputy who has not yet graduated from the academy. I predict you will love everything you learn at the academy."

"Do you have a parent or friend to pin on your badge after the swearing in?" Jenny asked, having been told about traditions earlier by Rich.

"No. I am afraid not. Would you do it, Jenny?" Polly asked.

"I'd be honored."

All three walked to the office after breakfast. Rich gave her the uniform blouses, ball cap, tactical vest and winter uniform coat. He included the thinner Kevlar vest to wear when not wearing the tactical one. Polly took a blouse and excused herself long enough to put it on.

She was sworn in uniform, since she already had starched, creased jeans on. Jenny pinned her badge on her and received a hug in thanks. Rich shook her hand.

"May I wear my .45 over to HR? I hate to wear a badge and no gun. It would be asking for trouble."

"I agree. Just don't shoot anybody until I qualify you later this morning," Rich said seriously.

"I will do my best!"

"You need to walk over to the County Courthouse. The administrative offices are on the first floor. I have a few bailiff deputies who work there instead of the street. Good people! Most are retired from other LE jobs. You won't have to pass through the walk-through metal detector in uniform. If there is a problem about the bailiff not recognizing you and you not having an ID credential, have him or her call me. I am not sure who's on duty today at the post."

"Okay, boss! Thanks. I will be back when I am on the payroll. It will be nice to meet the personnel lady I have been pestering for a year," Polly said as she walked out.

"She's a doll and really perky. I hope neither of those things gets her in trouble as a deputy," Jenny noted.

"Me, too. The doll part can be mitigated somewhat by her wearing her hair pulled back and pinned. It's also a safety feature I will remind her about. It lessens the chance of someone grabbing a fistful of hair during an altercation.

"I think—and hope—the perky part will fade quickly on the job. It gets real serious real fast out there, honey. You never know who or what you are going to face. Look at the drunk considering jumping from the steeple of the church yesterday.

"Her perkiness is an appealing part of her personality. I hope she keeps it. Just not on the job," Rich said.

"I am pretty sure she will. I have a late shift today. Think my little SUV will make it down the track to the camper tonight?" she asked.

"Other than tornadoes, there is not much weather this part of Oklahoma can throw at you the Subaru won't plow through. I will get you a small, but shootable revolver to carry. I'd like for you to get a concealed weapons license. However, Oklahoma is a Constitutional Carry state, so you are fine carrying it and keeping it locked in your car in situations like the hospital where rules prohibit it," Rich said.

"You have spent so much money on me with the beautiful necklace, Rich."

"You are worth every penny. And your safety is priceless. Once I find the right one and get you to handle it in the gun shop and make sure it is comfortable for you, I will train you so you will be confident," he said.

He walked her out to the secure lot to retrieve her car, kissed her and she headed towards the regional hospital on the edge of Warrior County. He stood watching until she was out of sight.

Rich had a busy agenda for this first "business" day of the year. Polly's orientation, qualification, and being turned over to her field training officer or FTO was first on the list. He had assigned the duty to his most seasoned deputies, Bob and Steve. Neither wanted to leave the road for the deskbound job of being chief deputy. As Rich himself had found it was a little more money for a lot less freedom.

He had two sergeant slots. Assuming both did well as FTOs, they would each be promoted.

Hank Custalow was doing a great job as acting chief

deputy. He had only been at Warrior County several months, but came with experience from Oklahoma City PD.

Rich planned on elevating him to the chief position at the same time he promoted the other two to sergeant.

Polly returned to the office, fully employed and ready for the next step. They got in the Responder and went back to his ranch. Rich had set up seven steel swinging targets.

He gave her a box of frangible target .45 ACP cartridges and had her load all three of her magazines.

She was to draw and fire all seven rounds in her magazine and do a combat reload and fire seven more. From the close seven yards, chosen because most gunfights happen within the distance. The frangible bullets would breakup upon impact and not splatter lead or ricochet back at them.

Polly put on shooting earmuffs and safety glasses and stood at the ready, gun in her holster.

"Now!" Rich yelled.

She drew and fired seven shots, hitting each plate but needing two shots on the sixth. The seventh stood unmarred. She loaded as fast as she could and repeated hitting all seven this time.

"Do it again with your third mag," Rich ordered.

She did and repeated her second performance.

"Did I fail?" she asked with some trepidation.

"No. You already qualified at the academy. This was to prove to me you can handle a .45 under stress. You pretty much already did it at Jack's wedding. You are good to go with a .45.

"I do have some recommendations, though" he said.

"After you finish firing, go to low ready and look left,

right and behind you and make sure there are no other threats. Try to reload as you do this.

"You did a good job keeping your trigger finger extended along the top of the frame and off the trigger when not firing. It's a mandatory safety practice."

"Thanks, Rich. What now?" she asked.

"You are going to field strip your pistol and clean it, then reload with these LE Gold Dot hollow points. I will give you several boxes of practice rounds and several of carry rounds. Try to keep a similar amount on hand. Also, one in your kit in the patrol vehicle. We will talk about the kit when we get back to the office."

"Will I go on the road with an FTO then?" she asked.

"No, you will be in the office for a week working with Tac learning how to handle the radio and dispatch. Urge him to teach you the county map over the radio console. The vehicles have navigation systems, which help in an emergency, but knowing which way you need to head will save crucial time."

"What kind of unit will I get?" she asked.

"A one-year old Interceptor. It's a really fast police model Ford Explorer. It has all-wheel drive. You don't have to shift into four-wheel drive as you do in this truck. I know you have been through the driving course at the academy. It's a good one. When I was there, we used clapped out old Crown Vics. Your vehicle is smaller and has considerably more horsepower, so you have to remember it at all times. You don't want it getting away from you.

"On this subject, pursuing or even running fast on a Code-3 call is not the fun you might think. You have to not just focus on who you are chasing, but also on your vehicle and surrounding traffic. In a pursuit or a fast run, you cannot depend on the public to just pull to the side and let you past. It is likely at least somebody will do something incredibly stupid. Swerve in front of you, slam on breaks. Slow down unexpectedly. You have to be ready for the unknown," Rich said.

"Will I be in the office all the time this week?" she asked.

"Probably not. I will get you to go on some patrols or fast runs with me."

"That will be fun!" she said.

"Maybe or maybe not. It really depends on the nature of the call. I talked a drunk guy planning suicide down from a tall church spire a few days ago. It was a success. I wrote the report. Had he jumped it would not have been pleasant. And, you would have done the report had you been there."

"Do you ever get used to the horrible things you see?" she asked.

"I don't know. I came into this out of some pretty rough combat in the Middle East and elsewhere. I was already almost used to the horror," Rich said as they pulled into the parking lot at the office.

Deputy Polly Antrim got through her several weeks with FTOs and in the office. She started and finished the state's academy with flying colors.

Rich was there, as were her parents, for her graduation. Her mother repined the badge on her Warrior Sheriff's Office uniform after the ceremony. Even her father, who had been against her going into law enforcement was proud. Not happy, but proud.

Polly returned to patrol and learned how to be a deputy in real life. Despite an expected number of mistakes, she became a contributing and respected member of Sheriff Rich Ammon's Warrior County Sheriff's Office.

CHAPTER TEN

JACK AND LILY spent their first Christmas at Cinco Peso, the family and Jess gathered around the large tree from the property after dinner. They exchanged gifts, mostly needed ranch-type items.

Jack looked over at his great uncle. He was sitting in a cowhide chair fifty years older than he was. Uncle Bud was snoozing with Jasmine curled up in his lap purring.

His mother was talking about some new foals with Jess and Lily was sidled up against him on a sofa which matched Uncle Bud's chair in both construction and age.

"I worried so long about us giving up our lives for this, Lily. But, all of a sudden it feels so right. This place has not felt like home to me since I was a little boy.

"Now you are here, it does once again. I am happier than I ever thought I'd be," Jack said.

"You are okay with being a gentleman rancher and a slightly more than part-time livestock agent?" Lily asked softly, wanting to keep the conversation just between them.

"I believe so, honey. The livestock agent job is interesting and allows me to serve my fellow ranchers in a real important way. It is far more of an action police job than I thought, though I worked with them on the Morgan horse theft ring which involved Julie's former brother-in-law and full time nemesis.

"Ranching is not in my heart. I admit it. But it is a lifetime obligation which came to me earlier than I expected. I have to do the right thing and I will."

"What if we don't have at least one son to inherit and take over Cinco Peso, Jack?"

"I truly don't know. I guess every owner has faced the possibility. I guess I will run it as long as I can and then… well, I don't know."

"Could daughters run it?" Lily asked.

"Without a doubt. Assuming they wanted to. They would have the Lily Landers, Georgia Landers tough woman DNA. I can't think of anything stronger."

"I know you and your Uncle Bud always wanted you to be a Texas Ranger. Is it still a dream?"

"No. Not for him or for me. For years now, to get selected as a ranger, one has to be an eight year experienced DPS trooper, or maybe also DPS investigator, but I'm not sure. The eight years patrolling the highways and then being among fifty or more trying for one slot thing…it's a crap shoot I didn't want any part of. Even if I did, it's too late for me now."

"Jack?" she asked.

"What Red Rose?"

"I am hearing an honorable man doing the best he can to be happy with what life has thrown him."

"Isn't it what we all do? I am trying to make the best of it. I do have one thing which makes me extremely happy. An aspect which makes it all workable," he said.

"What's your special thing?"

271

"You."

"I am only one part of your being, dearest. Your drive is to help others and be an adventurer."

"My sole drive now is to be with and take care of you, mom, and Uncle Bud. Nothing else in the world matters to me. Nothing."

She cuddled closer to him and closed her eyes. He knew she was not sleeping and wished he knew what she was thinking. From the drift of her questions, he suspected she had not reached any conclusive opinion. He would not push her. He knew his strong, intelligent partner would share her conclusions once they were formulated. It's one of the many things he adored about her.

WINTER BECAME SPRING. Brown turned green and the winds grew warmer in both Oklahoma and Texas.

Sheriff Rich Ammon grew into his job. He moved into his cabin. So did Jenny O'Neill, RN. She wore a new ring on her left hand.

Zack Bodeway's nuptials were delayed by a series of important cases for both him and his intended. It was beginning to look like a June wedding.

The state of Texas continued to seek the whereabouts of crime boss Frank Heinrich. He still had several felony warrants outstanding and more awaiting issue.

Dr. Lily Landers partnered with an existing female gynecologist instead of starting from scratch. The two got along well and the practice flourished with the second doctor. Lily's commute was only twenty miles each way.

The Cinco Peso Ranch grew. The injection of capital

from the sale of Doolin's Cave Ranch seemed just the boost it needed. The hardest thing they faced was finding a couple more hardworking and conscientious hands.

The arms remained placed strategically, but even Jack admitted the chance of Heinrich attacking them in retribution was diminishing geometrically each passing month.

For once in his life, Jack was wrong. Critically wrong.

HEINRICH HAD BEEN SCHEMING since the day he left his office and home behind and retreated with his family and a few close associates.

One of those associates was a very unlikely individual. His name was Rocky Cardarelli.

Rocky, born Rocco, had grown up in the Bronx. He was the gangly, blue-eyed, sandy haired standout in his Italian section. His mother was a seamstress, his father a stevedore.

Rock finished high school and joined the NYPD. He was a lazy, crooked cop. Finally, without enough to prosecute him, the NYPD fired him. He did the expected thing. He became a private investigator.

Cunning and the ability to become a virtual chameleon, he excelled. Until he violated every regulation the Empire State had for PIs. All on one case. He fled to Texas, where he crashed with a friend. The friend was another crook and worked for a man named Heinrich.

Frank Heinrich could pick the best talent out of any slime covered pool. He saw a lot of uses for having a former cop and PI on his team. He hired Rocky right away.

Since shortly after the raid on Heinrich's office and the cattle storage yard, Rocky had been surveilling Jack Landers and cataloging the members of the staff and household at Cinco Peso.

Looking for the world like a Texas cowboy in his jeans, boots and hat, he took photos of the people and their vehicles as they left and returned to the ranch.

Luckily for Rocky, the ranch road ran out onto a county road.

There was a truck stop with convenience store within a short distance from their intersection.

Rocky set up there, often with others of Heinrich's men. His operations officer, an ex-German military man hired for both experience and to further Heinrich's image as a Neo-Nazi, often accompanied Rocky on these *recce's*, as he called them.

It was a beautiful spring day in the Texas Hill Country when the ops officer, Karl Koleszar, took his five-man team and Rocky to meet with the boss.

The team Koleszar had assembled was a combination of former German and two Ukrainian soldiers. None had been special operations, but all had been combat infantrymen.

"I want Rocky and Karl to describe the ranch and its people we are going to hit. Maybe tomorrow. Rocky has done the brunt of the surveillance and Karl has done a lot of computer research on the occupants. Karl, fill us in on who and what we will face."

"Sure, boss. Jack Landers is the owner. He is a former sheriff and current agent for the livestock association. Which means he is a sworn peace officer here. He is the veteran of several widely reported gunfights and is likely a dangerous player.

"Boss, if he does not fall in our initial barrage, I think I'd better take him," Karl said.

"No! Hell, no! He's mine to kill!" Heinrich screamed like a madman.

"Your call, boss," Karl said, thinking *this idiot is going to die tomorrow, if he tries to take down a proven killer. He never killed a damn thing in his life.*

"The ranch manager is a man in his sixties. There is virtually no information online about this Jess Noland or his new ranch hand. I doubt they will provide much threat to us.

"Lander's eighty plus year old great uncle, Bud Carey is there. He may be a threat despite his age. He is a famous retired Texas Ranger. We cannot discount him, walker or not. He seems to be armed with at least a small revolver at all times.

"There are two women. Lander's mother is about sixty, his wife is a medical doctor in her mid-thirties. I cannot imagine they would represent any sort of threat.

"Boss, what do you want us to do with the two women and old man?" Karl asked.

"Kill them like the men, of course! This is retribution, and I want full retribution. If time allows, I want us to burn their damn house and stable and barn down, too!" Heinrich said vehemently.

"And, Karl. When this is done, you go straight to Austin and lay low. I will meet you there and we will kill the black woman ranger and the old ranger with the cane. He has made my life costly for the past five or six years.

"I want you men, other than Karl, to take the vehicles you use on the Cinco Peso raid and the money I will give you there and disappear. I don't want to ever see or hear from you again, got it?" The men nodded, none too happy about waiting for their money.

"Rocky, you go back to surveil at the truck stop. Report back to Karl or me if everybody seems to be in place. We may just hit them this afternoon.

"Karl, make sure the Suburban has the dynamite, fuses, caps and the several five gallon cans of gas in it to torch the place once we are through." Karl nodded.

An hour later, eleven-forty in the morning, Rocky called Karl and reported Noland and the ranch hand had left the ranch and stopped for Diesel fuel at the truck stop. They had then driven on towards the nearby town.

Karl reported to Heinrich, who yelled in his best commander voice, "It's a go! Mount up. Do not chamber until I give the order."

What an idiot. These men, unlike you, false Nazi, have really been in combat. They know what to do. You are the loose cannon here, fool, Karl thought.

They left, Rocky in his old pickup, three men in the munitions Suburban, and Heinrich and Karl in the former's Mercedes SUV.

"My instructions to the men for a daylight raid, which I don't like, is for Rocky to park away from the ranch house and sneak in on foot. He can be our cleanup man. Klaus, driving the Suburban, will make one machine gun pass at the house and then drop the Ukrainian, Igor with the gas and explosives at the stable. Klaus and Mark will make another machine gun pass in the Suburban, then dismount and continue the attack at close quarters. You and I will let the others soften them up, then move in for your specific target, Jack Landers. Since you want to take him, I will hang back and cover your six," Karl said.

"Fine. Let's go."

Jess and the new hand had already fueled up and were heading for the feed store. They would be five miles away when the attack occurred.

———

JACK FINISHED RIDING fence along his last unchecked section. He was not on Remington, but the Gator.

He pulled up near the house and parked it about thirty feet from the front door. His mother's Suburban, Lily's BMW, his company, personal, and ranch pickups were around back.

"Hey, guys! What's for lunch? I almost got warm out there riding the south fence. What a great day."

"I know I turned you down today, but maybe next time you take the Gator, I'll ride along," Uncle Bud said with Jasmine on his lap.

The sound of a front window breaking was simultaneous to the crack of two gunshots, followed by a full automatic machine gun volley.

Jasmine screeched and jumped seven feet to the sofa and disappeared underneath. Uncle Bud fell off his chair onto the floor, knocking over his walker.

"Everybody on the floor get whatever gun you can reach!" Jack ordered as more machine gun fire took out the remainder of the front windows and peppered the front of the house.

Georgia crawled on her stomach to her uncle. "I'm okay," he said. "I just fell."

Jack heard his great uncle say he was okay and heard the vehicle with the shooters turn in the gravel by the stable. He filed the fact it stopped and probably dropped somebody.

"Lily, stay down. Do you have your phone in your pocket? Good! Dial 911 and tell them we are under an automatic weapons fire attack and need deputies now!" She did not answer. She complied instead by immediately dialing.

Jack heard the vehicle near the stable gun its engine and head back towards the house. He knew he had a window of opportunity as it approached. The shooter could only fire out of the vehicle when it was passing the house. Jack could shoot into the windshield as it was approaching.

The engine noise grew and Jack crouched by a shot-out window with his .30-30. When he had a clear shot, he fired several rounds into the windshield. He knew he killed the driver and thought he hit one of the people in the rear seat.

Out of control and loaded with gasoline cans and explosives, the Suburban crashed into the Gator and burst aflame. Jack saw a man roll out of the backseat on the far side.

He aimed, but the fire ignited the dynamite and the Suburban exploded. The concussion blew Jack backwards onto the floor. His Winchester slid away.

Lily slid a M1 carbine with a twenty-round clip across the tile floor to him. He pursed his lips in a kiss. Both husband and wife chambered .30 Carbine rounds at the same time.

Igor, his explosives gone, approached the house with his MP-5 submachine gun. He went up the window closest to the stable and tried to see in. He could not, so he stood and shouldered the Heckler and Koch. Uncle Bud and Georgia both shot him with their revolvers at the same time. He went down screaming.

Uncle Bud looked at his beloved niece with pride and grinned the grin he had taught Jack thirty years ago.

Instead of reloading their two revolvers, Georgia secured two of the Shockwave shotguns. They crouched on either side of Uncle Bud's chair, the guns pumped and ready.

Karl knew his plan had gone to hell and they should make the best of a bad thing and withdraw. He told Heinrich who went completely berserk over the idea.

"I am going after Landers, you follow!"

Heinrich launched off towards the house with one of the H&K MP-5 submachine guns. Karl shrugged and followed.

With things quiet, Jack moved everyone into the dining room. All guns were recovered and reloaded. Jasmine appeared but was not happy with the goings on.

Armed with his holstered .45 and an M1 carbine, Jack slipped out of the back door.

He carefully rounded the house just as Heinrich did. Heinrich raised the MP-2 and Jack fired from the hip. He hit the fugitive in the gut with a controlled pair of shots and Heinrich screamed a high-pitched scream and dropped the sub gun and bent over.

Karl and Jack closed and a fight to the death silently began.

It started with a grapple. Both men went down and popped back up transitioning into punches. Karl hit Jack in the solar plexus folding him. As he moved in, Jack straightened and head butted the German. Karl staggered back, his crushed and broken nose leaking crimson down his face.

Karl moved forward to reach Jack. With painful effort, Jack punched him in the throat. He made some gurgling noises and died.

Rocky shot Jack in the back with a .32 automatic. Jack could feel the burn as the bullet penetrated deep into muscle, missing organs and lodged by the rear of his right shoulder blade.

Jack staggered forward and fell, reaching for his .45. Rocky aimed again and Jack heard a crack but did not feel pain. He looked up at Rocky. Rocky had a surprised look on his face. Lily was off to Rocky's right with an M1, aiming for a second shot.

Rocky had staggered from being hit, but still turned towards Lily. Jack shot him in the temple with the .45 Uncle Bud carried so proudly for years in the rangers. Jack leaned against the wall of the house filling a couple of the bullet pockmarks with his blood.

Lily rushed to Jack, but he waved her over to the gut-shot Heinrich, who was moaning in intense pain.

He covered as Lily did her Hippocratic responsibility, checking Heinrich.

They could hear sirens in the distance but approaching quickly. Otherwise, the Cinco Peso was amazingly silent.

"Is Jazz okay?" Jack asked.

"I think so. She is still under the sofa."

"There may be a wounded guy beyond the wreckage. I really liked the Gator," Jack said.

"There's another under the last window. He might have expired by now though," Lily said. "Your mother and Uncle Bud both shot him."

"Let's us cover from here and have the deputies check them in a minute when they arrive."

The arriving deputies called for supervisors and Texas Rangers. They also called for a coroner and several ambulances. By the time the first ambulance arrived, only Jack and Heinrich were still alive.

As he was not bleeding profusely and Lily determined the small non-expanding bullet from Rocky's mouse gun had missed organs. There was not much she could do for him.

When she had checked Heinrich and removed the guns from his reach, she knew unless he had immediate surgery, he would be dead within an hour or two.

The call to the rangers from the first arriving sheriff's sergeant had precipitated the request for a medevac helicopter. Its arrival and fast turnaround greatly increased the probability Heinrich would survive for a long life at Texas taxpayer's expense.

From the ambulance, Jack called Elliott and advised him what had happened. Elliott and Mary would respond immediately and charge Heinrich, if he survived.

Uncle Bud and his mother came out. They would be subject to hours of questions by deputies and rangers alike. They saw Jack and Lily off in the ambulance only after assuring Jack the tiny black and white cat was unhurt.

Jack was released from the hospital two days later. His whole family was in Georgia's Suburban, including Jasmine.

Frank Heinrich survived and is facing six felony charges. Others are pending. His future apparel is destined to be Texas prison white. Probably for the remainder of his time on earth. No one else on his attack team survived. The Cinco Peso Ranch did survive. As always.

RICH and his team flourished in Warrior County. The promotions occurred and Rich felt he had the right people in the right jobs. And, he was the right person to be living with his true love in their new cabin near the caves where the Doolin-Dalton Gang hid on the Cimarron River.

Jack and Lily grew Cinco Peso while Jack kept the agricultural business of his Hill Country district safe. Georgia became happy again and Uncle Bud continued to be the family sage.

In her mind (and everyone else's) Jasmine became the Black and White Rose of Texas.

A LOOK AT RIDE WITH THE RANGERS:
A WESTERN DUO

DOGGED MANHUNTER, LEGENDARY WESTERN LAWMAN – AND FAST GUNS!

Texas Ranger Zack Bodeway trails an outlaw into Oklahoma, in Indian Territory, and is bushwhacked. He makes it to a stagecoach stop and falls off his horse, almost dead, a beautiful young widow nurses him back to health. When everything is going well, Bodeway learns that life can have some unexpected twists...and he solves them with the fast .44 on his hip.

Follow Tilghman from his early days as a buffalo hunter out of Dodge City to serving as the Marshal of Dodge, and later the Deputy U.S. Marshal who became one of the Three Guardsmen of Oklahoma to his last arrest in 1924 at age 70. Tilghman wanted to be a successful businessman and tried and failed throughout his life. He always came back to what he did best – enforcing the law.

Ride With The Rangers: A Western Duo includes – Zack Bodeway Texas Ranger and The Legend of Bell Tilghman.

AVAILABLE NOW

ABOUT THE AUTHOR

G. Wayne Tilman is a full-time author. He is retired from the Federal Bureau of Investigation. Prior to the FBI, he was a Marine, bank security director, deputy sheriff, investigator, and security contractor.

He holds baccalaureate and master's degrees from the University of Richmond and has been an adjunct faculty member there and several other universities as he has moved around America.

Mr. Tilman holds the internationally-recognized Certified Protection Professional board certification, generally accepted as the highest in the security profession. He also earned a US Coast Guard 50 Ton Inspected Vessel Master Captain's license.

He writes espionage thrillers, mysteries, and Westerns. Mr. Tilman's impetus to write in those genres comes from both personal experience and heritage.

A direct ancestor was a sheriff in Virginia Colony in 1680. Another ancestor was the lawman who brought in outlaw Bill Doolin (Desperado of song fame) singlehandedly and helped to neutralize the infamous Doolin-Dalton outlaw gang.

Closer to home, his mother was a counterintelligence agent for what is now the Defense Intelligence Agency or DIA.